PRAISE FOR
ALL OF YOU

"Five words to describe this book (and you'll get this once you read it): hot, sweet, emotional, page-turner, awesome."
—Monica Murphy, *New York Times* and *USA Today* bestselling author of *One Week Girlfriend* and *Second Chance Boyfriend*

"With *All of You*, Christina Lee has crafted a fresh and fascinating twist on the classic love story. At its core, *All of You* is pure NA goodness, full of mistrust and hardened hearts, angst and anguish, hot and steamy scenes, and a satisfying HEA."
—*New York Times* bestselling author Jasinda Wilder

"A one-sitting read simply because I could not put it down. From steamy to sweet and every emotion in between, Christina Lee had me glued to the pages in her unforgettable debut, *All of You*. This is one New Adult you don't want to miss."
—*New York Times* and *USA Today* bestselling author A. L. Jackson

"Bennett stole my heart! If you like hot, sweet, sexy, caring good guys, he'll claim yours, too."
—*New York Times* and *USA Today* bestselling author Lauren Blakely

"Steamy, honest, and full of heart, *All of You* kept me glued to the pages and had one of the best heroes I've read all year. A fantastic debut!"
—Roni Loren, national bestselling author of *Not Until You* and the Loving on the Edge series

continued . . .

"Christina Lee's debut is a smoking-hot read. With a heroine who is real and unapologetic and a hero who made me swoon, *All of You* is a must read. Hands down one of the best I've read this year." —Juliana Stone, author of *The Summer He Came Home*

"Heat, heart, humor, and a hot guy who is toe-curling sexy AND actually a good guy, *All of You* has everything you could ask for. A fantastic debut I couldn't put down!" —Rachel Harris, author of *Taste the Heat*

"Lee's first novel is a wonder." —*Romantic Times*

"A good portrayal of two people with opposing desires falling in love. . . . *All of You* delivered." —Dear Author

"[A] beautiful story about how love and friendship can heal wounds . . . a hot New Adult novel with amazing characters and a sizzling romance." —Dark Faerie Tales

"I can't believe Christina Lee is a debut author. Her story was well-polished, drew me in completely, and didn't let me go the entire time." —A Bookish Escape

"This is an amazing story of hope. . . . Thank you, Christina Lee, for gifting us with this story and these characters." —Bookish Temptations

ALSO BY CHRISTINA LEE

The Between Breaths Series
All of You

BEFORE YOU BREAK

YOU

BREAK

The Between Breaths Series

CHRISTINA LEE

 New American Library

New American Library
Published by the Penguin Group
Penguin Group (USA) LLC, 375 Hudson Street,
New York, New York 10014

USA | Canada | UK | Ireland | Australia | New Zealand | India | South Africa | China
penguin.com
A Penguin Random House Company

Published by New American Library, a division of Penguin Group (USA) LLC.
Previously published in an InterMix edition.

First New American Library Printing, October 2014

REGISTERED TRADEMARK—MARCA REGISTRADA

LIBRARY OF CONGRESS CATALOGING-IN-PUBLICATION DATA:

Lee, Christina, 1968–
Before you break/Christina Lee.
p. cm.—(Between breaths ; 2)
ISBN 978-0-451-47087-4 (paperback)
1. Love stories. 2. College stories. I. Title.
PS3612.I.325B44 2014
813'.6—dc23 2014018896

Printed in the United States of America
10 9 8 7 6 5 4 3 2 1

Set in Bembo
Designed by Spring Hoteling

PUBLISHER'S NOTE
This is a work of fiction. Names, characters, places, and incidents either are the
product of the author's imagination or are used fictitiously, and any resemblance to
actual persons, living or dead, business establishments, events, or locales is entirely
coincidental.

To Evan.
You are the moon.
The stars.
The entire universe.

BEFORE
YOU
BREAK

CHAPTER ONE

ELLA

"Daddy, please. I . . . I need to see Christopher," I sobbed. "I need to be with him."

My father gripped the door handle and stood firm and resolute, despite the stream of tears tumbling down his cheeks.

"Nie, C . . . Corka." His voice cracked, so his Polish sounded jumbled. Strained. Mangled. Just like my heart. "You don't want to see him like this. Please . . . go back downstairs."

I fell to my knees on the carpet and buried my face in my hands. I could hear my mother's guttural wailing from the kitchen below, and it was a noise I wouldn't soon forget.

The sound of the siren sliced through my family's sorrow and then imprinted its glaring lights on our once peaceful home.

And that's when the realization struck me so hard that the air was *forced straight from my lungs. I gripped my stomach and wept so mercilessly that no sound fell from my lips.*

My brother was truly gone.

lined everything up perfectly on the small brown desktop. My coffee cup, my notes, and the psychology textbook I'd been studying from this semester. My fingers straightened the black picture frame behind my laptop before they traced over Christopher's soulful eyes, his quiet smile.

I'd been working at this hotline the past few weeks as part of my field hours at the university. So far it'd been a good experience, if not a bit sad and overwhelming. But if I wanted to become a psychologist, I needed to experience this side of it. My supervisor called it the underbelly. Those broken members of society reaching out for help.

I'd been told that I was a natural. Insightful beyond my years. That I had a knack for getting people to open up to me. Still, the notebook on my desk reminded me what I needed to focus on during my conversations. Like providing available community resources and figuring out if the caller had an actual plan to kill himself.

Desperate people called the hotline, sure. But there were the regulars, too, who just needed someone to listen. Maybe they were attention seekers. Or maybe they needed a stranger to unload on.

One man's pebble in the road of life is another man's boulder, my grief counselor said after Christopher died. You just never knew.

It was my job to figure out whether the caller felt the weight of that boulder and then decide how to proceed from there. Did they need medical attention or a willing ear? The simple act of listening was a powerful thing.

I checked the clock on the wall. No sooner had I placed the headphones over my ears than the red button lit up like a road hazard. I inhaled sharply, never sure what would be thrown at me.

"Suicide prevention line. This is Gabriella."

I used my full name at work for formality's sake, but my family and friends called me Ella.

I heard a clearing of the throat, and then a distinctly male breath filled my eardrums through the phone line.

This might have been his first time calling. I could have only guessed how scary this experience was. My job was to assess his needs, so hopefully I could get him talking.

"I can hear you breathing. And it's okay." I tapped my pen on the desktop. "Talk whenever you're ready."

Another intake of breath.

"Must be tough for you to speak to a stranger." I adjusted myself in my seat. "But there's a reason you called, and I'm here to listen."

Finally he spoke, in a low and defenseless voice that sent a chill straight through me. Maybe it was because he sounded young and vulnerable. Like my brother who died when I was in high school. "I . . . I don't know why I called. It was a mistake. I'm not . . ."

"It's never a mistake," I said, my voice strong and confident. "Even if you just called to hear someone's voice other than your own."

Would Christopher have stood a chance if he had called a hotline?

"I . . . um . . . okay." I could almost picture him exhaling and squeezing his eyes shut, like he was uncomfortable.

"Can you tell me your first name and what prompted you to call?"

"Okay." His voice was a quiet rumble. "It's . . . it's . . . Daniel."

"Hi, Daniel," I said almost breathlessly, relieved he'd relaxed enough to give me his name.

I could practically hear how difficult it had been for him to call. "Hi, um . . . Gab . . . Was your name Gabriella?"

I tried to find my confident voice again. "Yes."

"I have an aunt named Gabriella," he said, his voice sounding a little lighter at the memory. "Everyone calls her Gabby."

"I'm cool with Gabby, too." He could call me whatever the hell he wanted to. I didn't want to screw up this phone call. My stomach was in full-on clench mode.

Only one other person had called me Gabby. My brother Christopher. It was our little joke. He'd call me Gabby and I'd call him Chrissy. But then once, my twin brothers heard me and started calling him Chrissy the Sissy. He was pissed at me for days.

I shook the memory away and cleared my throat. "So, Daniel, why'd you call?"

"I . . . I can't stop feeling guilty about something terrible I've done." I heard him take a swig of something. Maybe a beer, liquid courage. "I don't know if I can live with myself anymore."

Crap! What could he have done that was so terrible?

Normally, phone calls came from people suffering from symptoms of depression. They felt empty and helpless and

4

useless. They were usually teary or could barely drag themselves out of bed to face life. But this guy didn't sound typical. He sounded tortured about something he'd *done*.

I took a breath and made sure I had my professional hat back on. "Let's talk it through."

"I . . . I can't." His breath was harsh. "This is stupid."

"No it's not, Daniel." I could feel it—he was going to hang up. "Please talk to me, tell me something. *Anything*."

"I . . . I'm sorry." And then the line went dead.

I sat there paralyzed, playing the conversation over in my head. What could I have said differently to keep him on the phone? What was he doing now? Hopefully not drinking himself into oblivion. Or worse . . .

The call line lit up again and my heart was in my throat. Maybe he'd decided to call back. "Suicide prevention line. Gabriella speaking."

"H . . . hi. Um, my name is Susan." Disappointment and regret waged a war in my chest. I looked through the open doorway to the two offices across the hall. There were three of us on tonight in separate rooms. We were to keep doors open in case we had questions or needed support. I now wondered if he'd called back and was on the line with either of the other two.

"Hi, Susan. How are you feeling tonight?"

"Lonely . . ."

Three hours later, I grabbed my purse out of the bottom drawer and trudged out to my car. I'd spoken to a cutter, a jumper, and a crier, but never again to Daniel, if that was in fact his real name.

I wasn't sure why I was even still thinking about him. It

was something about the tone of his voice, I decided. Something desperate, broken, hollow. Maybe that was how Christopher would have sounded the night he'd taken his own life . . . if anyone had been home to listen.

Daniel had wanted to tell someone what he'd done. Someone who might've helped. I didn't think he wanted to die. Not yet. And I hoped he found someone to talk to soon.

Just like I'd wished all those nights that Christopher had talked to someone. We were so close. Why couldn't he have confided in me? Asked me to come home? And why hadn't I read the signs?

As I was pulling up to my apartment building, I got a text from my boyfriend, Joel.

> Playing cards tonight. Can't get
> away. Come here instead.

My stomach tightened immediately. *Can't get away, my ass.*

Joel used to always want to be alone with me. He'd complain about being at the frat house so much. But lately, he didn't seem to mind at all. He was partying harder, getting more involved in campus life, and I definitely felt our relationship fraying at the edges. Hell, we barely even made out anymore.

I looked up at the brick building. The first-floor lights were off, which meant my roommate, Avery, wasn't home. She was probably already up at her boyfriend's place on the fifth floor. She and Bennett had gotten together in the fall and had been inseparable ever since. Which didn't bug me—until I realized that what they had was so much deeper than what I had with Joel.

So why the hell was I hanging in there with him?

Joel was my first adult relationship. The first guy to notice me—really notice me—next to my beauty-queen friends, Avery and Rachel. I liked having a boyfriend and a steady relationship. I'd dated the same guy on and off in high school for two years. But we'd drifted apart after Christopher died. I was a wreck, and he didn't know how to handle it.

By that time Avery was always sleeping over, trying to get away from her own crazy life, and I took comfort in that. There was something to be said for loyalty.

But I was probably loyal to Joel to a fault. Plus, my parents liked him. Joel was from the next town over and his family belonged to the same church. My father coached him in community soccer.

But there was also another connection.

Joel had known Christopher. Had mentored him in soccer as a junior coach. He knew a different side to Christopher— the competitive side. How much he loved the game and the travel team. Just knowing he'd been linked to Christopher in some small way brought me relief. Reminded me of happier times.

I scrolled down to Avery's name in my phone.

> Me: Hey, bitch, you up on 5? Heading to Joel's. See you in the morning.

```
Avery: Yep, I'm here. Heading
there again, huh? You know what
I'm gonna say, right? You & I are
gonna have a real conversation.
About what you're doing. And what
you need. Without mentioning that
asshead & what he's doing. Got it?
```

Here we go again. Avery was so protective of me when it came to guys. The funny thing was, she'd been one big player herself before she met Bennett. She didn't think guys were a necessity. Unless you fell madly in love with one of them, like she did. She'd had quite the adjustment.

```
Me: *eye roll* Later, bitch.
```

I pulled away from the curb in the direction of the frat house.

CHAPTER TWO

QUINN

I took a long pull of my beer and plopped down on my sheets. Why the hell had I called that hotline? And why the fuck had I given my real name? Sure, nobody called me by my first name anyway, but still, I could have lied. Yet there was something about hearing her say *Daniel*. It sounded solid falling from her lips. Like maybe she could actually help me or something.

Geez, enough already. If I'd wanted to kill myself I should've just driven off a goddamn bridge already. Maybe I wasn't totally serious—maybe I was a chickenshit—but some days I sure felt like I needed to disappear. The guilt I carried was like a goddamn heavy coat—prickly hot, itchy, and smothering.

"Quinn, get your ass down here!" I heard Joel's loud mouth through my door. If I didn't make an appearance with my frat brothers, I'd get harassed. One time they jumped me and pulled my ass out of bed. I sat up and reached for my shoes under my bed. The sneakers I changed into after baseball practice were still caked with mud from the field, so I slipped into my blue Cons.

The boys played poker most nights and got trashed just the same. I couldn't always bow out after an afternoon game or practice. But at least I had an excuse during baseball season not to hang out too much. We played three ball games a week, and spent a lot of time on the road. But it didn't help that my teammate Jimmy lived at the house and upstaged me with his partying.

As I headed down the stairs I heard distinctly familiar female voices. Same girls, different night. The guys referred to them as *frat brats* behind their backs. They were here every weekend night and always willing to do any number of favors for the guys, especially sexual ones.

I'd made the mistake of getting it on with a frat brat once before realizing what a mistake it was to hook up with these girls—they were always in your business. But I'd been pretty hard up by that time. Normally, if I was desperate, I'd head away from the frat house and up to the local bar where the townies hung out. I always came away satiated. It helped get my head back in the game. Literally.

I was at TSU to study, play ball, and live the frat life that my best friend always wanted. Sebastian had promised his dad that he'd pledge to the same house from his alma mater. And if he couldn't be here to do it himself—because of what I'd done—I'd honor him by doing it for him.

I was here for Sebastian, for his parents, and maybe a little for myself. As long as I kept going—living his life—the guilt was pushed to the side for a while. Until it bubbled up and consumed me. Like it had tonight.

I nodded to the guys at the table, scraped the metal chair across the floor, and sat my ass down. "Deal me in."

The girl sitting on Joel's lap had also been there the previous night. His hands were hidden beneath the table doing God knows what to her. Joel's gaze kept darting out the window, which meant his girlfriend, Ella, was on her way over.

Ella was pretty and had a smoking body, but was obviously too naïve to realize what a huge player her boyfriend was. I'd never seen Joel do more than cop a feel since he'd started hanging with Ella, but it wasn't like I had been watching him twenty-four-seven. These frat brats kept their mouths shut, just like the baseball groupies did after ball games. I didn't get the whole chicks-stabbing-chicks-in-the-back thing. I just knew I definitely wanted no part of it.

Hell, Sebastian had been doing the same thing to his girlfriend, Amber. But she hadn't been all that innocent, either. Then again, I'm not one to talk. I'd been playing games, too. I just hadn't realized it. Until it was too late.

I didn't know Ella all that well, but lately she'd been on the quiet side. Too quiet. She used to joke around more, had one hell of a truck driver's mouth, and could hold her own in a *Call of Duty* game with the guys.

Maybe her silence spoke volumes. I could feel the tension hanging in the air lately between her and Joel.

A lot of the guys accused Joel of keeping Ella around for free pussy. Joel always pretended to be into the chicks hard to get them to spread their legs. Sure, he'd kept Ella around longer than most. So maybe she *was* good in bed. I shook my thoughts away from Ella's nice rack and how her dark hair might look fanned around my pillow. I didn't need a boner tonight.

As soon as Joel spied Ella through the window, he pushed the girl off his lap and she plopped down on mine, pouty bottom lip jutted out. And there went my potential hard-on. But if she wiggled her hips a little more she'd be sure to bring it back.

She turned and whispered against my ear, "Want to head upstairs, Quinn?" I looked down at her sheer white T-shirt, her lacy bra peeking beneath, hiding her small but perky breasts.

The trouble with these frat brats was that they were around too much. If you just wanted to chill with the boys, it could get awkward. And if you brought home a date, it could even get ugly. So I stayed far away. Not that I brought home any dates.

"Hey, baby." Joel hadn't even bothered to stand up and greet his girl when she walked through the door. I glanced at Ella. Flushed cheeks, a hint of irritation in her eyes. Maybe she was getting tired of his bullshit, too. She had on a fluffy skirt that went to her knees with a fitted blue T-shirt. Her long brown hair was draped over her shoulders. She looked like she'd just come from work, because she wasn't in her usual attire.

"Hey, Ella," both Jimmy and Todd said, waving over their beer bottles. She glanced at me and then my visitor, who was now rocking her hips in my lap. For some reason, Ella's scrutiny made me want to push this chick off. I wouldn't be taking her upstairs, anyway. She knew that and so did all of the guys.

Did Ella?

I shook my head. Why in the hell did it matter?

Ella rolled her eyes right before they became blank. It was as if she'd literally flipped a switch and become numb. I knew that feeling all too well, but what did this girl know about feeling dead inside? I'd heard Joel talk about her large and boisterous Polish family and how her mom made the best dumplings from scratch. How could a girl with all that have any problems?

My mother served takeout from the local pricey restaurant and we ate it around an awkwardly silent table. And that was just on the two nights our maid, Louise, was off. On the other nights, I used to eat alone. I'd trade places with Ella in a heartbeat.

I'd bet she never lay awake at night wondering if her parents would ever forgive her. All because a huge-ass mistake almost ruined her father's chances of running for political office.

Joel tugged Ella down on his lap, where the chick in mine had been sitting just moments before, and a couple of the guys exchanged smirks. Had it been Brian's girlfriend, Tracey, in Ella's place, none of that would have gone down. Brian was in love with Tracey, fiercely loyal to her, and I admired him for that. He got razzed about it all the time, but he didn't put up with that frat-brat bullshit when she was around. Or even when she wasn't. Joel needed to take lessons from him or just let Ella go.

Sebastian should have done the same with Amber. They should have been honest with each other. Damn, we all should have been. My stomach started sloshing and rolling. Guess that was the end of my thinking about stupid-ass Joel and his naïve girlfriend. Who the fuck cared about what the hell they did? I had bigger things to think about, like spring break and whether or not I'd be going home over it.

I realized the girl in my lap was still waiting on my answer. I was hoping she'd just forgotten she'd asked me to go upstairs. She tried nibbling on my ear and I pushed her away. "Not tonight, Beth."

"Never *any* night with you," she huffed and stood up.

"Yeah, big Q-Man, what's up with that?" Todd asked.

Even Ella passed me a strange look before her eyes cleared. What the hell was that for?

"What's up with *what*?" I said. I knew exactly what they were getting at, but it wasn't any of their fucking business.

"You and chicks, man. You bat for the other team, or something?"

Here they go, giving me the business.

"I think Quinn's girlfriend might be his beloved car," Brain said, grinning. I wouldn't dispute that. I'd put a lot of hours into restoring my classic beauty and got pissed whenever I caught anyone leaning against her. Hell, sometimes I even covered her at night.

Before I could come up with some lame-ass excuse, Joel put his damn foot in his mouth and saved me the trouble.

"Have you guys *seen* the chicks who hang around after ball games?" Joel said, and Ella stiffened. "They are smoking *hot*. He could probably get his fill every night."

The table went completely silent as everyone stared at the floor or wall and avoided eye contact with Ella, who looked like she wanted to crawl inside a hole. Her normally bright blue eyes looked cloudy and worn. Talk about disrespectful. At least Sebastian had never done something as asinine as that in front of Amber. No, it was me who'd done something horribly wrong, while he had been only a few feet away.

I felt like punching Joel in the face and telling Ella to find a guy that respected her, but then the awkward moment passed, and Jimmy had to pipe in about the damn baseball groupies. "You hit some of that action, Quinn?"

I shrugged. Let them think whatever the hell they wanted to.

"What about you?" Todd asked Jimmy. The girl on his lap looked back at him, too.

"Of course," he said, and then resumed gnawing on her neck.

After a few more rounds of poker, I was down twenty bucks and ready to call it quits. By that point, Joel was practically falling off his chair. Even Ella had stepped up her drinking. About an hour ago, she had wandered into the living room, picked up a controller, and started playing *Skyrim*. She had a tall glass of beer sitting next to her, and now the contents of her cup were drained. She was probably still pissed off and hurt by Joel's idiotic comment.

I paused behind the couch and watched her play for a few minutes before saying good night and heading up to my room. I plugged in my headphones and lay down on my bed, hoping to fall into a less fitful sleep than the previous night.

About twenty minutes later, a loud clunk against my wall woke me from my reverie. I pulled a bud away from my ear and heard Joel's and Ella's hushed voices. It sounded like she was struggling getting him to bed.

Typical fucking Joel. I threw my headphones aside and strode out my door to help her out. Joel probably weighed twice as much she did.

"Whoa, there." I grabbed hold of Joel's other arm. "I got this."

"Thanks," Ella said, her cheeks pink and puffy from the effort.

I plopped him down on his bed a little too roughly and headed toward the door. "All yours. Lucky you."

When I got back to my room I changed the CD to something slow and soothing, hoping I could fall asleep for real this time.

But then I heard a gagging noise coming from the hallway. Regular Grand-Fucking Central around here. Coughing and then gagging again. I peeked out the door and saw Ella, hunched over and trying to make her way to the bathroom across the hall.

She was wearing an oversize white Sigma T-shirt. And nothing else. I didn't know what propelled me out the door again except that maybe I wanted to help her. What the fuck for, I had no clue.

But if I was being honest, maybe I wanted to stare at Ella's long-ass legs that were barely hidden beneath the bottom of her T-shirt.

"Hey. You okay?" I stood on the threshold of the bathroom door, wondering again what in the hell I was doing. "Need some help?"

Before I could get the words out, she dry heaved into the toilet.

That shit wasn't sexy at all, except her white T-shirt had

traveled up her ass and she was wearing barely there pink panties.

Ella wasn't a tiny girl. She had a large rack and nice, shapely hips. Seeing her practically bare ass in full glory stopped me dead in my tracks. I couldn't move my limbs or my lips.

What the hell was wrong with me? It wasn't like I hadn't seen a girl's ass before.

I adjusted myself in my shorts. *Shit.*

CHAPTER THREE

ELLA

This is so embarrassing. I was sick to my stomach but thankful that I hadn't actually puked my brains out. Nothing like blowing chunks in front of one of Joel's frat buddies.

"I'm okay," I said, the words like cotton in my mouth. My head was pounding like a steel drum band. "Th . . . thanks for asking."

Then I felt the heat of Quinn's body and his soft voice near my ear. "Ella, you need to cover up in case some drunk-ass busts in here and sees you."

Like him? Except he didn't seem at all drunk. He sounded . . . concerned.

I tried shrugging my shoulders but I wasn't even sure if they'd moved. Before I had time to register my next thought,

I felt his rough hands tug down my T-shirt. And then he took a quick step back, like he was afraid I'd think he was fondling me or something.

I laid my cheek against the toilet seat, praying nothing gross was stuck to it, while the room spun around me. Somehow I didn't even care. I just needed my stomach to stop sloshing around and for my brain to stop feeling like sludge.

Why the hell had I downed that last shot and then chased it back with a beer?

Oh yeah, because my boyfriend was an asshole and had made me feel like I wasn't even in the room. Maybe it was time I started being more truthful with myself *and* with Joel. Tell him how he made me feel and how he needed to cut that crap out. I didn't know why I'd let things that bothered me go on for so long.

"I'll wet a washcloth," Quinn said. I heard the faucet turn on and a vanity drawer slide open. "Might make you feel better."

Before I could protest, Quinn clunked down on the tile behind me and passed me the wet towel. My hand reached back but I had trouble grasping it; I was that squeamish. Instead, a low groan came out of my mouth.

"I'm gonna help you." His voice was low and raspy, and right then and there I wished this strange meeting were under different circumstances. That I could actually lift my head and look at him. Figure out what he might be thinking. Discover the true color of his eyes. Were they green or copper or a mix of both? Had he thrown on his university ball cap again or was his russet hair a mess of tangles?

I was pretty sure I didn't need anyone babying me, especially not mysterious Quinn. But I supposed it could have been worse. Jimmy, who always partied hard, might have tried to cop a feel alone in here with me. I didn't get that impression from Quinn. He was handsome and broody. It always seemed like he had a lot on his mind. Like he was pretty serious about baseball and school. And not about girls or partying.

"Okay?" he whispered. He was waiting for permission to touch me again. And, God, I appreciated that about him.

"Yeah," I said, another wave of nausea rolling over me. I swallowed the warm bile in the back of my throat and squeezed my eyes shut.

I felt Quinn's hot fingers lift up my hair and then smooth it from my shoulders. I attempted to hold in a shiver. His heat mixed with my clammy skin made my stomach do weird flips. Next, I felt the cool cloth against the nape of my neck and I let out a deep sigh. It soothed and cooled my skin.

"If you raise your head, I can wipe your forehead, too."

"N-not sure if I can yet." I swallowed back my nausea.

I felt his breath against my cheek. "Let me do it."

Why did this suddenly feel too damned intimate? I prayed that I smelled halfway decent and that my makeup was still intact and not beneath my eyes. I'd never been this up close and personal with Quinn and I felt like he could see all of my flaws. Hell, he'd already seen my ass. I wasn't petite like my two best girls. I had curves. Curves that Joel used to appreciate.

The question was: Why did I care?

Quinn was only being nice, and I was in no state to think it through more clearly. "Okay."

His large and rough palm slipped beneath my cheek and

gently lifted my head. He swiped the cool cloth over my forehead and then down the sides of my face.

"Hmmmm . . . so good." I sounded ridiculous, but I couldn't help it. It was nice being taken care of, even if it was by a virtual stranger. A cute, mysterious stranger.

"Can you sit up yet?" he asked, sounding a little breathless. "I can help you back to Joel's room if you want."

I shook my head a little too forcefully, causing me to pitch forward and dry heave again. I was suddenly glad I hadn't eaten any dinner. It might have ended up in Quinn's lap.

"Shoot." I lay down with my cheek against the cool tile floor. I could feel my T-shirt rising above my hips again, but I just didn't care. Besides, he'd already seen it all. "I'm just going to stay here for a while."

I listened to him inhale a lungful of air and then release it quickly. "Um, okay. I'm gonna bolt."

I heard him stand and mutter, "Fucking Joel," under his breath. "But I don't like the idea of you being in here all night. I'm gonna check on you again in a little bit."

"Wh . . . why wouldn't you want me in here?" I asked. "What's the big deal? I'll be fine."

"Ella, your shirt's riding up again." I heard him struggling for words. "You're in a house full of horny drunk guys and you can't stand up long enough to lock the door behind me."

Crap. I didn't think of it like that.

"But everyone knows me," I said, with some effort. "I'm Joel's girlfriend."

"Sure." He took a deep breath like he was contemplating saying something else. And then I heard him pace once, then twice. "No offense, Ella, but Joel doesn't exactly give the guys the impression that you're off-limits. Not like Brian does with Tracey. Not like I'd do . . ." Breathe in. Breathe out. "Never mind."

His words stung. But I wanted him to tell me more. To say everything. "No, don't stop. Finish what you were going to say."

"No, I better not." I heard his hollow steps on the tile floor. "I should go."

"Wait, don't go yet." What was I even saying? "Can you . . . can you wet that washcloth again?"

Why would I want Quinn to stay if I hardly even knew him? And why did he make me feel so protected, more than Joel ever did?

"Sure," Quinn said, and then swore under his breath. "But, Ella, you've got to pull your shirt down."

My eyes flew open. He sounded like he was struggling to keep himself together. To not have naughty thoughts about me. A strange emotion jammed in my chest. I was affecting have-nothing-to-do-with-girls Quinn? I'd admit, I was curious about his answers when the guys were grilling him at the poker table. Why *was* he never with any girls?

My hands struggled with my T-shirt. "Is that better?"

I was asking him to look at my ass again? *Brilliant.*

He let out a shaky breath. "Yeah, better."

I heard him run the faucet and then sit back down.

"Ready?"

"Yes, please."

He shifted my hair over my shoulder again and then I shivered against the coolness of the cloth. "Hmmm . . . feels nice."

I felt Quinn's fingers shaking and I wondered what the hell was wrong with him.

"Quinn . . ." I rasped out. He didn't answer me, just remained silent. But I could hear his harsh breaths, like it was taking some effort to contain them. Had I done something to upset him? Did he wish he hadn't stayed?

"I'm sorry. I probably shouldn't have asked you to stay. I just . . ." I struggled to get my thoughts out. "You can leave now. I'll be okay. You sound . . ."

"No, I'm cool," he said, and his fingers relaxed against my neck. We stayed quiet for another couple of minutes; the only sound was our breaths. It was a comfortable silence and I was glad to not be alone. He dabbed at my forehead and cheeks and then put the cloth back on my neck.

I wanted so badly to continue our conversation from before, but I didn't know him or his moods. Would he get mad if I pushed him about it?

"Quinn. Would you mind . . . if I asked you to finish what you were saying . . . um, before?"

"I shouldn't have talked about Joel like that," he said in a rush.

"Things haven't been right between Joel and me for weeks. And I'm sure it shows," I said, swallowing several times. "I guess I keep hoping we can work it out, make it what it once was."

"Which was what?" he mumbled.

"What do you mean?"

"I mean, what made it special?" His voice was low, soft. "What did you guys have . . . that's now lost?"

There was no sarcasm in his voice. Only sincerity. Honesty. Curiosity.

It made me wonder how many relationships he'd been in. Made me want to lift my head and see whether there was any emotion in his eyes. But I didn't want to risk puking on him.

All I had to go by was the sound of his voice.

CHAPTER FOUR

QUINN

"I don't know," she said, like she was thinking it through out loud. "Maybe it just felt like something more."

And then she went still, so I waited for her to finish her thought. I wanted to tell her that maybe Joel was the kind of guy who only made girls *feel* like there was something more, but I didn't want to hurt her feelings.

It's not like I knew anyway—I wasn't inside Joel's head. Maybe he'd kept her around as long as he had because they had something special together. Maybe he thought he'd try to take it to the next level, be more serious than he'd ever been with other girls.

Except, he sure had a hell of a way of showing it.

What the fuck was I still doing in this bathroom with Joel's girl? I was going to get my ass beaten. But shit, someone needed to be in here, protecting her. Taking care of her. Having a middle-of-the-night conversation with her.

25

And more. So much more.

She was only wearing a T-shirt and pink skimpy underwear. No bra. And her damn sexy voice telling me how good the wet washcloth felt against her skin almost made me come unglued.

And those legs. Strong and shapely. They could wrap around my waist so easily. With that dragonfly tattoo on her ankle that I wanted to know more about.

For a brief moment I imagined Ella being stone-cold sober, begging me to kiss her, touch her, and be inside her.

She'd have to be sober for me to touch her. She'd also have to ditch Joel. No way would I get myself involved in something like that again. Keeping things on the down low wasn't all it was cracked up to be. It hurt people. Even *killed* them. And you paid for that shit.

You paid every single day for that shit.

Fuck. I couldn't even believe I was entertaining thoughts like that about this girl.

Someone else's girl.

And then Ella started talking again. Her voice was soft and breathy. Like fingernails raking through my hair and then down my back.

I needed to cut that crap out.

Damn, I should've been glad she couldn't see my raging hard-on.

"You know that feeling at the beginning of a relationship with someone?" she asked. "When you're excited to talk to them, see them, and spend time with them? And you absolutely know the feeling is mutual? At least, at first?"

"Yeah, I do," I said, thinking about the couple of girls I'd dated over the years.

"Is that what you were hinting at before . . . before you stopped yourself?" She rolled her head to the other side and her hand came up to rub her temple. I reached over to do it for her before my fingers fell short. I needed to stop touching her before I started liking it too much.

"Maybe. I just think . . ." I rushed my fingers through my hair. "If you're going to be with somebody, then *really* be with them, you know? And if you have doubts or change your mind, don't string them along. Talk to them about it."

"Is that what you think Joel is doing—stringing me along?" She sounded hurt, like a wounded animal. And I didn't want to be the one to make her feel that way.

"Hell if I know," I said. "That's for you guys to figure out. I just know it should be him in here, not me. And maybe . . . maybe you should tell him that."

"How would *you* do things differently? If you were with . . . a girl." She seemed hesitant asking me. *Shit.* Did *she* wonder if I was gay, too?

Or maybe she just felt she was overstepping bounds.

If anyone had disregarded boundaries tonight, it was me. I hoped she'd stop asking me questions about Joel. Joel was *not* Sebastian. I just wished I'd had the courage to speak up to Sebastian sooner.

Before I ruined his life. His family's life. My life.

"First, I'd make sure the girl was *worth* it," I said, trying to hide the bitterness in my voice. It wasn't totally Amber's fault. I was just a weak-ass fool.

"What do you mean?" She sounded so sleepy. Good thing, because that was the extent of the talking I was willing to do about any of that.

27

"How about I tell you another time and you try to close your eyes for a bit?"

She mumbled something else and then all I heard were her soft breaths.

Before I knew it, my eyes drifted closed as well.

I jerked awake a while later. My neck was stiff from falling asleep against the wall and my legs felt tight and tense.

Ella had somehow managed to prop her head against my leg. And shit if my hand wasn't tangled in the back of her hair. It was soft and shiny, even though it looked like a long knotted mess in some spots.

What the fuck? Anyone could have walked in here and seen us. And I hoped to hell no one had. Or used their phone to take a photo or some other shit.

I carefully moved her head off my leg and then sprang to my knees. I should have done this an hour ago and been asleep in my own bed by now. I lifted Ella into my arms and then carried her to Joel's room. My forearm was beneath her ass, but I ignored the feel of her skin against mine.

The house was so quiet I doubted anyone had been up. I breathed a sigh of relief.

Ella shifted in her sleep and draped her arm around my neck. Her head was against my lips and hell if I didn't take a quick whiff of her hair. And damn if she didn't smell like almond shampoo.

Joel didn't stir when we inched inside the room. I slid her down next to him and got the hell out of Dodge.

CHAPTER FIVE

ELLA

Joel's loud snores woke me out of a deep sleep. How did I get back in his bed? I vaguely remembered being in Quinn's arms and fitting snugly against his hard chest. He smelled spicy and woodsy mixed together. Different from Joel, who, lately, smelled like beer and weed.

Heat crept up my cheeks when I remembered that Quinn saw me practically naked. I shot straight up in bed and then squeezed closed my eyes as the room tilted at a severe angle.

Quinn also said some things about Joel. Stuff I already knew but was afraid to admit.

I stood on shaky legs to gather my clothes. My stomach growled in protest at last night's events. I needed to eat something. And soon.

"Joel," I whispered in his ear while nudging him. "Want to get some breakfast?"

"Just wanna sleep." He smashed his pillow over his head. "You go. And bring me back something."

Anger flared in my gut. "I'll just go home to eat. I'll call you later."

I quickly changed and sprinted out the back door, thankful I didn't run into anybody on my way out.

When I walked through the apartment door, Avery was sitting in her blue scrubs on the couch, a cup of coffee in her hand. The distinct smell of nail-polish remover was in the air, making my stomach curdle.

Avery refused to let me pay rent. She'd convinced me to move in, telling me I'd be helping her out, since she was always at Bennett's place and her lease wasn't up for another few months. So I paid for the groceries and utilities.

She'd admitted she wasn't comfortable alone in her apartment anymore since her mother's ex-boyfriend had tried breaking in last fall. Even though he was now serving time on an attempted rape and assault charge, she'd said living here would never be the same.

"Thank God you made coffee." I sagged against the door frame.

"Good morning to you, too, bitch," she said, a mischievous grin on her face.

"Yeah whatever, dill weed, just tell me there's milk for cereal."

"Of course. You know I rarely drink it," she said, propping her brightly painted toes on the table in front of her. "You look like shit. What the hell happened last night?"

I stalked to the kitchen like a girl determined to eat after a week in the desert. "I drank one too many on an empty stomach and then got sick." I pulled down a mug and a bowl from the cupboard.

"What'd you do, puke on Joel?" she asked, admiring her paint job by wiggling her toes. "I would've liked to have seen *that*."

"Actually, Joel was passed out," I said, reaching for the milk. "But I did almost puke on *Quinn*."

"Quinn?" she asked, twisting to look at me. "Star-catcher-for-TSU Quinn?"

"Yep." My cheeks flushed remembering our night spent in the bathroom. The floor was gross, the lights dim, but Quinn's voice was warm, sweet, and all kinds of sexy.

She snapped her fingers and motioned to the cushion beside her. "Details now, asshead."

I moseyed toward the couch with a full bowl and propped my knee on the arm of the chair.

"I was struggling to make it to the bathroom," I said around a mouthful of cereal. Raisin Bran never tasted so damn good. "He kind of helped me. Even wet a washcloth for me."

"Seriously?" she asked, one eyebrow arched. "I can tell you're holding something back. Spill."

"It's just . . ." I huffed out a breath. "It was a strange night. He stayed in the bathroom with me and we kind of . . . talked."

She twisted her bottom lip, calling bullshit. *My* trademark tell. "That's all that happened?"

"Of course," I said, after gulping some milk from my bowl. "Do you think I'd actually cheat on Joel? Besides, it wasn't like that. It was sweet."

"Oh, I trust *you*. It's the other guy I'm not sure about," she said, folding her arms. "It's just that you sound kinda breathy talking about Quinn. Did we develop a crush on him while puking in the bathroom?"

"Yeah, like that'd be possible." It actually might have been possible, but I wasn't going to tell Avery that. "It was embarrassing."

Then my hands felt all clammy. "Know what else was humiliating?"

Avery went back to wiggling her pink toes. "What?"

"I only had on a T-shirt and underwear and I pretty much flashed him my ass a few times," I said, setting my bowl on the counter. "And *not* on purpose."

"Oh, I bet he got an eyeful. I *wish* I had your ass, girl." Then her mouth drew into a thin line. "Did he try anything with you?"

"No way. That's the sweet part. He told me to pull my shirt down and even pulled it down once *for* me," I said, plopping down on a kitchen barstool. "Said he didn't want to leave me in the bathroom alone with all the horny guys in the house."

"Really?" Avery said, dipping her head back to look at me. "Quinn just scored a few points on the good-guy meter."

"He also said some stuff about Joel." *Shoot.* Why had I let that slip out? Joel was already on Avery's shit list for acting like a douche the last few weeks.

She twisted to give me her full attention. "What did he say?"

My voice came out sounding strangled. Even I didn't want to admit it out loud. "He . . . kind of said that Joel wasn't that great of a boyfriend because he was passed out in the next room."

She aimed her nail file at me. "He's got a point, you know."

"I know how you feel about Joel," I griped. "We've definitely got stuff to work out. It wasn't always like this."

"I'll admit I liked him at the beginning. He seemed really into you. But lately . . ." She gave me a stern look. "The question is: How do you feel about him?"

I rinsed my bowl in the sink, feeling full and satiated. "I don't know anymore."

"Girl, you might be loyal to a fault. You need to take care of *you*."

"I know," I said, pulling down the dishwasher drawer.

"Out of all of us, you have your head screwed on straight," she said. "The way you worked through what happened with your brother . . ."

She stared at the wall, contemplating her next words. I leaned against the counter, wondering where she was going with this. Avery knew me better than anyone, outside of my family.

"I know I rag on you for your psycho bullshit, but I realize you take it seriously. And it's helped you work through stuff."

"Which reminds me . . ." I pushed off the counter and then plopped down on the cushy chair across from Avery. "There was a guy who called the hotline last night."

I laid my head against the arm of the chair, thinking about Daniel. "He reminded me of Christopher."

"Sometimes I wonder if the hotline is such a good idea," Avery said. "For Christ's sake, you had a brother who committed suicide in high school, Ella. Don't be such a fucking martyr."

My hand absently ran over the dragonfly tattoo that

Avery's boyfriend, Bennett, designed for me last fall, in memory of Christopher.

"You're wrong, Avery," I said, raising my head. On this fact I was emphatic. "Working there has been so rewarding. I want . . . I *need* to help people."

"Okay, okay," she said, lifting her hands. We'd had this discussion too many times to count. "I should know better than to argue mental health with you. I'm way out of my league."

A key scraped in the door, and I knew it was Bennett. The guy was pretty dreamy, I'd give him that. And if I was being honest with myself, Joel had nothing on him. Sure, Joel was cute and a decent kisser, but he wasn't straight-out sexy like Bennett was.

Or Quinn.

Where in the hell had that thought come from?

His height, his muscled forearms from baseball, his fit stomach and calves. I had always noticed him peripherally, but being in that bathroom with him had given me a more solid perspective of him. Not physically speaking, because I couldn't see him. But I certainly could feel him. His presence. He had a quiet kind of intensity that made me feel safe and warm.

In all the wrong places.

Joel was thin, without an ounce of fat on him. And it wasn't that I was fat, but I had hips and breasts and wished my stomach were as flat as Avery's. If I worked out like she did, I might get rid of it, but I'd never been one to love physical exertion.

I'd also never been one to care about body type, but there

was just something so appealing about Quinn. The way he moved, carried himself, with this gentle confidence. It was different from Joel, who was almost cocky.

"Hi, Ella." Bennett plopped down on the couch next to Avery and pulled her into a steamy kiss. Damn, they were annoying to be around. Hadn't they just seen each other a few minutes ago?

Avery pulled away, breathless. And then gave me a devilish grin. "What do you know about Quinn from the frat house, baby?"

I shot her a dirty look.

"The dude who plays baseball for TSU?" Bennett shrugged. "Why don't you ask your friend Rachel? Aren't athletes her specialty?"

My stomach twisted at his words. *Crap.* I hadn't thought of that. She did like her jocks, and she wasn't choosy.

Avery gave Bennett a pointed look that he seemed to understand. I wish Joel and I had a secret language we connected on. We didn't connect on much of anything lately. Maybe we never really had. I'd clung to Joel like he was my next breath, especially after I found out he'd known my brother. Maybe I shouldn't have done that so blindly.

Bennett mouthed *sorry* and then turned to me. "You know who would know? Nate. Ask him."

Nate was Bennett's friend. And he spent lots of time at frat house parties. But I sure as hell wasn't going to go around asking people about Quinn, like I had some lovesick crush or something. I had a relationship to worry about. To work out, if I could.

"No thanks. I am not on some mission to find out more about Quinn, for God's sake." I headed to my bedroom to jump in the shower.

I realized Joel probably didn't know a whole lot about Quinn, either, despite living with him. Which made him all the more mysterious.

CHAPTER SIX

QUINN

The bleachers were beginning to fill. I slid on my catcher's mask and headed to the batter's box to take more practice pitches from McGreevy. He was a damn good pitcher, had a killer curveball. But it was supposed to be Sebastian up there.

Bastian and I would practice for hours at Miller Park in our neighborhood after high school ball games. His fastball had probably been the best in the state, had even earned him a scholarship. I'd had to work a bit harder to earn my position on the team. I never had the kind of heart and natural talent for the game that he did.

Truth be told, there was a time that I would've rather been under the hood of a car than on a dusty field. It's not like baseball wasn't in my blood. It definitely was. The sound of the bat cracking, the murmur of the crowd as the ball hung midair over the outfield. You had to like baseball to play it so damn much.

I just didn't have a constant hard-on for it like my other teammates. I didn't want to make it my career. But I was good at it, and I could stand being on a team from season to season.

Working solo on an engine or a custom paint job had been my passion. My dream. My lifeline. Until the summer after high school.

"McGreevy, let Smithy take a few rounds of practice," Coach yelled from the dugout. Then he trained his eyes on me. "You good, Quinn?"

I stood to give my knees a break and nodded. Coach had complimented me privately on my dedication to the game. Said he admired my drive. If only he knew I was carrying the load of two players. Me, and one who should have been a star pitcher on his team.

I looked up at the stands just as my parents were headed to their seats. They came to a home game every few weeks. Not to actually see their only child play, but to keep up appearances. My father wanted it to look like he actually cared about his family while he tried to renew his seat in the House of Representatives. He was gunning for senator next and had some scary pipe dream to make it all the way to the presidency.

Mom loved being a politician's wife, so sometimes my only escape from that cold and empty home had been to go to Sebastian's house. His family was in politics, too. My father had helped Bastian's father win his seat in a landslide. The difference was: His parents were warm, open, *real*.

As Smithy took the mound, I gave the bleachers one last glance. Sebastian's mom waved at me and I tipped my head in her direction. The grief was still apparent in her eyes and the lines of her face almost three years later. She was hanging in there, trying to make it day-to-day, and that killed me.

When I saw Amber was with them today, my throat closed up. I struggled to swallow.

I hoped she wouldn't try to corner me again. I had no desire to talk to her, to have a powwow about what had happened that night. She insisted she needed to talk and I kept saying no. I knew she was only trying to alleviate her own guilt.

She was a pretty girl with her red hair and tight body. I may have had feelings for her a couple of years ago, but there was no way that I did now.

But she was still trying to keep up appearances with Bastian's parents. Showing up here, pretending like she and Sebastian hadn't been about to break up, that that one night hadn't changed everything.

Every single fucking thing.

Could I blame her, though? I was pretending, too.

Still, I wanted nothing to do with her.

I noticed my frat brothers on the other side of the stands as well. They attended the home games to show school spirit with our sister sorority. But this time I zeroed in on Ella, sitting next to Brian's girlfriend, Tracey. That was nothing new. She'd spent a few Saturdays at this ball field with Joel and his friends.

Her long hair was pulled up in a ponytail, showcasing her cheekbones, and she wore a red Titans T-shirt. I pictured her dressed in that top with nothing else on, except maybe those same pink panties. Shit, since when did I start fantasizing about Joel's sweet and innocent girlfriend?

I had always thought Ella was nice to look at, but something had changed that night in the bathroom. I needed to stop thinking about how she'd felt in my arms or the throaty noises she'd made when I'd placed the wet rag on her neck. I was being stupid. I knew she was off-limits. And if there was any bigger reminder of how unavailable she was, I had Amber here as a recap. She should have been a crude prompt to keep my thoughts and hands to myself.

Maybe Ella couldn't ignore how the air had become charged between us that night, either. She'd sneaked glances at me out of the corner of her eye, not wanting to appear too obvious. And she'd followed my gaze to Sebastian's parents, sitting with Amber. Maybe she was trying to figure it all out, and maybe she wondered if Amber was my girlfriend. She would be so wrong.

Ella was not Amber. And Joel and I were definitely not best friends.

But why the hell did I care when she was still dating that asshole? Besides, eventually she would realize she was worth more than that. And I certainly was *not* more. That thought was like an ice bucket being thrown at me.

Soon enough the first inning began, along with the music from the speakers. The lead batter was winding up in front of me, and I got lost in my job, gesturing to McGreevy which pitch to throw, based on Coach's signals and the batter's weaknesses.

But by the third batter, and no outs, I realized that McGreevy was being inflexible as shit tonight, calling off most of my suggestions. But I could be stubborn, too. I signaled for a timeout and jogged to the mound.

I placed my glove over my face so the other team couldn't read my lips. "What the fuck, McGreevy?"

"You want to know what the fuck's up? . . . You're calling shitty signals tonight."

"Yeah, then why are there runners on first and second?"

He toed the dirt on the mound in an angry pattern. "Because of your terrible calls?"

"My calls?" Man, he could be full of himself sometimes. "You're doing whatever the hell you want up here. Get your head out of your ass."

After a few seconds of our glaring at each other, Coach joined us at the mound.

"You two better work it out or I'm changing pitchers," he said. "McGreevy, trust Quinn's calls. He's good at his job."

That got McGreevy fired up. He hated how much confidence Coach had in me. To be honest, so did I. I was a nobody, lower than the earth under my feet. And someday he'd realize it. But for now I could pretend. I could forget how unworthy I really was.

After the game, which we won by two runs, my parents put on a show by waiting for me next to Bastian's mom and dad. I waved to a couple of my frat buddies and then walked over to the fence.

"Nice game, son."

"Thanks, Dad."

My mom leaned in and hugged me. She'd always touched me more when others were around. I'd desperately craved it from her as a kid. Thankfully, I'd been raised by nurturing nannies who gave a shit. And my mom's sister, Aunt Gabby. She was the best.

She'd pick me up and take me places with her own kids. My cousins' house was chaotic and loud and I loved every minute of it. It helped me blend in—even become invisible if I wanted—instead of standing out and acting appropriately as the politician's son. Especially when I was dragged to political events night after friggin' night.

Amber tried catching my eye but I refused to look at her. She attended a local community college and worked in her parents' bakery. I didn't know what I'd do if she attended the same university. It was hard enough avoiding her now.

The truth of the matter was: I was still angry with her about what went down. And frankly, I was afraid of what she wanted to say. That she'd blame me, like she did that night. I'd only ever read one of her e-mail rants before canceling my account. That had been enough for me.

"Thanks for coming," I said to Bastian's mom and dad. Damn, they were loyal to me and to this university. They still donated to the fraternity and Bastian's dad still attended alumni events. I knew they came to my games to try to hold on to some piece of their son. I could see it in their eyes, feel it in their hugs.

"Wouldn't miss it," Sebastian's mom said, and it cut me up inside. All I wanted to do was get the hell out of there and drink myself into oblivion or drive into a fucking ditch. But then who would they come see play? What would keep them going? "We'll come whenever we can."

After I showered and changed, I trudged to the team bus. Girlfriends and baseball groupies were lined up in their tight jeans and short skirts, waiting on different players. The guys looking to get laid that night would tell certain girls to head up to Zach's Bar near the university or they'd just meet them at their cars in the TSU parking lot.

"Great game, Quinn." I nodded politely at one of the girls, who had long blond hair and pouty pink lips. It was tempting to get lost in one of them for an hour. But I knew that feeling quickly passed and then I'd be alone with my pathetic thoughts again.

After exiting the bus in the college lot, I hopped in my car and followed the guys to the bar for a quick drink. I sat at my usual stool near the door so I could make a quick escape when my teammates got too stupid and drunk. Joel was there, at a table near the window with Jimmy, but Ella was nowhere in sight. I breathed a sigh of relief. I didn't feel like going home with blue balls again tonight.

I hadn't taken a leak since the beginning of the game, so I walked down the grimy hallway to the only bathroom in the joint. I didn't want to think about how many people had gotten it on in that bathroom. Once, I'd even let a girl go down on me in there and immediately regretted it afterward.

I waited impatiently against the wall, tapping my foot to the rock music blaring from the speakers, because the bathroom was occupied. The door swung open and I straightened as Ella emerged into the dimly lit space. I wasn't expecting to see her and my breath caught at about the same time as hers. Heat lapped at my neck as my body instantly reacted to her.

"Hey, Quinn," she panted out, shoving her hands in the back pockets of her jeans, which only made her chest stand out more. "Nice game."

"Hey," I said, trying to keep my eyes leveled on her face. But they kept swimming down to her full breasts and round hips. God, she looked hot in that baseball shirt. Even better if it had *Quinn #3* emblazoned across the back. "Thanks."

"I never thanked you for the other night," she said, breaking eye contact with me. A faint shade of pink stretched across her cheeks. "I kind of fell asleep on you."

"Not a problem, Ella." I noticed how snugly her jeans fit her shape, how she'd folded up the ragged bottoms to reveal her tiny red Converse kicks. Damn, she was cute.

"I should probably be embarrassed," she said.

My gaze traveled up her neck to her dark hair as I tried getting my thoughts in working order. "About what?"

She lifted her face and our gazes locked. Her blue eyes were mesmerizing.

"Seriously? I was hanging over the toilet. Wearing practically nothing." Her eyes widened like she hadn't meant to say that last bit and as soon as my gaze scanned down her legs, remembering how they had looked that night, her pale skin turned to gooseflesh.

I was surprised how affected she was by me, and I felt the urge to move closer so I could inhale her almond shampoo or lotion or whatever scent I'd smelled the other night. Warm and soothing and all kinds of sexy.

"Nothing at all to be embarrassed about." I took a step forward and noticed how she held her breath and curled her hands into tighter balls. How she looked at my lips and then at my eyes.

Then I heard a familiar voice. One I hadn't been expecting. "Quinn."

I squinted down the hall and saw Amber standing there, shifting on the balls of her feet. *What the hell?* No way had she ever tried to show up any place I'd been other than my baseball games.

"Gotta go," I said to Ella and stalked down the hall, swiping right by Amber.

"Wait." Amber followed me through the bar and out the door to my car.

I kept my back to her and picked up my pace. "What in the hell do you want from me?"

"Please, talk to me," she muttered. "Damn it, just give me one minute of your time!"

I turned to look at her, my fingers gripping my car keys. There was desperation in her voice. I'd heard that tone before. Whenever she and Sebastian had a fight. When she wanted to talk about what had transpired that night. When she called my cell incessantly the month after.

"Fine. Go for it," I said, leaning against my car door. "Although I'm not really sure what there is to talk about."

"I want to talk about what happened that night." I felt my whole body tense. It was enough to lie awake at night thinking about it. But to discuss it openly with her again? Hadn't we been through all of this already? I just wanted to shake her.

"What the hell about it? Just get it out already." I tossed my hands in the air. "You obviously have something huge to say."

She took a deep breath. "It wasn't our fault, Quinn. You have to start believing that."

"No, you're right, it wasn't *our* fault." I used my fingers for emphasis. "Just *my* fault. Mine and mine alone."

"Quinn, you've got to stop torturing yourself like this," she practically shouted. I looked around the parking lot, making sure we didn't have an audience. "I'm sorry I blamed you.

I was such an emotional wreck afterward—angry at the world."

I wanted to say she was right to blame me. That I was paying for it every day. But I decided to let her talk—get it out— so I could leave already.

"I can't help the feelings that I had for you. And I know you had them for me, too." She looked me in the eye, and I didn't deny it. "I . . . I need someone to talk to about everything that happened. You're the only one who understands."

"We've already rehashed that night, Amber." I folded my arms across my chest, maybe in an effort to protect my heart. "How many damn times can we do this? I need to move on."

"But that's just it. You're not moving on. You're . . . living *his* life. Not yours." She looked over my shoulder to my car. "What about your love of cars, your plan to own a shop someday?"

My fingers brushed against my 1966 Chevy Chevelle. She was black and sleek and the one thing I owned that I cherished the most. I'd helped my uncle Nick build her from the ground up. Now I regretted sharing that with Amber. She was throwing it back in my face.

"Things change." Whenever I'd stayed at Aunt Gabby's house, I'd wander into the garage and watch Uncle Nick work. Pretty soon I was holding a wrench and he was teaching me how to rebuild an engine or customize a paint job. My father bought my car off of Uncle Nick for my sixteenth birthday, after I begged him repeatedly. But I wasn't allowed to drive her until I went off to college. Dad didn't want me getting any crazy ideas in my head about being a broke blue-collar business owner. He'd been thrilled when I'd applied to TSU to become a business major. I focused back on Amber's face. "*Dreams* change."

"Not really. You tell yourself that they do." Her finger jabbed at my chest for emphasis. "That you need to pay your dues. That you *owe* him. But you don't."

I placed my hands on her shoulders to show her I meant business. "Don't do this, Amber."

Tears were streaming down her face, and she clung to my shirt for support. I felt terrible that she was such a wreck, so I pulled her against me and held her, rubbing her back in small circles.

"I need you, Quinn," she said into my shoulder. "And I . . . I still want you. I can't feel guilty about that."

I became rigid and then pushed away from her. She always knew how to twist the screw. How to manipulate me. I was naïve and inexperienced back then. She knew Sebastian was pulling away from her, so she went after me instead.

Probably because she wanted to make Sebastian jealous. And I fell for her. Fell damn *hard* for her.

"No, Amber. I won't go there with you. Not anymore," I spit out. "Go find someone else to fuck around with."

Then I wrenched open my door, cranked the key in the ignition, and pushed down on the gas. When I looked in my rearview mirror, she stood staring after me.

CHAPTER SEVEN

ELLA

I had my script ready to go at my desk. It was a slow night, which didn't happen that often. Usually the weeks preceding a holiday like Easter were the worst. They triggered all kinds of expectations and memories for people. But on sunny days like today, the lines were slow. The weather made people feel better somehow. At least momentarily.

My thoughts were all over the place tonight.

I couldn't stop thinking about seeing Quinn in the hallway at Zach's. How he'd moved toward me like he wanted to be nearer. I wouldn't have stopped him, either, even though my boyfriend had only been five hundred feet away. How messed up was that? There was just something about Quinn. Like being around him again had pulled me back into his orbit.

And that girl who'd showed up. Was she an ex? Did he still

want her? The powerful way he'd stared me down and then looked at her—pain mapped all over his face.

And then the way he'd held her in the parking lot. I couldn't turn away from that window. It was all tender and intimate, and it tied my stomach up in knots. But then he'd pushed her away and sped off, leaving her standing all alone.

Joel had done a fair amount of groveling after that night I spent in the bathroom with Quinn. I didn't mention what Quinn had done—which felt wrong, like he and I shared a secret. I didn't want Joel to get the wrong idea, because in truth, nothing had happened. Except that the atmosphere had somehow shifted between Quinn and me.

Joel wasn't a jealous kind of guy, and at first, I liked that about him. But after what Quinn had told me, I was beginning to think differently of him. Like Joel didn't quite care enough about me to be possessive. To make me feel like I was his and he was mine.

I imagined it felt amazing to have someone want you so much that they staked a claim on you. Like Bennett and Avery. Maybe they hadn't spoken it out loud, but it was obvious. They were all over each other all the time and no one would stand a chance getting between them.

I'd wondered on more than one occasion if Quinn was that impassioned with his girlfriends, and I had a pretty good idea that maybe he was. It seemed like he'd been holding himself back in the bathroom. He'd stopped himself from saying everything he had wanted to about Joel. Like his raw emotions had been right under the surface waiting to be unleashed.

He was so intense in the hallway at Zach's. It had been like he was crawling beneath my skin, trying to get inside me. Unless I'd been imagining it and my crush was purely one-sided. I mean, the guy watched me dry heave, for fuck's sake. How sexy could that have been?

I wasn't sure why I kept thinking about that gorgeous boy. It was stupid and dangerous. Besides, he was never with any girls—at least not recently—and even if he was, I was pretty sure he wouldn't choose someone like me. I was probably too tame, too straitlaced for him. I liked things orderly, tidy, with few surprises.

What I saw in Quinn—beneath the surface of his eyes—was something wholly uncultivated, despite his smooth exterior. Something passionate and undisciplined. And it made me want to throw all my rules out the window and feel wild and untamed with him.

All of these fantasies about Quinn were keeping me from facing some hard truths about my own relationship. I always knew Joel had been a bit of a flirt, but based on his "hot girls" comment the other night, I wondered if he'd cheated on me, too. The problem was: We'd never truly had a conversation about not seeing other people. It was just assumed. He knew I was a loyal girlfriend and so maybe he'd never felt the need to tell me he wanted me and me alone.

And here I was six months later, not even sure where I stood. I knew he enjoyed our sex life, because he'd told me it was some of the best he'd ever had. He denied up and down that he was screwing around with other girls when I'd asked him, but there was something in his eyes that said different.

I thought about telling him that we should date other people to see if he would take the bait, but ultimately, I decided I didn't want to play head games with him. Besides, if I was fantasizing about this other guy, did I really feel that deeply for Joel in the first place?

My phone line lit up and snapped me straight back to reality.

"Suicide prevention, this is Gabriella."

"Hi, um . . . Gabby?" The low drawl of his tortured voice made my heart practically crash straight out of my chest.

It was him, the guy I'd been wondering about. The one who I'd hoped was still alive. "Daniel?"

I heard him let out a gasp. "You remembered my name?"

"Well, not too many people call me Gabby," I said. I needed to continue talking to keep him on the phone this time. "I'm glad to hear your voice. Last time you called . . ."

"Yeah, I hung up, sorry about that," he said. His words were a bit slurred, and I wondered how much he'd had to drink. "I just wasn't ready to talk. And I'm still not sure if I am. But tonight I had . . ."

"Had what, Daniel?"

When he didn't respond I tried filling in the words for him. "Suicidal thoughts?"

"Yeah, sorta," he said. "I just figured . . . things would be so much easier if I weren't around."

I'd heard this same sentiment from many of my callers. They just wanted to know someone cared. Needed them. Would listen. "Easier for whom?"

"For the people I hurt. And for me," he said. "But I'm also not sure what's waiting for me. On the other side. Probably some form of hell. And I'm a chickenshit."

My heart clenched for him. He thought he was worthless. Bad. Would go straight to hell. What had this guy done?

"Why do you think you'd go to hell? Everyone makes mistakes. We hurt people when we don't mean to. Or sometimes, we even *do*." I'd had to convince my parents of this fact, because suicide was a sin so ingrained in their religion. A religion I couldn't stand behind any longer. Not when my brother would be condemned for taking his own life after having longstanding mental health issues. "It's a part of being human, Daniel."

"Not this kind of mistake. I don't think I can ever be forgiven." And then more quietly, he said, "Or even forgive myself."

"I'm here to listen, Daniel. And I'm not going to judge you." My fingers gripped the phone so hard my knuckles turned white. I was desperate to hear his story. For him. And for me, too. So I could help him heal. Or direct him to someone who could. "You can pour it all out and never worry about running into me. We don't even know each other. We're just on the phone. You're safe to tell me."

"Shit." His voice came out gurgled, like he was on the verge of tears. And then with one big huff, the floodgates opened, and he let them flow. He was sobbing and panting, so I kept silent, my heart lodged in my throat.

"It's okay," I whispered after several long minutes. "It's good to get those emotions out."

When his breathing finally slowed and he pulled himself together, he said, "Thanks."

"No problem," I said, my words clogged with emotion. "I'd like to hear your story, Daniel. We all have one, you know."

I heard him shifting and wondered where exactly he was.

I figured inside somewhere because I hadn't heard any car horns or other people in the background. I pictured him in his room, much like Christopher had been that fateful night. "If I tell you, you might not think I'm such a nice person after all."

"What could you possibly have done to make you think that?"

"My best friend." He choked on the word. "I betrayed him and then . . . I killed him."

What the hell? Killed him? I was out of my league here.

Am I talking to a murderer? No, I couldn't believe that. This was Daniel. The person who somehow evoked memories of my sweet brother whose life ended too early.

He was calling the hotline because he was hurting. Desperate. In agony.

"Killed him how?" I tried to make my voice sound level. I gripped my pen cap and it left an indentation in my palm. "Was it an accident?"

"That's what people think, yes," he muttered. "But I should've been more careful, been paying better attention."

My hand went to my eyes, rubbing them to keep my emotions at bay. I needed to stay strong. For him. "Oh, Daniel."

"Don't you dare say it." His voice was like a soft growl. Like he'd been clenching his teeth. "All those things the therapist would say. That no one decides in a split second to take someone's life. That I need to forgive myself, or my life will feel meaningless, too."

So he'd been to therapy over this. He was carrying guilt around. Wearing it like a suit of armor. "Okay." I was trying to remain neutral, to allow him the chance to talk.

"What the therapist didn't know was that I didn't give two

shits about my own life," he rumbled. "That I was already thinking of ways I could end it."

But he hadn't ended it. Which told me he needed to unload all of this. Unburden himself. That's why he was calling the hotline. To talk to someone he felt safe and anonymous with. My instincts were usually right. But what kind of guilt was he lugging around? Survivor's guilt or just self-loathing?

"What do you think of me now, Gabby?"

His voice was shaky, laced with fear. As if by knowing his truth I'd have the power to ruin him, take him down, or call him the filthiest names in the book. Like that would be any worse than what he was already putting himself through.

And that's when I realized just how vulnerable Daniel was.

I felt a longing in my chest to hold him, comfort him. Like I might have done with Christopher that night.

"I wish I could see your face," he said, never allowing me the chance to respond. His voice was fueled with anger. "I'd be able to tell what you thought of me just by looking in your eyes. Just like what I saw in everybody else's eyes. Pity. Disgust."

"No, Daniel. Not disgust. Not even close."

"What, then?" His voice became soft and timid.

"The truth is," I said, finally finding my voice, "I'd only have to look in *your* eyes to see a person filled with an overwhelming amount of guilt and pain. So much hurt that it's coming out of your eyeballs."

I heard him clear his throat like maybe it was jammed with grief.

"But there are layers to you, Daniel, that make you deep and complex and *good*. Under all that agony is an inherently good person," I said. "That's what I believe."

"You don't even fucking know me," he spat out. "I'm not *good*."

And then the line went dead. Again.

Damn it to hell!

Like last time, Daniel had called from a blocked number, so I had no way to get him back. Only in the case of an emergency did we involve the police or put a trace on a call.

Even still, I had trouble sleeping that night thinking about Daniel sobbing into the phone and hoped against hope that he believed there was good inside of him.

And maybe that's what kept him going. Kept him alive.

I wondered what Christopher had said to himself in the still of the night. The night he took his own life. What truths did he tell himself? And what lies—as he downed that bottle of prescription pills and chased it with vodka.

CHAPTER EIGHT

QUINN

I woke from a fuzzy night filled with vodka and rum dreams. I'd cried my sorry ass to sleep and hopefully my goddamn wussy tears were muffled by my pillow. Otherwise the guys would totally razz me or get on my case about being too stinking drunk.

I'd made the hotline call instead of playing poker with those jokers again. No way could I stomach any more pussy jokes—because I sure as hell wasn't getting any—or losing any more money.

Had Brian been home, he'd have played video games with me, but he'd been out with Tracey. Even Ella would have played, but she hadn't been around last night, either. Besides, being around her would have felt different. I'd have been too tempted to sit closer so I could feel her thigh brush mine and her breaths against my arm. Maybe get to know her better. I needed to get her out of my system, already.

I'd considered driving my drunk ass out to the cliffs last night and then maybe going over, but I didn't want to kill anyone else in the process. Sometimes, I parked there and stood on the edge, peering into the stormy water, hoping it would somehow swallow me up.

What Gabby had said to me on the hotline was probably standard. Possibly something she had to say to all the fucked-up people who called her. Regardless, it had touched something raw inside of me.

It was the way she'd said it. It reminded me of something my aunt and uncle once said to me, after Mom and Dad had left me home alone for hours. Nick and Gabby had shown up at the house to rescue me. I'd been old enough to stay home by myself but not legal yet to drive. I was shoving my clothes and toothbrush into a bag so I could stay with them for the weekend.

"It sucks that you can't pick your family members," Aunt Gabby said, standing at the doorway to my room. Uncle Nick stood behind her, his hands on her shoulders in a show of support. "But you *can* choose who you surround yourself with and how you handle what you're dealt in life. I hope you know how much we love you, even on days you don't feel supported."

"You are good, through and through. You hear me, Daniel?" Uncle Nick had said. "Don't ever forget that."

I'd pushed them away these past couple of years. I couldn't look them in the eye. They were like surrogate parents to me and I was terrified to see the disappointment etched in their faces over what I'd done.

Talking over the phone felt freer somehow. Gabby had been right about that. The person on the other end couldn't see you struggle through whatever you were telling them.

I knew there was good buried deep inside me. Otherwise, I wouldn't have been able to keep up this farce for Sebastian's parents. My intentions were good, even though I kept lying through my teeth every time I saw them.

So what did you do when all the good inside you was yanked deep into the abyss of your soul because of one big event? Was it possible for one act in your life to ruin everything else—to mar it, weaken it, poison it, make it sour? It had been for me.

Today was the fund-raiser car wash event with our sister sorority. I needed to get my butt up, especially since I was in charge of rags and bucket supplies. I had gone around and collected old clothes from the guys the other night and torn them into rags with Lucy from Sigma Tau.

I got my ass in the shower and then pulled on a worn pair of cutoff jeans shorts and a shitty T-shirt that I knew would come off when the sun beat down on us. It was an exceptionally warm spring day, the temperature already in the seventies, which meant more traffic would be sent our way.

When I walked downstairs, my chest tightened at the sight of Ella playing *Call of Duty*, and Brian.

As I stepped into the room Ella looked up and said, "Hey, Quinn."

I nodded and sat on the arm of the nearest chair.

"I was just dropping off bagels and coffee for the fund-raiser," she said. "But Brian practically begged me to play the zombie version with him."

"If you say so." Brian laughed and then shoved his controller at me. "Dude, take over. I gotta make a beer run."

When I looked at the screen, Ella was totally obliterating all the zombies in her path.

"Take *that*, sucker," she ground out through clenched teeth.

"You might not need me, after all," I said.

"I totally do," she said, her voice suddenly elevated. "Hurry, I've been hit. I need you to revive me."

I plopped into the chair Brian had vacated to save her from total apocalyptic failure. For the next ten minutes we yelled, laughed, and swore at the screen until finally being overrun by the zombie population and suffering fatal blows.

"That's the highest level we've ever gotten to," Ella said, holding her arms up in triumph.

We sank back into our seats high on our small victory. She was smiling ear to ear, and the way her blue eyes were so unguarded and sincere right then made her look angelic.

Yet sexy as sin.

I tried to channel my thoughts about what it would feel like to kiss her into something tamer. She must have noticed the change in my features because the smile slid from her mouth and she worried her bottom lip between her teeth.

I wanted to tug that lip into my mouth and suck on it long and hard. She looked down at her feet, a line of red creeping up her neck as if she could read my thoughts. As though she wouldn't object to what I had in mind, either.

I needed to rein in my goddamn imagination before I did

something irrational, and who better to help me with that than fucking Joel. He walked in the room holding a beer in one hand and a CD in the other. I looked away as my stomach clenched tight.

"Babe, weren't you running home to change?"

"Oops, got too caught up gaming. Okay, I'm out." Ella threw one last demure grin in my direction before hopping up. And I latched on to that smile like it was my goddamn lifeline or something. "Be back soon."

Fifteen minutes later, five cars full of sorority sisters showed up blaring pop music from their speakers. They were loud and rowdy as they put the finishing touches on the huge signs they'd made to hold up on both corners of the street. They wore bikini tops and short shorts and would have no problems getting boatloads of cars to pull in and donate money to our cause.

And ironically enough, the charity the fraternity had chosen to donate to was a fucking national foundation to combat child and adult depression. So maybe we'd be contributing directly to Gabby's salary after today.

The car wash always took place in the parking lot next to the frat house so there was room to spread out. I gathered up my buckets and towels and then came back to yank the hoses over there.

The next thing I knew the car wash was under way and cars were lined up around the corner waiting to pull in. I was so busy getting buckets filled with soapy water that I hadn't noticed that Ella had returned with her two friends.

One was a petite blonde with a tight little body. She was dating the tattoo artist all the guys in our frat used. They'd pushed me to get a tattoo also, but there was nothing I'd want stamped on my body except maybe something that reminded me of Sebastian. But then I'd have a literal daily reminder of my guilt. Not that I wasn't reminded every day, anyway.

Besides, I wasn't worthy enough to wear his name anywhere on my body, especially since I was the one who had taken his life. What scumbag would do such a thing? Did murderers on death row wear the tattoos of their victims, for Christ's sake?

Now I wondered if Ella had gotten her ankle tattoo from him. Bennett, I think his name was. I knew the other girl with Ella. Her name was Rachel and she'd hooked up with half the baseball team. She'd tried to make the moves on me twice before. She was gorgeous—I'd give her that, with those green eyes and full lips. I'd made out with her once at a party but didn't take it any further. Same reason as always. I'd rather mess around with someone who didn't hang out with my friends.

Ella's legs looked a mile long in those tiny cutoffs she wore. The straps of her black bikini top peeked out from under her pink tank and I wondered if she'd take off her top when she got hot enough. I imagined how she'd look standing in front of me in nothing but those damn skimpy shorts. Fuck, I was attracted to that girl.

Her hair was pulled up in a messy kind of bun and my fingers itched to reach up and release her brown waves. Our eyes met across the parking lot as I was soaping up a car bumper and I nodded at her to be polite. But she didn't give me one of her secret smiles again. Her blond friend eyed me, too, and then looked back at Ella with a smirk. Had Ella told her friend what'd gone down in the bathroom between us?

Joel certainly hadn't said a word, so I figured it had stayed between us.

And even if Joel had, I would've given him an earful about always being blitzed out of his mind when his girlfriend was around.

Joel stood behind Ella with his arms locked around her waist, yet he made sure to eye every chick in a bikini top. What an ass. Ella had to notice how he ogled other girls, and either didn't care or didn't care enough. *Which was it, Ella?*

Or maybe she was more insecure than I'd given her credit for. Why else would she put up with that shit?

Soon enough I got lost in the mind-numbing car wash assembly line. I was on wash detail and Ella was rinsing the cars with Joel. Her blond friend was helping with the cash drawer and Rachel had gone up front with a poster to flash her nice tits to the passing cars.

I heard a high-pitched squeal and looked in Ella's direction. Joel had the hose pointed at some of the girls and before they could scatter, he started spraying. He got Ella in the face and her clothes became soaked. She manhandled the hose out of his hands with a couple of other girls and got him back good. Her laugh was infectious, and I found myself listening for its sound as I continued to work.

Fantasizing about Ella was stupid, but it also let me forget for a little while. I was pretty damn sure I could easily get lost in that girl. And some days that was all that I wanted. But it wasn't what I needed. And neither did she. Not with someone like me.

We were running out of dry rags, so I ran next door to the frat house to gather more from our basement floor. I went inside and bolted down the steps. I waved to two girls who had emerged from the bathroom on the other side of the room. The bathroom was dank and grungy but did the trick for parties and events.

I heard the screen door creak open at the top of the stairs, letting in a sliver of sunlight. Ella came bounding down the steps wringing out her tank top, too busy to notice me. She stood in front of the bathroom door and lifted her wet shirt over her head. I saw the smooth skin of her back, her delicate neckline, and how the baby hairs from her bun had gotten tangled in the knot of her black bikini top.

All I could think about was sliding my hand down the soft skin above her shorts, on the small of her back. I stepped closer and cleared my throat so she'd know she wasn't alone.

She turned toward me, eyes wide.

"My bad," I said, my voice coming out hoarse. "Sorry if I scared you."

Her tits looked fucking amazing in that bikini top and I couldn't help my jaw from hanging open as I tried to rein in my dirty thoughts.

She stood stock-still as my eyes roamed over her body.

Like she welcomed it. Wanted it. Needed it.

Her breaths became harsher and when my eyes met hers, she held me there, transfixed. I couldn't have looked anywhere else even if I'd tried.

"You always seem to catch me in some state of undress," she mumbled.

I moved nearer and noticed how water had beaded in her cleavage. I imagined my tongue lapping up each drop, and my hard-on strained against my zipper.

"I'm not much better this time," I said, referring to my shirtless torso and wet cutoffs.

Her eyes skated over my shoulders, down my chest, to the front of my shorts. If she hadn't had a clue how much she'd affected me, she would now.

Gazes pinned on each other, we both seemed to lose the ability to form coherent sentences. I was close enough to draw her into my arms and kiss the hell out of her, but I restrained myself.

The air between us was charged. It was obvious and imposing. My knees quivered as my urge to hold her amplified. To press my nose along her collarbone and taste her skin.

Ella was biting her lip so hard, I wondered if she'd draw blood.

Looking into her bright blue eyes, I noticed her dark and thick lashes, the pretty rose color splashed across her cheeks, and the dainty hoop earrings she wore in her ears.

Both of our fists clenched tight, it was as if time stood still. Waiting on something to happen. For one of us to make a move. For someone to walk in and spot us huddled so closely together.

My own breaths were broken and rough and all at once Ella squeezed her eyes closed and inhaled sharply.

"Ella . . ." I closed the distance between us and placed my fingers on her warm arm. "Are you . . ."

I didn't even know what I was asking. I was lost in her earthy smell, her soft skin beneath my touch, and her lips, moist because she had run her tongue across them.

I noticed how her nipples had pebbled beneath her swim top.

"Do you want . . ." I skimmed my hand up her shoulder to the nape of her neck and she shivered against my touch. She gazed into my eyes and took firm breaths through her nose.

"Say something, Ella," I mumbled.

She shook her head and then slid her fingers to my waist. Her hands felt like they were on fire and my skin prickled like it might burst into flames.

The anticipation of this moment coiled tight in my stomach as I glided my hip against hers and pinned her to the wall. I was sure she could feel how aroused I was through the thin material of my shorts.

A moan tumbled from her mouth and her head fell back against the brick wall.

I leaned forward and dragged my nose along her jawline, resisting the urge to lick her skin. When I pulled back, the burning desire in her eyes was as palpable as mine.

I knew I shouldn't take it any further. Not since she was dating Joel. And I figured she knew it, as well.

But now I understood without question that she wanted me. And fuck, I wanted her.

When I heard the screen door slap open upstairs, I took several steps back and turned away. Ella locked herself in the bathroom before two sorority girls came springing down the steps. I grabbed a pile of rags off the floor, moved them to the front of my shorts, and headed back outside.

CHAPTER NINE

ELLA

didn't know what the hell happened to me down there, in the basement with Quinn. It was as if I'd become immobile and couldn't get unstuck to save my life.

My body was burning for him and all I had wanted was for him to kiss me, touch me, and claim me as his. Never in my life had I wanted that from someone the way I'd wanted it from him.

And that's when I knew I needed to break things off with Joel. That it wasn't right.

That it had *never* been right.

Even if Quinn and I never ended up together, it was wrong to be dating one person and lusting after another. Joel and I hadn't had sex in a couple of weeks. We hadn't even made out. I wasn't sure why he was hanging on, either, when he could be free to hook up with whomever he wanted.

Despite his dark shades today, I still noticed how Joel reveled in checking out all the skimpy-clothed girls. How he'd always done it, without regard for my feelings. And for the first time, it didn't bother me. It hadn't made me feel like I couldn't compete, like I wasn't skinny or pretty enough.

In one minute flat, someone else had made me feel like the sexiest woman on the planet.

Something Joel had never been able to do.

I'd get through this day with Joel and then decide the best way to walk away from him.

I made sure to avoid eye contact with Quinn the rest of the morning. I needed to get my thoughts in some semblance of order. Quinn shouldn't have figured into this decision, anyway. Sure, he may have been the catalyst, but that didn't mean I was breaking up with Joel for him. He'd only helped me see what was right in front of my eyes.

Besides, Quinn didn't date. So if anything, I'd need to decide if I could withstand a onetime fling with him. Could I walk away satisfied with the experience? Would I be able to get him out of my system? I'd never been that kind of girl. But maybe it was time to channel my friends Avery and Rachel, who were experts at that sort of thing.

For the first time, I was thankful that Joel was already buzzed, so I didn't have to talk to him about anything of substance. Instead, I tuned in to bits and pieces of conversations that involved Quinn, and I realized that despite being quiet and brooding, he also was fun and had a charming sense of humor.

And other girls obviously liked that about him, too. He had a parade of admirers swarming him during the car wash.

Maybe they realized he wasn't the type of guy to try anything. And maybe that's what made me feel so protected in the bathroom that one night. There were no expectations. I could just be myself. My very pukey, sick self.

And even in the intimate moment we'd just shared in the basement, he hadn't tried to kiss me. I knew he wouldn't do anything without asking permission. I think he might have been trying to ask, but he couldn't get the words out. And neither could I.

"There's a line of cars around the corner!" Lucy shouted. "We need more help up here."

I handed the hose over to Joel and headed toward the front of the line along with Tracey and a couple other guys.

"Where can I find a spare rag?" I asked, looking around.

"There's one in the bucket behind you." Quinn pointed and then got started soaping up the passenger side of a blue sedan.

I hesitated for only a split second before joining him near the rear bumper. "I'll start up front and meet you in the middle."

"Sounds like a plan," he said, stealing a quick glance out of the corner of his eye. My stomach swooped just from that small contact.

I began soaping up the front panel and despite our distance I could feel Quinn's gaze press on me like a wall of heat. My skin tingled with anticipation. I thought of something to say. Just regular conversation. It had been so easy with him this morning when we had teamed up against the zombies.

But the exchange in the basement had been wholly different, and so my nervous energy had gotten the best of me. All

I could think about was his mouth so close to my lips and how it would feel to be wrapped up in his embrace.

Thankfully Quinn had the wherewithal to break through the tension. "So, how long have you been a gamer?"

"Uh . . . not sure I'd call myself a gamer." I stopped the motion of my soapy rag to look at him. "But I know a thing or two."

"A thing or two?" He smirked. "You can totally hold your own, Ella. In *Skyrim* the other night you defeated Alduin at the Throat of the World. That's damn impressive."

I stifled a gasp. Maybe he *had* been paying attention all along.

"Guess I've been outed." I grinned and dunked my rag in the soapy water again. "I grew up playing with my brothers. They loaned me their first-gen Xbox for my apartment—you know, the white console? Suppose it's kinda what I do . . . in my spare time."

When I looked up at him, he was watching me intently, his rag barely slopping over the dirty sections on the passenger door.

"You missed a few spots," I said, and stepped forward to help him out. To be closer to him as well. "I figured you'd be way more anal given that hot rod you drive around."

His eyes lit up in a way I hadn't noticed before. "Maintaining a vintage car is way more exciting than soaping up these cookie-cutter versions."

"It sounds like it's your hobby," I said, tilting my head sideways as if that would give me a clearer view of him. "Do you restore cars, too?"

"I . . . I used to." His eyes took on this faraway look, and

I instantly wanted to know more. Way more. "But with classes and ball and stuff, it leaves little time."

"Oh, I don't know about that," I said. "Seems like it's your thing. And if I'm right about that, then you should *find* the time."

His bottom lip hung open as if he was considering what I'd said. Before he could respond, Lucy started shouting again. "Guys, we need to move faster. We've got five cars waiting."

"Guess we'd better step it up," Quinn said, and then rounded the car to finish the back windshield.

As the day wore on and the cars stopped coming, some of the guys fired up the grill and brought out the keg. We cleaned up the parking lot and brought the party back over to the frat house. We dried off, ate burgers and hot dogs, and drank some more beer.

Jimmy and Quinn took off for baseball practice. Quinn hadn't had a beer in his hand all morning, which told me how dedicated he was to his sport. Jimmy, on the other hand, was cut off about an hour ago. Quinn had to remind him that Coach would kick him off the team if he showed up drunk.

I walked home to change out of my wet clothes with Avery and Rachel. I hadn't had to twist Avery's arm too hard to help out today. She knew the cause was close to my heart. In fact, she clamped her mouth shut the moment I said the words *childhood depression.*

Avery was heading off to work at the nursing home and Rachel was coming to the frat house with me. They were having another party—a bonfire—that night and she hoped to hook up with one of the ballplayers once they returned from their practice. Jimmy had said he'd bring back some guys from the team, and she had her eye on the third baseman, Sam Riggins.

I considered not going to the frat house and saving my talk with Joel for the morning, when he was sober. But it was tough to dissuade the melancholy rising up in my throat at the thought of saying my final good-byes. And deep down I knew that I needed to see Quinn again.

"So, what's going on, bitch?" Avery asked as we turned the corner to our street.

"What do you mean?" Damn, she was observant. Almost to a fault.

"What I mean is, your stupid-ass boyfriend is drunk again and he was checking out all the other half-naked chicks at the car wash," she said, and I cringed. "And you're busy checking out tall and gorgeous Quinn."

"Quinn?" Rachel asked, and I almost murdered Avery for saying it out loud. I wasn't ready to discuss it yet. "Damn, that boy is hot. Made out with him at the Fall Fest last year. He's got a pair of lips on him that would—"

"Okay, TMI, asshat," I said, shutting her down.

Rachel raised her brows at me. I'd never cared when she spoke of her conquests before. She always told hilarious and sexy stories, but hearing that she'd kissed Quinn brought out the green-eyed monster in me. Where in the hell had that come from?

"See what I mean?" Avery said. "Did something happen between the two of you?"

"No!" I said a little too quickly. But I couldn't shake Avery's penetrating stare. "Well, kinda. Sorta."

"What?" Rachel said. "Ms. Loyal-to-a-Fault has something

going on the side with Quinn? The hot guy who never hooks up with anyone? Now I'm jealous. Spill it, bitch."

"Nothing happened," I said, almost tripping over a branch in my path. "I can just tell there's something between us. Ever since he helped me that one night in the bathroom a couple of weeks ago."

Both of my friends remained silent, waiting on more juicy details. I sighed. "Every time we see each other there's so much damn tension between us. At first I thought maybe it was just one-sided. But not anymore."

"Then do something about it," Rachel said, hooking her arm through mine as we strode toward our building. "Break it off with what's-his-face first, since I know you're not the cheating type."

"How *are* you feeling about Joel?" Avery asked, sliding the key into our lock. "I know I've been vocal about him lately. I just care about you, girl."

"I know," I said, slipping inside and yanking off my shoes. "I'm starting to feel . . . indifferent. Kinda numb."

Avery tugged her hair from her ponytail and shook out her blond locks. "If Quinn weren't in the picture, taking up room in your thoughts, how would you feel?"

"I don't know," I said. She'd brought up a good point. "You know things haven't been right for a long time."

"Then why are you hanging in there when there's plenty of hot-guy ass all around you?" Rachel asked, wagging her eyebrows at me.

I threw her a look. She knew that was nothing like me.

"Okay, okay," she said, folding herself into the couch. "Just *Quinn* ass."

"Why *are* you hanging in there?" Avery asked, grabbing us bottled waters from the refrigerator.

"I don't have a good answer. Been asking myself that question for a while now." I took a long swig of water. It helped wash down the anxiety bubbling in my throat. "He knows my family. And he coached Christopher."

"That's not a reason to stay with someone, ass," Avery said. "Even Christopher would be shaking his head at you."

I knew she was right. Somehow I had veered way off course in the last couple of months. I may not have been as bold or outspoken as my two friends were. But in my own way, I knew how to stand up for myself and go after what I wanted.

Avery sat down and placed her arm around my shoulder. "Joel may have been his coach, but that doesn't mean he makes a good boyfriend for you. Or for anyone. You know that."

I nodded, tears stinging my eyes. Letting go was way harder than it looked. Even when everything felt wrong. That was the reason I looked for constants in my life. And I should've known better by now.

"You can't just do this for Quinn, though," she said, smoothing my hair with her fingers. "You do this for *you*."

"Obviously, dill weed." I playfully yanked a piece of her hair. "Besides, he may be attracted to me, but that doesn't mean he'd actually go through with it. Or that he's dating material, either."

"Oh, to get that boy in my bed for just one night," Rachel said dreamily.

"It *would* be pretty epic." Avery winked at me. "You should try it sometime."

CHAPTER TEN

QUINN

Thankfully, Coach said this would be a short practice followed by a team meeting.

This breather away from Ella gave me a good chance to get my head screwed on straight.

She had a boyfriend, for fuck's sake.

I had already messed around with someone in a similar situation and it had ruined my life.

Lots of people's lives.

It had *ended* a life.

Still, I was so drawn to her and I didn't understand why, except for the fact that Ella was smoking hot. She turned me on in ways I hadn't felt with other girls. And so far as I could tell, Ella was cool and kind and real. Being around her not only revved me up but filled a quieter place inside me that I didn't quite comprehend yet.

Damn, I wanted to pound her boyfriend's face into the ground. The way Joel strung her along reminded me so much of what Sebastian had done to Amber. And it pissed me off. It brought out the caveman in me. The need to protect her, save her, show her what she was worth. Ella seemed like a smart girl, so I didn't understand why she was putting up with his shit. And it just made me want to take care of her even more.

I needed to stay the hell away from her.

Besides, what could I possibly offer her? I needed saving myself.

At Coach's whistle, the practice ended. The outfielders ran in while the first, second, and third basemen pulled up the bases to stack in the corner of the dugout for the equipment manager to put away. It was hot as hell out, and I was glad to wrench the suffocating catcher's mask off my face.

I helped retrieve a couple of bats off the ground and placed them in their rack. Then I sat my ass down on the bench between McGreevy and Smithy, wiped off my face with a towel, and waited for Coach.

"You threw some nice pitches out there," I said before taking a long swig of my Gatorade.

"Thanks," McGreevy mumbled. He was always so damn moody.

A hint of a smile appeared on Smithy's lips. He never showed jealousy toward our star pitcher and he could hold his own on the mound, along with the five other pitchers in the rotation. Besides, McGreevy only pitched once every few games unless it was playoff season, so most of his fandom was only in his head.

McGreevy was also pissy because he thought Coach relied

on me for team stuff even though Phillips, our shortstop, was the captain. He was like that damn princess with the mattress and the peas. Everything bothered him, no matter how small, and Coach refused to kiss his ass. It became tiresome.

Normally, smart pitchers like McGreevy called their own pitches during games. But he was so temperamental that Coach started asking me to study up on players the week before a match. Coach and I had gotten into a good rhythm of calling signals together and as a result we were up a few games on our biggest competitor in the league.

I couldn't help rubbing it in when McGreevy was especially irritable. "And I'll have some nice fucking bruises on my thighs to show for it."

McGreevy pulled his hat lower on his head and leaned back, jutting out his legs. "Fuck you, Quinn."

I took off my hat and pushed my hand through the mess on the top of my head. I'd never admit just how many knots I'd gotten in my shins and thighs from stray pitches. Some of them hurt like hell for days. "Hey, just taking one for the team."

"Maybe you should learn to catch better," he mumbled as he leaned his head against the wall.

I toed the dirt with my cleat. "Maybe you should aim better."

The other guys on the bench howled with laughter. They enjoyed our banter, and I'll admit, it helped me blow off some steam. Smithy was way easier to deal with and certainly not as uptight as McGreevy. He called his own pitches and didn't complain when I called some, too.

I had nothing to lose as far as baseball was concerned. Most of these guys were hoping to make it into the minor leagues and then to the big time from there. I enjoyed the game but not enough to want it as a career. I just didn't let any of these guys know it. I pretended to be just like them—like I could jack off to seeing my own stats and shit like that.

The laughter died down the second Coach entered the dugout, and a few of the players straightened on the bench. All eyes were trained on him. You didn't mess around too much when he was there. He'd bench your ass quicker than McGreevy's hardest fast pitch.

"We'll be on the road the week after spring break," Coach said, meeting each player's eyes. "I'll be checking the log to be sure you showed up to train before school is back in session. And I better not hear about anyone partying hard. That's an automatic suspension."

He paced up and down the dugout, hands on his hips. "But be ready to come back here and play some good ball. We've got LSU up next and then Michigan State after that."

He spit some chew into his red cup. That habit was some nasty shit. "They'll both be tough to beat, and we need to kick some ass, you hear me?"

The energy on the bench immediately changed as the guys began pounding their cleats in a rhythm that reverberated up and down the bench. We all put our hands in the center, yelled a Titans cheer, and were on our way.

"Joel said he'd replace our rum when we got back to the house," Jimmy said, plopping down on the bench in the locker room. "He's been making himself rum and Cokes all afternoon."

Just hearing his name fired me up. I slammed my locker door shut harder than I'd intended. "Fuckin' Joel!"

Jimmy placed his hand on my shoulder. "Whoa, where is that coming from?"

"Sorry, a little on edge, I guess," I said. "He doesn't do shit around the house anymore. He's only interested in partying."

"Yeah, dude's been partying harder than me, and that's saying something. Drinking for days on end," Jimmy said, removing his cleats. "I don't know how that girlfriend of his puts up with it."

"Yeah, me neither." My heart clenched at the thought of Ella being around Joel when he'd been drinking. Joel was more of a happy drunk, so he probably just passed out most of the time.

"Pulled that shit with the last one, too." Jimmy tugged a clean shirt over his head. "Last year, before you moved into the house."

I'd commuted to classes last year, but it had gotten difficult between the ball schedule, classes, and frat house events. I missed living at home, only because it allowed me the option to rebuild that engine in our garage. The reality was, I hadn't picked up a wrench since the crash. I'd tried a couple of times, but I just couldn't do it. I questioned whether I had it in me anymore. But something about what Ella had said to me earlier today about *making* time had sparked a longing inside me.

Right then and there, I promised myself I'd get back out there during spring break week. Or at least I'd give it a good shot. I'd go home, put up with my parents' bullshit, and get busy on the one thing I used to love most. As long as I pretended it was a hobby, I didn't catch any flak from them. Besides, I needed to finally finish the candy-apple-red paint job on the classic that I'd been restoring for years.

I wasn't sure I was ready to hear what Jimmy had to say about Joel, but I asked anyway. "Pulled what shit?"

"When he wants to get rid of some chick but he doesn't know how, he acts like an idiot," Jimmy said. "The other day, he hooked up with this hot piece of ass from the bar and I told him not to bring her back to the house because he—"

"Wait a minute, so he's full-out cheating on Ella?" My fists were clenched so tight, my nails were digging into my skin. "That's some messed-up shit."

"Whoa, man. What are you so uptight about?" I had Jimmy's full attention now as he looked me up and down, from my fists to my tight jaw. "If I didn't know better, I'd say you've got a thing for his girl or something."

"Nope, I just have a great dislike for cheaters," I said, trying to deflect his thoughts away from Ella and me. All I needed was a rumor to start that I was messing around with her on the side or something. She'd be crucified. But I wouldn't mind the pleasure of kicking Joel's ass.

"Been burned that bad by somebody, huh?" he asked, but I didn't respond. Let him think what he wanted. They all wondered about me, anyway.

"I hear you, though," he said, spinning the combination on his lock. "Ella seems like a cool girl."

"Yeah." I shook my head. "What a douche."

"When it comes to chicks, yeah," said Jimmy, heading toward the exit doors. "But it ain't my problem. I just want our booze replaced."

CHAPTER ELEVEN

ELLA

By the time Rachel and I headed back to the frat house, everyone looked spent. The sun had been blazing hot and everyone had ended up inside with the fans pointed toward the large family room. Some of the sorority sisters had stayed and Brian's girlfriend, Tracey, sat next to me on one of the couches. Rachel found her ballplayer and was sitting with her legs crossed on the floor next to him. Jimmy, Quinn, and a couple of other players had joined us on the periphery of the room.

Joel was on the other side of me, sweaty and groggy from the sun. I found myself staring at him—really looking at him—trying to remember what it was about him that attracted me in the first place. Sure, he was cute and charming. But could he and I really talk about things on a deeper level? Could I trust him with my feelings?

The answer came as a resounding no.

The longer I hung in there, the less respect I was starting to have for myself. Maybe others were respecting me less as well. Like Avery and Rachel. And Tracey. And *Quinn*. That thought alone propelled me forward.

As I took in the Sigma crest painted on the far wall, it hit me that I wouldn't be hanging at the frat house anymore after I broke it off with Joel. I had never truly felt like I belonged here, anyway. Come to think of it, Quinn didn't seem to belong, either—not that it mattered. It was bound to make things awkward all the way around.

All breakups were awkward, weren't they?

"Let's play a game," Lucy said. We were spread out on the couches and chairs, looking worn and tired, and Joel's eyes were slits.

At least those *other* girls weren't here tonight. The ones that hung around the frat houses all the time. The ones that made me just a little bit suspicious of Joel. Had he hooked up with any of them?

"Like what?" Tracey asked. "As long as it doesn't involve heavy drinking. I am spent."

"How about Truth or Dare or Would You Rather?" Lucy said.

"Ugh, sick of those games," a sorority girl named Katy said.

"I know a game," I piped in. "We played it in high school. It's called Five Fingers."

I hadn't played the game in years. Avery told me that she'd used the game to get to know Bennett on a weekend trip to one of his art shows.

"How do you play?" Quinn asked as he squeezed himself into an empty spot on one of the couches. Our gazes crashed for the first time in a couple hours. His eyes lit me up from across the room and sent the butterflies in my stomach into a drunken tizzy, slamming them against my sides.

"You ask someone a question and they have to answer in five words or less," I said, looking at Lucy instead of Quinn. "The more you drink, the worse you become at counting the words."

"Never heard of it before," Joel mumbled as if he was suddenly aware I was next to him. He reached for me and attempted to pull me across his lap. My whole body went rigid. Joel was on the verge of being sloppy drunk, so when he thrust his tongue in my ear, it had the opposite effect of what he was after.

"Stop it." I pushed away from him. "Not here, in front of everyone."

He tried shoving his hands beneath my tank top and I yanked them from under my shirt.

"You're never any fun," he slurred.

"If I'm not fun," I hissed in his ear, "maybe you should find someone who is."

"Maybe I will," he said a little too loudly.

Everyone in the room went silent, their eyes on me, seeing how I'd respond.

Quinn's jaw ticked and his hand balled into a tight fist. Jimmy jutted his arm out as if to hold him back. All at once Quinn yanked a pillow off the couch and flung it across the room at Joel. "Why don't you go sleep it off, man?"

The other guys piped in, calling him a drunk and a douche, and I was saved from crawling into a hole in the ground.

"Let's get back to the game," Lucy said, puffing out a breath.

"We can do boys versus girls," I said, swallowing roughly,

trying to make things seem normal. "One side asks the question and everyone on the other side takes a shot at answering."

Quinn looked longingly toward the stairs like he was going to call it a night, and I held my breath while he decided. I wondered if he would have gone after Joel had Jimmy not held him off. Was that because he disliked Joel or because of how Joel had treated me?

I needed to break it off with Joel sooner than later. No way did I need to be considered some damsel in distress who couldn't take care of myself.

"Cool," Lucy said, and all the girls moved over to sit by me on one side of the room. Joel was too tipsy to move, so he stayed put. But at least a few girls were crammed between us now.

"Ready?" I looked across the room. Quinn had decided to stay and I gave him the hint of a smile.

I thought of a question I'd want him to answer. I was curious about so many things. Who he'd dated. How he'd grown up. *Where* he'd grown up. Just . . . everything.

"Okay, five words or less. Describe your first kiss," I said.

The guys groaned, but Quinn's eyes met mine in a challenge. And suddenly I wished Quinn and I were all alone in the room, so I could ask him any question I wanted.

"No talking it out beforehand, just go ahead with your answers," I said.

"Why don't you go first, Joel," Jimmy said. "Before you pass out on us."

He nodded and I held up my fingers to count the words.

"Sexy redhead . . . behind the bleachers . . . tongue in my mouth before I could . . ."

I mimicked the sound of a buzzer. "You went over five words, dude. Not so easy, is it? Take a sip of your beer."

I rolled my eyes. *Like you even need it.*

The guys went down the line, using words that would only be found in some erotic novel—and in their wildest dream. *Boobs, short skirts, hot, tongue action. Full of shit* was what I thought. Nobody's first kiss could be that good. The girls surrounding me were reduced to giggles, and most of the guys had to gulp their drinks.

Then it was Quinn's turn. His eyes focused in on me. He looked sure of himself, in control, and hot as ever.

"Cousin's friend . . . backyard . . ." Then he shrugged. "Sloppy mess."

"Finally, someone with a reality check," I said, and motioned toward him for a high five. His eyebrows drew together right before his hand met mine in midair.

"No one's first kiss could be that great," he said. "You have to practice to be good at it. And not with your pillow, either."

That opened up the floodgates for his frat brothers to pounce.

"Quinn, my boy," Joel said. "Just how much practice have you had?"

"Probably not as much as you, asswipe," Quinn spouted off. "Besides, that's not something I talk about in front of the ladies."

His scalding gaze remained locked on Joel. And then he seemed to rein himself in by taking a very deep breath.

"Come on, guys, it's your turn to ask us a question," Lucy said. She settled into the couch cushion and crossed her legs beneath her.

The guys on the other side of the room congregated together. And before we knew it they were smirking and grinning like damn fools.

"We can ask *any* question?" Jimmy asked.

Uh-oh. I shrugged. I didn't want to egg them on.

Todd cleared his throat. "Describe your first time giving a guy head."

The girls groaned in unison. This was a bad idea.

"I'll go first," Rachel volunteered.

We made eye contact and silently agreed to come up with ridiculous answers.

"Gross, disgusting, horrible taste . . . puny." Rachel high-fived all of the girls while we busted up laughing.

"You guys are cheating," Jimmy said. "We gave honest answers."

"Yeah, right," Lucy said. "All of your first kisses sounded like they were straight from porno movies!"

After two more rounds where the answers got even more absurd, we decided to quit while we were ahead. Quinn's responses left an indelible impression on my brain. He'd described his last girlfriend as funny, smart, tall, blond, and older. That certainly didn't portray the redhead who'd showed up at Zach's bar. And I'd wondered whether he'd made it up just so the guys wouldn't razz him anymore.

"I'm heading up to bed," Quinn announced, standing up. "Got an early practice in the morning."

He didn't look my way and I was half-relieved. I didn't want anyone thinking we'd made too much eye contact. As he made his way toward the stairs, something gleamed from the couch he'd just sat in. I moved over to where he'd been, complaining about needing more room. I shoved my hand between the cushions and my fingers closed around a set of keys.

I'd take them to him before I left. I definitely wasn't sleeping in Joel's bed tonight.

Everyone else began moving outside to the bonfire.

"You heading out there?" I asked Joel as the room cleared. His gaze had been fixed on a blond sorority girl moving out the door. The same girl who'd sat on the other side of him during our game. He didn't answer me. "Joel?"

"Hmmm?" He turned to the sound of my voice, barely even registering me, and right then and there, I decided I'd had enough.

I was dating him for all the wrong reasons.

When I'd asked him questions about my brother, I'd gotten this sense that my time was limited before we needed to move on to lighter things. More fun things.

And maybe that was what it had been about all along. Maybe I was hanging in there until the next time he'd allow me an opening to talk about Christopher again. To permit me to live in my brother's world, for brief snatches of time, where we were both on the same page. Where we both could reminisce about the person I'd loved most in the world.

So maybe I was using *him*.

And, whoa, that realization struck me so hard that I had trouble keeping it contained inside me any longer. My lips trembled and my fingers clenched Quinn's keys even tighter.

"It's okay, you know." The words rushed from my lips. I needed to get them out.

"What is?" His eyes were bloodshot and scarcely focused on me.

"If you want someone else." I said it so low I wasn't even sure he'd heard me.

His eyes became round and wide. "I don't want anyone else."

"You certainly haven't wanted *me* lately. At least not when you're sober." My stomach was churning, but I needed to keep levelheaded. "We can talk about this like two adults. We've been drifting apart for weeks."

I realized I was trying to have a conversation with a drunken person. But sometimes alcohol could bring out the truth. And I certainly had my own truths to own up to.

"S . . . sorry, Ella. You're a good girl," he garbled. He leaned forward and placed his hands on his knees. "Didn't want to disappoint you. Or your family."

Tears stung my eyes. Damn, he was being honest.

This may have been the most candid conversation we'd ever had.

"I wanted to be an upstanding guy for you." He relaxed against the cushions and covered his eyes with his forearm. Maybe he thought I was going to slug him one. "I did. But I'm just not a good boyfriend."

"I know. I see that now," I said, more for myself than for him. I realized how much I'd neglected or ignored about him. Avery had tried to warn me. But I didn't want to listen.

And now I was attracted to someone else who might not *want* to be boyfriend material. So who was to blame here for poor decision making? But I knew in my heart that Quinn would never disrespect me like Joel had done. And I was at fault for allowing it to go on for far too long.

"I wasn't a good girlfriend, either, Joel. Because I was dating you . . . for reasons you probably wouldn't even understand."

I stood up, my knees wobbling a bit and my eyes welling up with tears. The shock of this honest conversation had left me feeling a bit off-kilter.

"It'll be okay, Joel. Maybe we can still be friends." I leaned over to give him one last hug. He grabbed my face and tried shoving his tongue down my throat.

"Joel, stop." I pushed at his shoulders. "You can't kiss me if we just broke up."

It was then that I realized he might not remember this conversation in the morning.

He tried thumbing beneath my shirt. "I'm going to miss these fantastic tits."

After I'd wrenched myself from his grasp, I straightened myself and smoothed down my T-shirt and shorts. I took the beer from his hand and dumped it down the drain. "You're cut off for the night."

Looking out at the blazing fire in the backyard, I noticed the same blond sorority girl close to the glass doors, watching our display. When I motioned for her to come inside, she stiffened like she'd been caught.

The girl timidly stepped inside the room. "Yeah?"

"I'm going home and wondered if you could give me a hand," I said. "I think Joel wants to head out by the fire and I don't want him falling in."

Not unless I pushed him myself.

Her eyes widened like she couldn't believe I'd be naïve enough to give away my boyfriend so easily. Joel stared at me with mournful eyes.

But when he looked at the blond, a devilish grin crossed his lips.

And that's when I knew he'd be just fine without me.

He threw his arm around her shoulder, practically mauling her chest. I watched them move out the door together.

"He's all yours," I said. She looked once behind her as tears pricked my eyes again. "Good-bye, Joel."

I sagged against the wall and played our conversation over in my brain.

I'd thought that by saying good-bye to Joel, I'd be leaving a piece of Christopher behind, too. But I was wrong. He'd always be inside me. Joel had just given me more memories of him. And for that, I was grateful. And right now, Christopher would probably be telling me that it was about damn time.

I gripped Quinn's keys and turned toward the stairs. I considered leaving them on the kitchen counter and going home. I felt sad. But I also felt relieved. And brave.

And those emotions thrust me forward.

I still had a burning desire to see Quinn. Even though I knew it might head nowhere good. I was leaving one fire behind and walking into another.

But this one was already consuming me.

I stood in front of his door and gathered myself before knocking.

"Come in." His voice was muffled and throaty, sending a shiver straight through me.

I nudged open his door and stepped inside. The only light on in the room was from a bedside lamp. Quinn was lying on his back, in only his shorts, atop a navy-blue comforter. As soon as he saw me, he sprang to a sitting position and yanked the earbuds away from his head.

"Everything okay, Ella?" I most likely looked a mess.

There were lingering tears in my eyes. And possibly some residual hurt.

I nodded and held up his keys. "I found these in the couch cushion and thought you'd probably need them."

He stood up and stalked toward me, shutting the door behind us. He grabbed the keys and tucked them in his pocket. "Did something happen?"

"Not really." I shrugged. "Just your run-of-the-mill college breakup."

"You and Joel?" His eyebrows slammed together. "I'm . . . I'm sorry."

But he didn't look sorry. He looked relieved. And that lit a firestorm inside me.

"Don't be. It was a long time coming." I toed the hardwood floor as if there were something interesting there. "You know that."

He sighed, most likely recalling our earlier conversation.

"You actually helped me realize some stuff." My eyes slid up to meet his. "Decisions I needed to make."

Quinn took another step and was standing so close to me now I could see his pulse pounding at his neck. I wanted to touch the smooth skin on his chest and work my way down to his flat stomach.

"Will you be okay?" He swiped a strand of my hair behind my ear. "Do you want to talk about it?"

"No, I don't. *Really.*" And I meant it. Besides, having him so near didn't help organize any lucid thoughts in my brain. "I'm good."

"Where is Joel right now?" His eyes stole to the door, as if Joel would come busting through any minute now.

"Out by the fire with some blonde," I said. "And before you ask, I'm fine with it. I basically handed him to her. Since I walked away, he can do whatever the heck he wants to now."

"I guess that means you can, too," he said, his voice deep and his eyes hooded.

I offered a slight nod, all I could muster with him standing so near. "I was with him for all the wrong reasons."

We stood staring at each other and the splash of moonlight through his window illuminated the intensity in his eyes. Specks of green and gold sparkled in his irises. He had stubble along his jaw and I imagined its roughness against my skin.

He flexed his fingers like he didn't know where to set them. And I wanted nothing more than for him to place them around my waist. Or in my hair.

"Why . . ." he said, and then swallowed. "Why did you come up here, Ella?'

"I told you," I mumbled. "To return your keys."

"You could have given them to one of the guys." He leaned forward and his body heat enveloped me. "Why did you come up here, Ella?"

"Because," I whispered. I reached out and traced my thumb along his full bottom lip. I had no idea what I was doing, just that I was desperate to touch him.

A quiet growl emerged from the back of his throat and all at once he backed me against the door. "Tell me why."

"I . . . I don't know." Suddenly I was scared. Of my desire for him. Of the chance I'd taken coming up here. I was being careless, which was something I'd never done before. I'd broken up with my boyfriend and was now standing in this other boy's room.

Quinn's fingers reached out to mine and he laced our hands together. "You *do* know."

I felt drunk on his gruff voice. On his touch. I was hyper-aware of how his calloused fingers were tracing lazy circles along my palms.

"It's because I . . . I like you, Quinn."

"You like me," he said, parroting my words. He positioned his knee between my legs, pinning me in place. And then he slid my hands above my head and braced them against the wall.

I felt vulnerable. Exposed. And completely electrified.

He dipped his lips toward my collarbone. "What else?"

I could barely concentrate while his mouth and nose skimmed along my jawline, up to my earlobe. "Tell me," he whispered in my ear.

"And . . ." I stifled a whimper. "And I can't stop thinking about you."

"Been thinking about you, too." He nuzzled his lips in the crook of my neck and an electric current hummed between my legs. His hips rested against mine and I felt how turned on I'd made him. It was heady.

"You smell so fucking good, Ella."

I pretty much melted like hot wax right on the spot.

"Tell me what you want," he rasped against my hair.

Then his wet tongue darted out and licked my earlobe. This time, I couldn't stop the moan that escaped my lips.

You, I wanted to say. *I want you.*

CHAPTER TWELVE

QUINN

This girl was driving me out of my fucking mind. I wanted to wrap myself up in her. Get lost in her for days. She'd broken up with Joel. And then she'd come to my room.

But I wasn't the solution. I was the problem. A big-ass problem.

If I couldn't even live with myself, how could I make someone else happy?

She'd start to hate me after a while. Just like I hated myself.

She was making the sexiest damn noise in the back of her throat and tilting her hips against mine, driving me insane. I couldn't remember the last time I'd wanted someone this badly. Maybe I never had.

I still had her hands pinned to the wall and I could feel her soft breasts bumping up against my chest. I wanted to strip her naked and run my tongue along her skin. Taste her everywhere. Hold her until the sun came up in the morning.

"Quinn," she breathed against my hair. "I need . . . I want . . . *please*."

I pulled back to look at her. There was desperation in her eyes. She wanted me just as badly as I wanted her. I released her fingers and cupped her soft cheeks in my hands.

"I'm not going to kiss you, Ella. Not tonight."

She sagged against me, her forehead landing on my shoulder.

"Kissing you would be too easy," I whispered in her ear. "And you're not a girl I want to be easy with."

"I get it, okay? You don't date. I remember you said . . . you said that." She said those words into my shoulder. But now she raised her head to meet my eyes. There was determination in them. "I knew that coming here. And I'm okay with whatever happens."

She was telling me that she knew she might be a fling. And that didn't sit well with me. This girl needed more. She needed someone to give her everything.

And I couldn't do that. I wasn't good enough for her. I wasn't strong enough to give her anything more.

"Is that what you think? You think someone as incredible as you wouldn't be worth my time?" I pushed away from the wall and sat down hard on the edge of my bed. "I don't date girls because . . . I can't . . . I'm not . . ."

Her eyes were round and shiny. "Because of that girl in the parking lot at Zach's?"

My back straightened. Had she been spying on Amber and me?

That was the cold splash of reality I needed.

"Yes and no. Not because I still want her. But she's part of my past and it's a past I'd like to forget," I said. "And you bringing her up reminds me of why I shouldn't be doing this *again*."

She knelt down in front of me. "Doing what again?"

I didn't respond. I wasn't going there with her. With anybody. I'd already said too much.

"I'm sorry. I'm not trying to pry," she said. "I'm just trying to understand you."

Had anyone ever said that to me before? Had anyone even taken the time to care?

"Look, I've never done this before," she said, gesturing between us. "I've never been so reckless. Here I am throwing myself at you and you don't even want me. I must look like an idiot."

She stood up and balled her fists. Her hands were shaking.

And she couldn't have been more wrong.

"You think I don't want you?" I reached for her waist and yanked her toward me. I gripped her sweet ass and tipped my head to rest on her stomach. Her fingers fisted my hair and I felt her harsh breaths against my neck.

"If I kiss you, Ella, I won't be able to stop," I said. "I'd want more, and that can't happen. I'm just not . . . it just . . . can't."

I felt her stomach quiver and then her fingers loosened their grasp in my hair. "I don't know you very well, Quinn. But I'd like to."

She cupped my chin and forced me to look at her. "I don't understand why you're fighting this so hard. God, I made it so

95

easy for you." She leaned her face toward mine and I felt her warm breath on my lips. "So for whatever it's worth, I think you're amazing."

My chest squeezed into a tight fist and I bit my lip to keep my emotions in check.

She backed away from me, turned, and walked out the door.

Worst of all, I let her.

CHAPTER THIRTEEN

ELLA

t was the night before spring break, and I was volunteering at the suicide hotline. In the morning, I would be headed home for a long weekend. The phone lines were lit up tonight, as I knew they would be right before a holiday.

It helped keep my mind off Quinn and what he'd said to me that one night last week. Avery thought it was cavalier of him to push me away if he knew he was fucked-up. Her words, not mine. She'd done much of the same when she'd started crushing hard on Bennett last fall. It was nice to have her perspective. But it didn't lessen the want. The need. The desire to see him.

To make matters worse, I didn't miss Joel all that much. I'd seen him around campus with different girls. Like he'd unleashed himself on the female population again. He was free and raring to go.

It was strange to not have an excuse to go to the frat house anymore. Tracey had called to ask what happened between Joel and me and I'd been tempted to question her about Quinn. To spill the beans and see what she knew about him. I also considered showing up at his ball games, but I didn't want to look like a stalker.

A student volunteer named Lizzy gave an exasperated huff across the hall. "I'm getting a lot of hang-ups tonight; are you guys?"

"Nope, I haven't. But it's almost spring break, so it makes sense," I said. Steve, another volunteer on with us tonight, was busy on a call. Sometimes, hang-ups meant people were just too scared to go through with the call. It was frustrating on both sides.

I couldn't even finish my thought because my phone line lit up again.

"Suicide prevention. Gabriella speaking."

"I was beginning to think you weren't working tonight, Gabby."

My heart vaulted into my throat. "Daniel."

Had he been hanging up on the other lines until he reached me?

I swallowed several times before answering. "You having a hard time tonight?"

"How'd you guess?"

"I figured you wouldn't want to chill on the phone with me if you weren't." I was going for humor, but I wasn't sure if he'd appreciate that. So far, he'd been unpredictable.

"True. But I like talking to you, Gabby," he said. "You make me feel . . ."

"Feel what?" I had no clue why I hung on this guy's every word. He brought out some protective instinct in me.

Long silence. This time I could hear the wind in the background and the sound of cars swishing by. "Like I . . . matter."

"Oh, Daniel." An emotion I didn't recognize slammed into my chest and I tried not to vocalize it. All I could think about was whether Christopher had felt like he mattered. Had I told him enough times how much he'd meant to me? I knew from experience that what-ifs were useless and that loving homes didn't necessarily dissuade suicidal acts.

We had a loud and active family, and maybe Christopher had felt lost in the shuffle sometimes. He was the quiet and reflective sibling who spent lots of time alone in his room. But it would have helped to know that Christopher had felt loved before he'd decided he was ready to die.

"Gabby?"

"I'm here," I said. Shit, I didn't want him to think that I'd abandoned him. "What you just said made me feel . . . emotional."

I heard his uneven breaths.

"I do think you matter, Daniel. To a lot of people." I recognized the honk of a car horn and I imagined him sitting in a public park or maybe pulled over on the side of the road. "And to me."

"How could I matter to *you*?" His voice had pitched. "I'm just a voice on the end of a phone line."

"You're much more than that, Daniel," I said. "Don't you realize that every time you've hung up I've wondered for days if you were all right?"

"You have?" His voice was hoarse, as if he'd been gulping in air.

"Of course I have. Sure, this is my job," I said, "but I have feelings, too."

"Oh." His voice sounded incredulous. "Yeah . . . yeah, of course you do."

Did he have someone in his life who told him that he mattered?

My supervisor stood at the door listening, checking whether I needed any assistance. He used to stay in the room at the beginning of the semester, and then gradually allowed more independence and responsibility. I gave him the thumbs-up that all was okay and tuned back in to Daniel.

"Do you have anything you'd like to talk about, Daniel?" I asked, hoping that he finally felt safe enough to confide in me.

"I . . . uh, maybe. I'm not sure."

"Why don't we begin slowly. About that night. The night of the accident," I said, hoping my voice sounded soothing instead of nervous. "I mean, if you feel ready to tell me."

"I . . . I think I do."

"I'm here. You can trust me to listen." I realized I'd been bracing my knuckles so hard that I'd left indentations in the sides of my paper cup.

"We went to a party that night." He blew out a long breath. Like he was gearing himself up. To bare his soul. "I was the designated driver, and I drove my best friend and his girlfriend."

I tried picturing what Daniel might look like. I also wondered why he hadn't taken his own girlfriend with him that night. Did he hang out with only the two of them a lot? Like a third wheel?

"My best friend was being a dick to his girlfriend that

night. They'd been fighting lately. And what he didn't know was I'd been crushing on her *hard*." He said that last part in a whisper. That answered my question about why he wasn't with anybody else. "And she knew how I felt. I think she played me because of it. She and I had been sharing looks all night. I thought it was something intimate, but in hindsight, I wondered if she'd wanted to make him jealous."

"Why would she do that?"

"He was a huge flirt and had been in his element that night. All the girls loved him. Would've wanted their chance with him. He was into his girlfriend, but I noticed he had been getting bored." He huffed. "It was his pattern."

My heart was slamming against my rib cage. Even though I hadn't heard this story before, it felt too close. Too powerful. Too personal.

"How do you know she didn't have true feelings for you?"

"I didn't really. I just knew the effect Bas . . . um, my best friend had on the ladies." *Bas.* The beginning of a name or a nickname. He'd chosen to keep the names private. And I understood that, so I let it go. This was his story to tell.

"How were you different from your best friend?"

"I was always more quiet. Kept to myself. He was the life of the party." Something about the way he described himself reminded me of something else. Of someone else. It felt so familiar. I shook the feeling away to listen to his story.

"My best friend got trashed and his girlfriend and I got him in the backseat of the car, where he passed out." I heard him sniffling, and I wondered how many different emotions this stirred in him. "The last words he said to me were 'I . . . I love you, man.'"

A keening sound I'd never heard before tumbled from Daniel's lips, and a chill shot straight down my spine. My stomach was clenched so tightly into a ball that I needed to stretch my spine in order to loosen the dread that had taken hold.

And then Daniel let himself go. He let it all pour out—like a wound ripping open and bleeding—as he sobbed into the phone. I stayed silent, giving him the time to work through his emotions. Sometimes the noise sounded muffled like he'd put down his phone or held his hand over the speaker.

I knew from experience that crying was healing, purifying, cleansing to the soul. I'd done my fair share of crying over Christopher—gut-wrenching, heart-splitting, can't-catch-your-breath kind of bawling. I never would've been able to move forward without fully experiencing that hell—it was the only way out.

Finally, Daniel sniffled and caught his breath, composed again. "I'm . . . I'm sorry."

"You have absolutely nothing to be sorry about."

"I'd forgotten he'd said that to me," Daniel said, his voice raw from crying. "Do you think he knew?"

"That he was going to die?" I said, my voice light and pensive. "Some people believe that. But I'm not sure."

We fell into a comfortable kind of silence, and I waited for him to tell me more.

"His girlfriend sat in the front seat next to me while he was laid out in back. On our way home, she slid her fingers over and placed her hand in mine." He paused, maybe to reminisce about that moment in time. "My palm was sweaty and my heart was all erratic and, man, I had it so bad for her."

I pictured this scene in my head, how it might have felt for your crush to respond to you, to like you back. Even though it might have been bad timing, it didn't mean it wasn't real.

"You said that your best friend was passed out in the backseat. So she couldn't have been putting on a show for him—not right then."

He didn't say anything for a long moment, considering my words.

"Unless she was just setting me up for later," he said.

He had built up these walls, not allowing any positive thoughts to seep inside. He would only accept that he was bad, that he was wrong, that he didn't measure up.

"It seems you so easily believe there's no way she could've liked you for *you*," I said. "Am I right?"

CHAPTER FOURTEEN

QUINN

held in a gasp. *Fuck, that was a loaded question.*

Here I was pouring my heart out to a perfect stranger and she asked me the one question I'd refused to ask myself. Never thought I was worthy enough to ask myself.

How come this stranger got closer to the true me than anyone had in a long time?

Except maybe for Ella. We were drawn to each other. It was natural. Hypnotic. Magic. And Ella had the same soothing tone as Gabby, like I could tell her anything. Except telling her everything would make her loathe me. And telling Gabby was what she was trained to do.

"I . . . I don't know. All this time, that's what I'd told my-self." I thought about what Amber had said in the parking lot that night. About still wanting me. I thought she'd been mess-ing with my head.

"I guess I've always felt like I was only an obligation or a chore to people," I said.

"Is that why you put so little stake in yourself?" Her voice was soft, soothing.

How in the hell had she guessed my deepest secrets?

"Maybe." She'd pretty much hit the nail on the head. I immediately thought of my parents and maybe even Sebastian. I never stood up to him; I just fucking worshipped him. He had everything I didn't. He was everything I wasn't.

Maybe in the back of my mind I was glad he was dead.

"I just think . . . I just know . . ." I was having so much trouble getting the words to line up on my lips because they were so shocking, so mind-boggling. Could I even voice them out loud? "Maybe I would have done anything to get with her that night. What if I . . . did I . . . kill him on purpose?"

I'm sorry, Sebastian. I didn't mean that. My head was so messed up. *Fuck. Fuck. FUCK!*

I heard Gabby take a deep and meaningful breath. "Do you honestly believe that, Daniel?"

"Fuck, I don't know," I whispered. "No, that's not true. I do know. And the answer is . . . no. At least not consciously."

"Of course not, Daniel." She said it so resolutely that even I might have believed her. "Besides, thinking it and doing it are two different things. Maybe you wanted him to disappear for a while, so you'd have a chance with this girl. But you didn't want your friend dead."

"Yeah, okay."

And then I was lost in my own thoughts for long moments. And she let me be lost.

Until finally, I repeated, "Yeah, okay."

"So how did your night end?" she asked. "Your best friend was in the backseat and the girl you were crushing on was holding your hand in the front seat."

"I got distracted. By her. And my own thoughts. I kept thinking he was going to wake up any minute and see that I was betraying him," I said, sharing what I had never once uttered out loud. "I should have said no, let go of her hand. Told her to break up with him first."

I thought of me and Ella. How close we'd gotten with our flirting. I told myself I wasn't going to cross that line again, and I wouldn't have. Even in the basement, when I was desperate just to touch her.

But then she broke up with her boyfriend, showed up in my room, and called my bluff. I was out of excuses. It was just me and Ella, free to act on our feelings. And I chumped out on her. Because still, somewhere deep inside, I didn't believe that a girl could like me—really like me—for me. Just me. *All* of me.

"What happened next?" Gabby broke me from my self-pity.

"I don't know exactly. To this day, the details are still shady. There was a truck in the next lane over, hauling ass. I must have veered over the line, and we sideswiped each other. I lost control of the car—we were sent into a tailspin."

I shut my eyes and relived that moment. The brunt of the impact. The sound of crunched steel, shattered glass. Losing control of the wheel. Amber screaming.

"My best friend flew out the side window. My air bag

went off, and his girlfriend . . . she smashed her head against the dash, but her seat belt saved her."

"So it *was* an accident," she said very quietly.

I felt my anger building up but not to an all-consuming intensity this time. "I was being careless, not paying attention, and my best friend paid for it with his life."

I placed my head in my hands and rocked back and forth. "He died and I'm still alive."

"And that kind of devastation is the hardest to bear," she said with such empathy in her voice. "I know."

She said it like she really did know. Like she'd been through it, lived it, carried it inside her.

"What happened to the truck driver?"

"He survived," I said.

I wouldn't tell her that my parents had paid him off.

I had shared so much with her tonight, so why was that one piece of information so hard?

Because it was humiliating.

The truck driver had said he was sketchy on the details as well—who had swerved into whose lane. But then my parents became involved, spoke to the police, to Sebastian's family, to the driver, whom they paid off, to make it all go away in a neat and tidy package. Like it never happened.

Except that one person was gone forever.

And another was broken and lost, possibly for eternity.

I should have yelled and screamed and told the police to put me in jail. Even Amber had blamed me. Asked me why I hadn't seen the truck sooner as she cried over Sebastian's body on the side of the road, a huge knot protruding from her forehead.

It was the worst sight I'd ever witnessed in my entire life. One I'd never forget. Like it had been singed into the backs of my eyelids. I'd felt so horribly responsible that I'd retched right there in the grass near a blanket of shattered glass.

But a couple of nights later, my father came into my room, slapped me across the face, and told me to get hold of myself. Said I would not ruin my life and his chances of running for office. Said the driver agreed to take the lesser plea and get the hell out of town. That Sebastian's parents agreed it would all be for the best and wanted to put it behind them.

They never blamed me and they never would. The driver had taken responsibility.

Didn't my father realize that by paying people off, he was already blaming me? Me, his only child. It was the same as saying, *You're a fuckup. I don't believe in you. I'm going to pay off someone to make sure it remains a secret—the real you remains a secret.*

The following day, Aunt Gabby came over while I continued to barricade myself in my room. I listened to their muffled argument through the door. She told her sister that I deserved more. And then Mom kicked her out of the house.

Their relationship had been strained ever since. Not that it hadn't been before that. Aunt Gabby and Mom were different as night and day and sometimes I'd lie awake in bed and wish I'd been born into Aunt Gabby's family instead.

"What keeps you going, Daniel?" Gabby asked in a dreamy, faraway voice. "You *haven't* ended your life, and I'm thankful for that. So what is it that makes living worth it?"

"I . . . I don't know." I thought about how I was trying to

make it up to Sebastian's parents. My drive to do that had replaced my desire for my parents to see me succeed.

"*Sometimes* . . . I mean, really, *all* this time, I've been trying to keep myself alive for his parents."

"For your best friend's parents?" she asked, with an incredulous tone in her voice.

"Yeah, I mean, so that I guess . . . so they'd have someone to check in with. So that I hadn't abandoned them, too."

"Wow, Daniel that's really . . . selfless."

"Selfless? I just . . . I've been filled with so much guilt, I figured it's the least I could do," I said. "But that doesn't really answer your question. It certainly doesn't make my life worth living. Not really. I don't know what the fuck does anymore."

"I hope when you figure it out you'll call back and let me know," she said, like she wanted me to make a promise. And maybe in her mind, it was a promise to keep me alive. Even still, for the first time in a long time, it was one I was willing to keep.

She gave me the names of a couple of therapists in the area. She asked me to at least set up an appointment with one of them. I wasn't sure if I would, but I took the information anyway.

"Oh, and Daniel?" she said. "Thank you."

"For what?"

"For letting someone in. I feel privileged that you chose me."

It was as if the noose around my neck had been loosened. And I'd been allowed a few clean breaths. Maybe going home for spring break would be tolerable after all.

Yeah right. I might need to have Gabby on speed dial.

. . .

flipped the light on in my parents' garage and inhaled deeply. It was the smell I'd come to love most—besides a certain mysterious almond scent. It was like a mix of oil, metal, and paint—and, fuck, how I'd missed it.

I stepped farther inside and allowed my fingers to grasp the sheet that covered and protected one of my greatest accomplishments. I gently hauled the cloth over her bumper and my breath caught in the back of my throat. She was a beauty and I'd helped restore her.

And it had been too damn long since I'd laid eyes on her.

I squatted down, picked up the can of paint near the rear wheel, and blew the thick layer of dust off the top. I'd had such big plans for her. Had I continued my renovation the last couple of years, I'd be taking her for joy rides by now.

But after the accident it just seemed wrong to refurbish the same kind of machine that was instrumental in my best friend's death. And for me to find any kind of solace in it. All I could see was Bastian lying in the wreckage on the side of the road. The desire to rebuild anything, especially cars, had been zapped away. As if my livelihood, my spirit, had been vacuumed out of my soul.

But standing here now, I couldn't keep the foreign feeling welling up in my chest at bay. As if it couldn't be contained any longer or it would consume me. Permeate my skin, latch on to my bones, and flow through my veins.

I'd been too damn afraid all this time. Terrified it would taint Bastian's memory. Make me a disgrace.

Instead, it was slowly killing me. I was withering away to nothing. A hollow shell.

As I rolled up my sleeves and reached for the screwdriver on the worktable, I allowed a singular emotion to take hold and it was so fucking potent that I felt tears burn the back of my throat.

I didn't bother to swallow them down. I just knew I had to do this. Take this first step.

In order to *survive*.

CHAPTER FIFTEEN

ELLA

The two days I'd been home, I'd been busy with an endless list of chores to help my mom ready our house for Saturday-night dinner. We always celebrated with relatives the day before Easter because my parents believed Sunday should be reserved for church and immediate family. The Easter Bunny didn't figure into our traditions anymore, but there was plenty of food and sweets to keep us satiated.

One of the reasons I'd decided to leave home to live with Avery was because our family was close. Too close. Like know-all-of-your-business close. And they'd always set high expectations for us. And that's why I didn't know how Christopher could have slipped past us undetected. We were very involved in one another's lives.

My father admitted that he sometimes suffered from bouts

of depression. I wished he hadn't been too proud to come clean earlier. Maybe Christopher wouldn't have felt so alone. According to the journal I'd found after his death, he'd been depressed for a long time. He'd felt like he didn't belong to our family. The only thing that had made him feel halfway sane was playing soccer. Because he'd found something he was good at.

My parents had certainly changed since Christopher's death. Especially my father. He was more quiet, introspective, and protective of us.

One of the reasons I'd become a psychology major was because I'd wanted to understand why my brother had taken his own life. And in the process, I had helped heal my family. As much as a family could mend when one member was lost to you forever.

That morning, I was helping my mother prepare dinner. We were having all the Polish fixings—sauerkraut and kielbasa, cabbage and noodles. Each year, Mom made pierogies from scratch by rolling out her own dough at the kitchen table. One of my jobs was to add flour whenever the consistency became too wet. And later, to indent the dough with the bottom of a drinking glass, so it could be formed into soft pillows of goodness.

This was our routine, and some days we performed our tasks in silence. Today, Mom wanted to know all about my classes. I hadn't told her about Joel and me yet. I'd just said that he wouldn't be coming for dinner because of other obligations. She hadn't pressed me and neither had my father. Maybe they already knew. They could always read me pretty well.

My twin brothers, James and Jason, were in the garage

helping Dad change the oil in my car. My father insisted on inspecting my vehicle each time I came into town. It was his way of making sure I was safe.

"You bring Avery the leftovers," Mom said. "And tell her I expect a visit from her and her new boyfriend soon."

"I will, Momma. She already told me she'd miss your cooking."

The past several years, Avery and her brother, Adam, had come for Easter dinner. But this year they were headed to celebrate with Bennett's family for a couple of days. Adam would be attending TSU next year, and Avery was relieved to have her brother closer so she could keep a better eye on him.

Even though Avery's mother was having a better year in the parenting department, she wasn't up for any mom-of-the-year awards yet. She still shacked up with different guys, but at least she had curbed her alcohol and drug usage, according to Adam. She had even kept a decently paying job.

Two hours later, a couple hundred pierogies were pinched at the seams and ready to be boiled. They were filled with sauerkraut, ricotta, plum jam, and my favorite—potatoes and cheese.

After we cleaned off the table and washed the dishes, we headed out the door to Aunt Karina and Uncle Roman's restaurant. The diner was busy, and Aunt Karina had called and asked me to pick up dessert along with a side dish she'd made, in case they were running late.

Basia's Diner sold freshly baked pies, and I was glad that Mom had decided not to make hers from scratch. Truth be told, I liked Aunt Karina's pies the best, even though she and my mother used the same recipe—my late grandma Basia's. She taught them everything they knew about cooking.

The diner was located in the next town over on a busy thruway, and, no surprise, the lot was full. It was always packed during the holidays as people passed through town to get to their destinations.

I spotted a familiar car taking up two spots in the far corner of the lot. I don't know my classic cars like my father did—or like that *other* person did. The one who I was trying extra hard not to think about.

We were greeted by Aunt Karina as soon as we stepped through the door. She wore the same light blue apron with purple embroidered flowers that she refused to retire no matter how many replacements we'd bought. It had once belonged to Grandma Basia.

"Look at this beauty-queen niece of mine." Aunt Karina pulled me in for a strong hug while my mother walked behind the counter to greet Uncle Roman.

"Hi, Auntie." Our parents were so close, she'd almost become a second mother to me. "Been craving your banana cream pie for weeks. I can't wait to get my hands on a slice."

She kissed the top of my head. "I loaded it with extra whipped cream just for you."

She grabbed my cheeks and pinched lightly. "How are things?"

I looked into her bright blue eyes and saw myself in thirty years' time. "Good, Auntie."

She peeked over my shoulder to make sure my mother wasn't listening before whispering. "How about with that boy?"

I shrugged. "It's all right."

It was nearly impossible to lie to my aunt. She'd always had excellent radar for boy troubles. "You'll tell me all about it tonight?"

I nodded and looked around. "You guys have a crowd this afternoon."

My eyes scanned across the red and silver booths in the restaurant, landing on a lone diner in the very back. I nearly fumbled over my own feet trying to get a better look.

Quinn wore a black baseball cap and a dingy white T-shirt with black smudges across the front—like he'd been working in the yard or maybe on his car. When he looked up, our eyes met and he jerked back, visibly shaken.

Like this was the last place he'd ever imagined seeing me. On spring break, at Basia's Diner.

Yeah, no kidding. The feeling was mutual.

"What the hell?" I said, louder than I'd intended.

"What is it, honey?" Auntie asked, following my gaze. "Ah, that handsome boy at table twenty? He comes in every now and again."

"I . . . um . . . I know him," I said, trying not to sound so thunderstruck. I would have never guessed I'd see Quinn while I was home, let alone in my family's diner. "I'll be right back."

Walking over, I raked my fingers through my hair to remove any flour residue and silently cursed myself for not changing out of my faded jeans and T-shirt.

A cup of coffee and a piece of cherry pie sat in front of Quinn. Upon closer inspection, I saw a few days' worth of stubble had grown on his chin.

"Is that your favorite flavor pie?" I tried to control my quavering voice at the thrill of running into him.

His eyes roved over the landscape of my body from the top of my head down to my worn red sneakers. "From here, it is."

"So you've been here before?" I looked around to make sure I hadn't said that louder than I'd intended.

"Yeah, a few times," he said, adjusting his cap on his head. I noticed how his russet strands curled around his ears. My fingers itched to touch them. "You know the owner?"

"We're related," I said. "My aunt and uncle own this joint."

"Small world, huh?" he said as he looked around the place, as if for the first time—taking in the old-world fixtures, the menu on the chalkboard—and something seemed to click in place in his mind. Maybe Joel had told the guys about my family background.

"Tell me about it," I said while he studied the kitchen and counter staff. "How come we've never run into each other before?"

"Good question." He turned his warm gaze on me and it heated me from the inside. "So, how long have you been home?"

"A couple of days," I said. "You?"

"Same." He was playing with the saltshaker, making wide circles, like he was trying to work something out in his brain.

I heard the clucking of my mother's tongue behind me. She could make her presence known just by walking through a room. Her thick black hair was always worn in a bun, and she asserted an ample figure. I'd always prayed I'd get her boobs and not her hips. But I'd been blessed with both. Not that my mother was overweight. She was just all woman.

The only girl in a family of boys, it'd been hard dealing with my brothers' relentless teasing about my bra size. Unless someone outside the family tried it. Then they were protective to a fault—especially Christopher. He'd gotten his ass beaten once defending me when a senior tried to cop a feel in front of the lockers at the gym.

"Darling daughter," my mother said, rolling her *R*s dramatically. I used to be embarrassed at our eastern European background, because we didn't sound anything like my friends' parents. Now I cherished how unique our family was. "Who's your friend?"

"Quinn, this is my mom," I said. "Ma, I know Quinn from TSU. He plays baseball for the university. And he, um . . . is also Joel's frat brother."

"Nice to meet you, dear," Mom said, extending her hand. "A friend of Joel's is a friend of ours."

Quinn's eyebrows shot up and I gave him the slightest shake of my head.

"Thank you," he said, recovering quickly. Before reaching out to shake her hand, he apologized about his appearance. "Sorry, I've been working on my car all morning. It's hard to get all the grease from beneath my nails."

Mom gave him a warm smile. I could tell she liked his manners. "Does your family live nearby?"

"Yes, just over in Jefferson."

"So you're home to celebrate the holiday with your family?" I almost nudged Mom with my foot for prying too much, but I had to admit, I was curious myself.

Besides, Mom wouldn't have listened anyway. She loved to interfere in other people's business. Especially my friends'.

That's why she'd allowed Avery to practically live at our house the last year of high school. We were all in the haze of grief, and having Avery there broke us out of our fog from time to time.

"Actually, my parents were called away on business last minute, so it'll just be me and my pie." His head dipped down, discomfort and irritation in his eyes. Something lurched for him deep in my gut. "My father is the state representative for district eighteen, so there are always fund-raisers to attend. I chose to take a break from it this year."

Before I could open my mouth my mother beat me to the punch. "Then you'll come celebrate the holiday with us."

Quinn's cheeks flared red. "Oh, no, ma'am, that's okay, I'm just going to—"

"I insist," Mom said before he could get his sentence out.

She must have felt the same way I had. It wasn't pity, just sadness. Quinn was a private, mysterious guy. Did his parents' political status have anything to do with it? It must have been tough growing up with expectations, maybe equal parts from your parents as from the public. It felt like pieces of the puzzle were beginning to fall into place.

"Um," Quinn mumbled, staring at me as if he was checking whether or not I thought it was an okay idea.

"Why not?" I shrugged. "Besides, we're bringing home lots of dessert from the diner."

His cheek quirked into a grin. "I do love these pies."

"Plus, my mom has been slaving in the kitchen all morning creating a feast," I said, trying to sell him on the idea. I didn't want him to be alone. At least I told myself that was the only reason. "I think you'll enjoy it."

"Okay, sure," he said. "How can I pass up great food?"

"Then it's settled." Mom placed her hand on my shoulder. "How about you help your friend find our house? I'll meet you back there."

She didn't even wait for a response. Figuring she had the details all worked out, she walked off, proud of herself. I sighed and looked up at the counter where my auntie stood, spying on the conversation. She gave a quick wink before turning back to load the coffee machine.

"My mom didn't give you much choice in the matter," I said, slinking down in the booth. "But is it okay if I drive with you? If not, I can always catch her in the parking lot."

"Actually, it would be great if you joined me," he said after eating the last bite of his pie. "It'd be better than me walking in alone. I'm guessing you have a large family?"

"Yeah, it's pretty big," I said. "Sorry she put you on the spot. You might not like being around a bunch of rowdy relatives speaking two different languages."

"Nah, it'll be cool. Just not something I'm used to," he said. "My family is small. And we don't get together with relatives all that much anymore."

I couldn't imagine how that felt; I was so used to the chaos of my own family.

"Listen, I'm still dirty from working on my car," he said, looking down at his T-shirt. "Mind if I go home and change real quick?"

"Not at all," I said. My stomach got all fluttery thinking about how I'd be spending time with Quinn. And it had all happened by chance.

"So you finally found time to get back to your hobby,

huh?" I said, recalling our conversation about restoring cars at the fund-raiser event.

He ducked his head as he dug out his wallet and a hint of a smile outlined his lips. "Something like that."

Quinn laid a ten-dollar bill on the table and we headed out the door. I gave my auntie a little wave before leaving. She'd be sure to drill me later.

I hopped in the passenger side of his car, noticing the polished leather seats, the spotless floor and dashboard. "I get the honor of riding in your classic car. I see you take very good care of her."

A spark of pride flashed in his eyes as he backed out of the space. "This one's my baby."

I pulled the seat belt over my chest. "Does she have a name?"

He laughed. "Isn't naming your car kind of lame?"

"No way, you need to call her something," I said, checking out the vintage door handles. "Give me time to come up with one."

"Not making any guarantees that I'll use it, but go for it." Quinn seemed to light up talking about his car. The faint redness in his cheeks just made him more beautiful. Like he was glowing from the inside.

"It'll be my special name for her," I mumbled. When I looked over, something had softened in his eyes.

Quinn was a vigilant driver, staying several car lengths behind on the road and never riding anyone's tail on the freeway. I wondered if it was because of how much he cherished his car or if there was a different reason. Had something else happened to make him so cautious?

He seemed to be careful in other ways as well—like making a move on me the other night. He said he needed to make sure that things didn't happen between us just because it was easy. But I couldn't deny the current tethering us together now. Our legs rested just inches apart on the seat, and he'd looked at my thigh more than once, his Adam's apple bobbing up and down.

His hand tightened against the steering wheel and I noticed the leftover grease beneath his nails. But other than that, his hand looked soft, his skin smooth, his nails trimmed. And I longed to hold it now.

I remembered the rough calluses on his palms when he'd touched my face in his room, and my chest squeezed tight. What would it have been like to be snuggled against his side, with his arm around me, music blaring, road-tripping it together?

I tried to push the thought out of my head and focus on just getting to know him. I had this opportunity to spend time with him, and I wanted to make the most of it.

CHAPTER SIXTEEN

QUINN

"So, how bad does it suck that your parents are gone for the holiday?" she asked while staring out the window, almost as if she was afraid to meet my eyes. Maybe she was nervous she was overstepping bounds again.

I looked down at her knee, jiggling away on the other side of the console, and it mimicked the restless beats of my heart. I had Ella alone in my car and all I could think about was wrapping her in my arms and kissing the hell out of her. Being with Ella somehow gave me hope that one day, I could feel something real again.

Like I could hang all my worries on a hook by the door.

"Honestly? It happens all the time," I said. "I'm used to it. But don't tell anyone that."

I could see Ella's frown in my peripheral vision.

Ella's mother thought I was a friend of her boyfriend's, and I figured she'd kick the shit out of me if she knew I was entertaining dirty thoughts about her daughter. If her mother was that intimidating, I wondered what her father would be like.

My own father used to scare the hell out of me when I was younger. He'd only have to say one sentence in his imposing voice and I knew it was his way or the highway. I couldn't wait to be finished with college, done with having their money influence my decisions, just so I could take off somewhere the hell away from them.

I could have done it when I turned eighteen. I'd even planned it, but then everything happened. I was in shock, grieving, scared shitless, and had made the decision to do something for Sebastian and his parents. My parents never even asked what the hell I was doing and why, they were just glad I'd chosen a major good enough for the child of a politician.

Over the years I'd been asked countless times if I had similar political aspirations as my father. *Fuck no.* I didn't have any damn desire to be like my father.

"Do you have other family in the area?"

"My aunt and uncle," I said. "But . . . it's a long story."

I was hoping she got the hint that I didn't want to talk about it.

She must've because she changed the subject. "So, where do you work on cars?"

I pulled into my long driveway. I was almost embarrassed by the size of our home. It was a shell of an empty house, anyway. Too many bedrooms, and all for show. I had sent the housekeeper home for the weekend. No need for her to stay and make me dinner when she had a family of her own to be with over the holidays. Besides, I just wanted to be alone.

"I'll show you," I said, jerking the car into park. I walked to the passenger side and opened the door.

That small action had surprised her. "Thank you," she said, a shy grin lifting the corners of her lips.

She stepped out and looked up at the monstrosity that was my house. "Wow. Impressive."

"Not really." We walked through the side door of the garage and I flipped on the light.

Car parts were littered around the spacious cement floor. Portions of an engine I had abandoned the other day, in favor of fixing the brakes on my car. The canister of candy-apple-red paint stood tall against a brush. I walked toward the driver-side door of my latest project. "I'll be able to drive this baby someday. I've been restoring her for years."

She knelt down to inspect the paint canister. "That color kicks some serious ass."

"It does." I couldn't hold back my grin. "I finally got the right mix for this paint job."

She stroked her hand across the car bumper. "Where did you learn to work on cars?"

"My uncle. He taught me everything I know," I said, making sure the lid on the can was secure. I'd planned on coming back and painting more tonight, but my plans had obviously changed. Probably in the only way that could possibly be better. "He owns his own shop here in the city."

"How come he hasn't snatched you up yet?" she asked, now inspecting my worktable, as if truly interested in spark plugs and lug nuts.

"Ha, don't think he hasn't already tried," I said, carrying the paintbrush to the slop sink. "But my parents would have something to say about that *and* their college funding."

I twisted the hot-water handle and watched as the red paint washed down the drain. "Instead I'm learning about how to be a businessman. That keeps them quiet."

It was brief, but I saw anger pass through her eyes. "I hope it comes in handy for you someday."

"I plan to make sure it does," I said, stepping toward her. She was in my sacred space, and it was hard not to want to grab her hand and show her all of my treasures and toys, but I shoved my fingers in my pockets to restrain myself. She was probably bored to tears here.

Ella was staring at me, a ghost of a smile on her lips.

"Why are you looking at me like that?"

"You just . . . I've never seen you like this," she said, replacing a wrench she'd been inspecting. "There's this fire in your eyes when you talk about cars. It's . . . amazing."

I felt open, on display, like she could see inside my soul. I turned away and pretended to put a stray screwdriver back in the toolbox.

I cleared my throat. "What's so amazing about it?"

"It's your joy, your passion . . ." she said, then slanted her head, studying me. "Maybe even your lifeline."

"Never thought about it that way," I lied. Of course I had, a million times. I just didn't know I wore my heart so openly on my sleeve. It must have just been Ella. She saw inside me, through me. Brought my passions out of me, even. Little did she realize she had influenced me to resume this project after our conversation at the car wash. To be brave. My fingers had been itching to get started since the last day of classes. "I guess in a way, it is."

She moved closer, determination blazing in her eyes. "So why not do something about that?"

"I . . . don't know," I muttered. "I had planned to . . . but then everything went to shit."

I turned away again because it all became too real. Having Ella here at my house, inside my garage, around all the things I loved. I hoped she understood how overwhelming it was. I needed to move us along.

"My father will be thrilled to see your car," she said, and I breathed a sigh of relief at the change of topic. "He's an aficionado."

"I'd be honored to show him," I said, meeting her eyes, silently thanking her for not pushing the subject.

"Come inside?" I said, moving toward the door. As I passed her, I reached for her hand and she took it willingly. It felt so natural to lead her through the kitchen and offer her something to drink.

I leaned against the counter, a water bottle in my hand. It was time to put Ella on the hot seat. "So, you didn't tell your parents about Joel?"

"You noticed that, huh?" She bent her head, pink splotching her cheeks. "Just wasn't ready to yet."

"I think I can understand that," I said. Recently, conversations with my parents consisted only of perfunctory facts.

"My parents are very involved in our lives, and even more so since . . ." She stopped suddenly and shook her head. "Never mind."

"No, wait." I reached for her arm, feeling like she needed me close, needed my support. "Since what?"

"I don't want to be a Debbie Downer." She smiled, but it didn't reach her eyes.

"I'd like to hear," I said, never feeling more like I wanted to know Ella. Really know her. After all, she was in my home, had been in my intimate space, and I felt almost as vulnerable as maybe she did in that moment.

"My brother Christopher." Her voice was soft. As if she was revering his name. "He committed suicide when I was in high school."

I felt a strong slice to my gut, almost like a laceration. "Damn it. I'm sorry, Ella."

"No, it's okay," she said, meeting my gaze. "We've worked through it as a family. And I have, too. Well, as much as I can."

I couldn't help myself. I grabbed her and enveloped her in a tight embrace against my chest. She hesitated at first, but then wrapped her arms around my waist. Her skin was soft and warm and she smelled like almonds. In that moment, I felt like we were both in a safe and protected bubble, even though it was only supposed to be me comforting her.

My chest also ached with an insurmountable guilt. I'd been thinking about offing myself forever, and here this girl had someone close to her who had actually done it. In the most fundamental sense, the most basic of truths, we had something in common. Grief, sorrow, pain. We both knew what it felt like to lose someone we loved.

Except I'd *killed* the person I loved. Even though it may have been an accident in some small way, I was still mostly to blame. What would she think of me if she knew the truth? Or if she discovered that I'd wanted to take my own life too many times to count? Would she understand or run for the hills?

Part of me wanted so badly to unburden myself and hope for the best. Right here and right now, while I had her in my arms. But in reality, I was still a chickenshit. I couldn't stand the thought of losing her when I was just getting to know her.

"My parents are protective about me and the twins. We've always been a close family, but since that night . . . It's understandable, really." She pulled back to look at me. "It's one of the reasons I'm living with Avery. I tried to stay in the dorms the first year, but I was still grieving and finding my way. So I moved back. But recently, I decided it was time to live at school again."

I couldn't live anywhere that first year, either. I'd chosen to attend classes and then come home to barricade myself inside my room. It wasn't until I'd had a conversation with Bastian's father about his beloved frat house that I'd decided on a more solid plan. If I was going to live his son's life, I needed to stop hiding every part of me and just act like I was him—all the way. Like that saying—fake it until you make it.

"So you're afraid to tell them about Joel because you don't want to disappoint them?"

"In a way, yes," she said.

"I can relate to that, too." I'd felt like a huge disappointment to my parents my entire life. Nothing I'd done had ever been good enough. So I just went through the motions, trying to find my own way. Dad would have loved a son with political aspirations. But as soon as he clued in early on that I had no such intentions, he treated me more like a guest in his house than a son.

"Joel knows my family. My dad used to coach him, and Joel used to play soccer with my brother," she said, and I began connecting the dots a bit more. She had had a hard time walking away from Joel because it'd be like walking away from her brother.

Kind of how I had to wrench myself free from Amber after seeing her all the time proved to be heartrending. She reminded me too much of Sebastian.

"So I realized one of the reasons I hung in there so long with Joel was because we had that connection." I could feel her warm breath against my shirt and my heart flapping inside my chest. "And recently, I really started to see what a flimsy connection it had been."

I wanted to tell her that I wasn't a fan of Joel's, that he had been cheating on her, but she didn't need to feel any worse about their past relationship. There was enough guilt in this room to go around and then some. We could mop it up and fill buckets with it.

"Thanks for telling me about your brother." I pulled her close again, ran my fingers through her waves, and heard her sharp intake of breath. "And about Joel."

She stayed perfectly still against my chest, her hands gripping my shoulders.

"You're better off without him, you know."

"Yeah?" Her body tensed as she waited on my response.

"Absolutely." I pulled back and winked at her. "Okay if I take a quick shower before we go?"

"Go for it," she said, backing away dramatically. "You *do* smell like a grease monkey."

"Hey!" I grabbed her from behind and lifted her off her feet, sending her into a fit of giggles. Her laughter was infectious, and I couldn't help grinning from ear to ear. "Just don't let my father, Mr. Serious Politician, hear you say that."

I carried her down the hallway to the threshold of my room. She was a petite thing who just happened to have a set of tits on her that would make any man lose his breath. And damn if I didn't dream of seeing them someday. I bet they were perfect. My forearms rested on the underside of her breasts and I pushed that thought away before she could feel how quickly a simple idea like that could arouse me.

I set her down and stepped inside my room to grab a clean pair of jeans and a button-down shirt from my closet. I figured I should dress a little nicer if I was going to Ella's house for dinner.

I looked at the clock and stepped up my pace. "I'd offer to kick your ass in *Mario Kart*, but we don't have that kind of time."

Ella was busy looking at some books on my shelf. "I'll take a rain check."

"Be right back." I strode into the bathroom and closed the door behind me, not realizing I was allowing Ella into my bedroom with my personal belongings until I was under the showerhead, soaping up. The idea of her spotting something I wasn't ready for her to see made me wash myself a little more quickly.

As I was drying off, the thought of me behind this door

completely naked with Ella on the other side made the blood rush straight to my dick.

Wasn't that exactly what Ella had wanted to happen the other day in my room at the frat house? If I walked out there in just this towel, would she still want me like she had then?

I hadn't been ready to make any moves that night, but today felt more intimate. She'd trusted me enough to confide in me, to let me see her vulnerable. I felt closer to her, even more attracted to her, if that were possible. And if I didn't stop having these thoughts, I'd have to walk out there with a raging hard-on.

Somehow, I felt lighter, freer, having her here with me. I actually allowed the possibility of getting to know her more intimately enter my mind. I hadn't dated anyone in a very long time and I wasn't sure if I even knew how to be with someone, or let them in. But somehow Ella made it easier to open up. I looked forward to spending the rest of the day getting to know her and her family.

When I stepped inside my room, my muscles instantly contracted. Ella stood in front of my dresser, studying snapshots in frames left over from high school days.

Ella pointed to a picture of Sebastian and some other ballplayers. "Who are the people in this picture?"

"Just old high school friends," I said, trying to control my breathing. I hadn't banked on her zeroing in on anything related to Sebastian.

"And this is that girl from the parking lot at Zach's."

My stomach bunched into a hard ball.

Shit. Maybe bringing her here wasn't such a great idea.

"Uh-huh," I said, trying to sound nonchalant. The picture

was a generic one: just a bunch of us huddled together at a party.

"Were you in love?" Her voice was so soft I wasn't sure if I had heard her right.

"With Amber?" I asked, having never considered the question. Sure I'd had a major crush, but the idea of being in love with her was pushing it.

Ella was still turned away from me. Like she couldn't meet my eye as she awaited my answer. Probably because she questioned whether I still had a thing for Amber after seeing us together.

And she couldn't have been more wrong. I didn't have feelings for Amber.

I had feelings for *Ella*.

And I didn't know what the hell to do about it. Ella was mesmerizing. A force so captivating she was difficult to resist. Like a powerful tide washing over me, pulling me under, and compelling me along a path that was terrifying and exhilarating all at once.

"No, I wasn't," I said, coming up behind her. "I've never been in love with anyone. Not yet."

Her shoulders relaxed and her fists unclenched—as if she'd allowed all of her uncertainties to roll off of her.

"Look at me, Ella."

She turned around and her eyes widened as she took in my appearance. I had on a pair of dark jeans and had draped my shirt over my shoulder, ready to be pulled on and buttoned up. My hair was combed away from my face and her eyes roamed over the curve of my jaw, down my neck and chest, making my stomach flip completely over.

Damn, she mouthed.

I cleared my throat. "What?"

"Did I say that out loud?" she said, parting her pouty mouth.

I smirked. "Either that or I read your lips."

"It's just . . . I'm sure you know that you're hot, Quinn," she said, her gaze generously roaming over me. "You have an amazing body."

Ella's words turned me on like no one else's. I'd felt girls up with less provocation. And this girl had only uttered a simple sentence and I was already there. "So do you, Ella."

She shook her head like she didn't believe me. I closed the distance between us and gathered her face in my hands. "Don't you realize how gorgeous you are?"

Her breaths were broken and rough as her gaze aligned with mine. I felt myself tipping, plunging—falling headlong into those ocean-blue eyes.

I ran my thumb along her bottom lip and just as I was about to throw all caution to the wind, her phone chirped— loud and insistent—penetrating our perfect little bubble.

CHAPTER SEVENTEEN

ELLA

Leave it to my mother to be a romance wrecker. It was almost like she knew I wasn't being honest about Joel, so she was messing with me. She was the one who'd told me to bring Quinn to our house for dinner and now she must have been tapping her foot wondering where the hell we were.

"We're on our way, Momma," I said into my phone.

Quinn finished getting dressed and ready to go in his button-down shirt and black shoes. "I don't want to piss off your parents—let's get a move on."

I lamented the loss of his hands on my face. The whisper of his deep voice. And the sight of his sculpted chest.

No man, besides my own father, had ever called me gorgeous. That moment between Quinn and me felt sincere. Real. Heartfelt.

Despite the building urge to kiss him for weeks, in that instant, it felt like we had something more together. Like I had penetrated the wall he had carefully crafted. Had been let inside a tiny crack in the façade.

And it only confirmed how much I wanted him. *Damn*, I wanted him.

And now we were back in Quinn's hot rod and I could hardly believe we were headed to my house for a family dinner.

When Quinn pulled in the driveway, I spotted my father outside, smoking cigars with Uncle Roman and Uncle Martin. It was their tradition whenever our families got together. Mom always banished them away from the house because it stunk up the joint.

Now they stood alongside the flower bed in a heated discussion in their native language. Most likely about politics, the economy, or their jobs. My father was a building contractor and complained that the younger generation didn't appreciate his work ethic. It was the same argument, different decade.

We exited the car, and I introduced Quinn to my father and uncles.

"I understand you're one of Joel's frat brothers?" my dad asked.

Quinn didn't falter at hearing Joel's name. "Yes, sir."

Quinn twisted his car keys round and round his fingers as my father and uncles studied him, and I was beginning to understand what he meant about not being used to large family gatherings. Being publicly scrutinized as the son of a politician was probably totally different from being judged by the members of an extended family.

He'd mentioned an aunt and uncle but didn't seem to want

to talk about them. I couldn't help wondering what kind of parents traveled during a holiday rather than making time for their only child. Was that the reason for the meticulously built structure Quinn had erected around himself? Maybe he'd been disappointed too many times to let anyone in.

When Quinn had confessed at Basia's Diner that he'd be alone all weekend, my heart lurched. I'd also entertained the thought that maybe he'd made plans with someone else, since he was adamant about not wanting to kiss me the other night.

So why had he seemed so ready to kiss me just an hour ago?

He was still a mystery and it made me want to get to know him even more.

"Quinn's a star catcher for the Titans, Tata," I said, and Quinn dipped his head as if embarrassed by my gushing statement.

Dad gave me an odd sort of look. Did he know I'd been lying about Joel?

Baseball was the only American sport my father understood. If it wasn't baseball or soccer, he just wasn't interested.

My brothers darted out of the house, one with a Nerf football in hand, and went into insta-worship mode with Quinn once I told them that he played for the university. The twins participated in football, basketball, and baseball and revered any local sports team. To Quinn's amusement, they even spouted off TSU's stats.

Christopher had only played soccer, and he was the son you'd most likely see out in the garage with my father working on cars. My father had lost his little buddy. I certainly couldn't replace him, and neither could the twins.

Quinn tossed the football around with my brothers while

he answered their questions about his upcoming schedule on the road.

"Enough with the sports talk," my dad said. "Show me this little classic beauty." He patted Quinn on the back and then headed toward his car for a thorough inspection.

"I have to see if my mom needs help in the kitchen," I said, watching my father's excitement build the closer he got to Quinn's car. "Will you be okay?"

"I'm good," he said, his eyes sparkling with amusement.

Before I turned toward the house I said, "Wait, I think I got it."

His eyebrows slammed together. "Got what?"

I tipped my head toward my father and uncles. "The names of your cars."

"*Cars?*" he said. "As in plural?"

"Of course. There *are* two of them, right?" I said, as if it was the silliest thing in the world for him to question my logic.

"I guess." He appeared unconvinced that I hadn't lost my mind.

"That one is Fury because she's dark and foreboding." I pointed to his black beauty in our driveway. "And the one in your garage is Fire. Red and feisty."

"Hmmm," he said, rubbing the stubble on his chin as he contemplated the names I'd chosen. "I think I approve."

I was mesmerized by how his fingers worked his jawline. "Yeah?"

"I like them." His gaze landed on my lips before sliding up to my eyes. "I like them *a lot.*"

He turned to join my father and uncles as his double

meaning swept over me, like a salve. I stood there in a stupor, watching his tight backside move in those dark-wash jeans.

My father was already rubbing his hand along the side of Quinn's black, shiny paint job and I giggled to myself as I stepped inside to help my mother.

Mom was busy setting the tables. There were always two for these types of dinners. The formal one in the dining room was for adults. And a smaller foldaway table set up in the living room was for the kids. My two older cousins were helping align the chairs while their children played in the backyard with bubbles and fake swords.

"What took you so long, *Corka*?" My parents had spoken half Polish, half English my entire life, so I understood the language better than I communicated it. I would've been more fluent had I practiced, but my parents didn't push it. I was more interested in appearing as Americanized as I could in front of friends.

Avery was the only friend who got on my case about it. Said I should feel lucky and embrace the language. But I wasn't as confident or strong-willed as she was. I'd actually cared about being popular and fitting in. Which seemed ridiculous in hindsight.

Besides, after Christopher died, I'd never fit in again. Nobody had gone through what we had and none of my friends besides Avery had seemed to understand. So I'd stood out like a sore thumb even more. And that's when I'd decided to focus on healing rather than being popular.

"We weren't that long, *Matka*," I said. "He wanted to change his greasy shirt."

"That was polite," she said, and gave me a knowing look. "He's very handsome, that one. Just make sure the other one knows you're finished before moving on, you hear me?"

My cousin Andrea wiggled her eyebrows, and I felt my cheeks heat up.

"It's the right thing to do," Mom said, placing her hand on my shoulder, forcing me to look at her.

I had trouble meeting my mother's searing gaze. "So . . . you wouldn't be upset if that were to happen?"

"Upset?" she asked, her eyebrows bouncing together. "*Proszę*, I only want you to be happy."

I nodded and felt my stomach unclench. Relief washed through my limbs.

"And right now, your eyes are dancing for that boy."

I heard my cousins snickering in the kitchen as they separated utensils for the place settings. Aunt Karina wasn't here yet, and I was grateful to not also be under her direct scrutiny.

Soon enough we were all packed into the dining and living rooms. Quinn and I were at the kids' table, and he seemed relieved about that—kids didn't dissect you the way adults did, though they were honest to a fault. So far my little cousins were smitten with Quinn, one asking him to sit next to her. Apparently she saw his appeal even at her young age.

When Quinn helped my cousin cut her kielbasa so that her mother could stay seated at the grown-ups' table and then wiped her spill when she knocked over her apple juice, I felt my heart swell in my chest. He was surprisingly good with kids—a natural, in fact. Aunt Karina nodded her approval across the room.

After a couple plates of food each, we sat back in our folding chairs stuffed to the gills.

"That was so good," Quinn said, nudging me with his knee. "You get to eat like this all the time?"

"Not all the time. But, yeah, I guess so." I realized that I took all of this for granted. What kind of meals did Quinn have to look forward to?

"What favorite thing does your mother make?" I asked, figuring he had *something* to be nostalgic about.

"*My* mom?" He nearly choked on the soda he'd been sipping. "I could tell you my favorite restaurant takeout menu. Or about the spaghetti and meatballs our cook used to make."

I bit the inside of my lip to contain my reaction. "Oh. Sorry."

"No sweat," he said. "It's how I grew up. I didn't know any different—unless I stayed with my aunt and uncle."

And that's when I finally saw a wistful glint in his eyes. Or maybe it was regret.

"My father's a career politician, and for us, that meant another way of life," he said.

Before I could ask him exactly what he meant, he took the conversation in a different direction. "How do you say *thank you* in Polish?"

Something unlocked in the very center of me. I'd tried teaching Joel how to say a couple of words to impress my parents, but he'd never seemed interested enough to try. Besides, he'd already known my family well enough from church and sports.

I leaned across my seat to whisper it to him as gratitude and admiration lodged in the back of my throat. When my lips closed in on his ear, I felt him shiver. "*Dziekuje*. I'll say it slowly for you. Jin-ku-yeh."

"Jin-ku-yeh," he repeated two times, and it was the sweetest sound to my ears.

He walked over to where my parents were sitting and then he cleared his throat. "Mr. and Mrs. Abrams, jin-ku-yeh. This food was amazing."

The whole table went silent at his rough pronunciation. My cousin Andrea's eyes twinkled at me and my aunt Karina looked taken aback and pleased at the same time. She tapped my mother's hand.

"That's a lovely thing for you to say, Quinn," my mother said. "*Proszę bardzo*. You are very welcome."

Quinn smiled and then patted his stomach. "Gosh, I don't think I've eaten this well in maybe, *ever*."

My mother's eyes flooded with sadness. She could tell how sincere his thank-you had been as well as I could. She must have been already deciding which leftovers to wrap up for him. He had just opened up the floodgates for my mother to gift him with endless amounts of food and bakery items. I was never going to hear the end of it.

"You come back anytime," my father chimed in, rendering me speechless. "You hear me, son?"

I knew my father had enjoyed Joel's company and thought he was funny, but I could tell he thought Quinn was special . . . sincere . . . genuine. As much as I did.

Having my father's approval meant more to me than he'd ever know. Even if Quinn and I only remained friends. In his own way, my father was giving me permission to pave my own path, choose the people I surrounded myself with. My foot had stepped outside of his protective dome, and he had trusted me to explore the world a bit more on my own.

We gorged on Aunt Karina's cream pies and my mother's powdered-sugar *pizelles* while we played two games of *Mario Kart* with my brothers in our basement rec room. Afterward, I helped Quinn carry out four containers of leftovers, including some dessert.

My mother had gone as overboard as I'd expected her to, given the amount of Tupperware loaded in our hands. But I didn't complain. I knew Quinn's statement had touched her as deeply as it had me.

"Now I see where you get your gaming skills," Quinn said, carefully placing the containers in his backseat.

"You mean my brothers?" I asked. "Nah, I taught them everything they know."

Quinn laughed. "Yeah, you probably did."

He leaned against his car, his keys dangling in his fingers, and I tried thinking of anything to say to prolong his visit. I wasn't quite ready to let him go yet.

"Hey, how far is Seymour Park from here?" he asked. "Used to have games there in high school. Sometimes we'd hang by that cool waterfall afterward."

"Not far at all, just around that bend." I pointed down the street. "You could walk there from here."

"Seriously?" He straightened himself and glanced at the sidewalk leading in that direction. The park was a regular hangout for us in high school. It boasted a fishing pond, a mini waterfall, as well as a playground, and a baseball diamond.

"Would you . . ." He looked down at his feet, suddenly unsure of himself.

But I didn't let him finish. I didn't want the night to end, either.

"Yes. I'd love to take a walk to the park," I said. "If anything, to work off this food."

As we started down the street, he reached for my hand and laced our fingers together. My palm tingled from the contact. So I didn't question it—just let my heart lead me.

"Ella?" I sucked in a breath when Quinn traced his thumb along my palm.

I peeked at him from beneath my eyelashes and my cheeks reddened. "Yeah?" I wasn't sure if he realized how his finger outlining my skin was affecting me. He seemed lost in deep thought.

"Did . . . um," he fumbled, hesitant to ask. "Did your brother Christopher used to play video games, too?"

"A little," I said. "He liked solo games more, like *Skyrim*."

"Sorry, didn't mean to pry," he said, his voice soft. "It's just . . . your family seems so tight. So I found myself wondering where he fit in."

"I think about that all the time. I mean, he and I were close, definitely. But there was this other side to him that he kept hidden," I said. "That's . . . that's the only way to describe it. It's hard to explain."

"I get what you mean," he said, and I realized that Quinn probably shared that quality with Christopher. He kept things close to the cuff, whether he realized it or not. I wondered how much it would interfere with getting to know him, even as a friend. "So does that mean you, um . . . didn't know . . . he was planning to do it?"

"I definitely didn't know. It's probably one of those things that will haunt me for the rest of my life," I said, and I felt his hand stiffen in mine. Maybe he had something he lamented, too. Or some*one*. "Guilt and regret are powerful things. They can destroy your life. Somehow you have to learn to forgive yourself so you can move on."

Quinn stopped walking and turned to me. Sorrow laced his eyes. What was he thinking?

"I'm sorry that this is a heavy conversation," I said, concerned I had brought up some sort of painful memory for him.

"No. I started it, remember?" he said, moving forward again. "So how is it that you . . . got past that?"

"I got help. We all did. Grief groups, grief counseling, individual therapy." It wasn't something I was ashamed of. If I had been, how could I become a psychologist someday? It was part of being human. "I'm a pretty optimistic person, I'll admit. One day it hit me that Christopher was somewhere looking down on us. And we were wasting all of this time. Always sad and quiet and crying. He must have been saying *Move on already*. So I did."

"That's . . . impressive, really." Quinn's gaze was so intense, I had to look away.

"Yeah, well. The pain never truly goes away, so you have to . . . file it away. And then get busy living your life."

He looked up to the sky, lost in deep thought, and then to the tops of the pines where the stars hung so low they were like the toppers of Christmas trees.

I wanted to change the subject but I also wanted to ask him who was haunting him, too. I could see it in his eyes. But maybe he wasn't ready to share it with me. For some people, it took time. I'd always been open about it, wanting to share, talk things through. I knew that it helped. But some people were more resistant.

"So, here we are." I motioned to the sign. "See how close it is?"

As we walked through the park entrance and found the trail that led to the pond, I said, "Today wasn't too bad, was it?"

"Meeting your family?" We came upon the water's edge and Quinn picked up a stone to skip along the water. "It was great, actually."

"I'm glad," I said, letting out a breath.

The pond was surrounded on all sides by tall pines, lending a feeling of privacy, outside of a couple of walkers across the way. I tossed a rock in the pond as well but could only hear its splash. The crickets chirped their nighttime lullabies and there was a gentle breeze in the air that did nothing to cool my heated skin.

"My mom likes you," I said, biting my lip. "I can tell."

"Yeah?" He turned to face me, his voice softening. "You think she can tell that I like her daughter?"

My breath caught in the back of my throat. Something had shifted in the air between us. It was heavy and heated. Something so commanding I felt it down to my toes. My heart was thrashing so loudly against my chest, I was sure he could hear it.

He moved closer than any two friends should rightfully stand and his spicy scent enveloped me. Oh Lord, if I didn't get a taste of those full lips I would die on this very spot.

Right this very instant.

When I looked up into his face, his eyes had become hooded.

Words were shouting inside my skull. And then they worked their way onto my lips. They were hanging there, dangling for dear life.

Just take a chance, damn it. Take a gamble, Quinn.

Kiss me and let's find out what this magic is between us.

He'd been the one who'd held back that other night, so the ball was in his court.

"It's not just me who feels this, right?" Quinn mumbled. His fingers curled around my neck, his thumb mapping patterns in the hollow of my throat. "I'm not crazy?"

The words that had been so readily available just moments before had flitted away on the wind. I'd wanted this moment for days. Weeks. Maybe even *years*.

"There's something here, Ella. Between us," he whispered. His lips were a breath away and I momentarily shut my eyes to gain control of my erratic breathing.

"I don't know what this is or what the hell might happen," he said, rubbing his finger along the edge of my earlobe. "But I do know one thing."

Still, I couldn't move or even speak. I was motionless—hypnotized by his eyes, his lips, his words. Finally, my hands became unstuck and I slid them up his chest to his shoulders as he shuddered against my touch.

"I know I need to put my mouth on those pretty lips and kiss you," he said with so much conviction, it felt like a swarm of butterflies had been let loose in my stomach. "Do you know that, too?"

His eyes now held me prisoner and all I could do was mouth the word *yes*.

Then his lips closed over mine and I hummed against their

warmth. His hands shifted upward and clutched at my hair, essentially holding me captive.

We stayed that way—lips joined, gazes locked, and breaths stolen. As if the world had stopped spinning while we branded the memory of each other's mouths and eyes and hands.

And then his tongue fluttered against my lips, demanding entrance, and I was lost.

Entirely over-the-moon lost.

He groaned as his tongue slid past my lips, filling my mouth so completely, as he explored every inch in a languid rhythm.

And he tasted . . . *God*, he tasted like the best kind of dessert. Like banana cream pie and fried dough mixed together. As he caressed my tongue, my teeth, the roof of my mouth, I was sure the rush I felt had nothing to do with sugar.

I slid my hands down his biceps to his waist and pushed firmly against him. I wanted to get as near as I could in case this was the first and last time I'd have this opportunity.

He released my mouth and dragged his lips along my jaw and then down to my neck. I felt his hot tongue against my skin as he bit and licked his way to my ear.

His hands slid down my back to cup my ass. "Damn it, Ella. You're sexy as hell." He hauled me tightly against him and my entire body thrummed. We fit so snugly together that I could feel his arousal pulsing against my stomach.

I couldn't help the noise that erupted from the back of my throat.

He paused in his perusal of my neck and looked up at me, his eyes dark. So damn dark.

"You drive me insane when you make that sound." Then

his lips crashed against mine, hard and insistent, as my fingers clawed at his shoulders. His wet tongue probed the seam of my lips and I parted them so he could deepen the kiss.

His hands released my ass and slid back up to my hair. "Did you even realize what you were doing to me that night in the bathroom?"

He pulled my bottom lip into his mouth and sucked it hungrily as I whimpered against him. "Ella, you make me fucking crazy."

Then he gave me a melting kiss, his tongue slowing us down to its drugging rhythm.

And this kiss. *This* one.

It made me swoon so completely that I nearly turned liquid and slid onto the ground into a soggy mess. I knew we were in public but I didn't even care.

No guy had ever told me I was sexy. Made me feel this desirable.

I was the sweet, cute, good girl.

Never gorgeous. Beautiful. Sexy.

But with Quinn, the reckless part of me had transformed into this vixen I had only ever dreamt of becoming. If he'd wanted to lay me down on the grass and rip off my clothes, I would have let him; that's how incredibly turned on I'd become.

But the saner part of me—the rational part—knew that we'd need to stop. Eventually. Before we put on an erotic show for the world to see.

But for this singular, mesmerizing moment, as the moonlight filtered through the gleaming pine needles, I wanted—I *needed*—this final, toe-curling kiss.

CHAPTER EIGHTEEN

QUINN

"Suicide prevention line. This is Gabriella."

I tried finding my confident voice. "Gabby."

Even though I didn't feel like driving headlong into a tree tonight, I still found it tough to dial this number. Gabby had sort of become a salvation for me, and for that I would be eternally grateful.

"Daniel," she said, her voice laced with worry. Maybe she thought I was holding a damn revolver to my head or something.

"Hi." I had driven out to the cliff again tonight and now sat perched along the edge.

"Hi." I heard her swallow. "How are you feeling tonight?"

"That's kind of why I'm calling." This time as I looked down into the shadowy water below, I didn't feel the urge to jump.

"Okay," she said. "Go for it. I'm here to listen."

"The last time we spoke, I told you what happened that night," I said. "The night that changed my life. Changed a lot of people's lives."

"Yes, of course. I remember," she said, and it sounded like she took a sip of something. Coffee, soda, water.

I didn't know anything about her. What she looked like, how old she was, where she lived. Only that she was this calming voice. This peaceful force that permitted me to spill my guts. Spill my soul. There was something about her that felt so familiar to me, but it may as well have been her gentle demeanor, her insightful advice that made me feel so comfortable.

"I've been thinking about the power I held in my hands that night," I said. "I mean, I shift my car one way, crash into a truck, and everybody's world is turned upside down."

"And how did that make you feel?"

"Power*less*." I took a deep breath. "It's so crazy, but that's exactly how I felt. Because of everything going on inside of me. And inside of the car."

There was a long silence as Gabby considered what I'd said.

"You were just trying to get your friends home. And struggling to figure out how you felt about a certain girl. Typical stuff that happens in a teenager's life," she said. "See, Daniel. That's why you're a *good person*. You couldn't help everything that happened; it was just an accident. You weren't trying to mess with anybody's life."

This time when she told me I was good, I didn't even flinch. I didn't try to fight it. I'd thought about it long and hard since the last time she'd told me the same thing.

She paused and I heard her chair squeak as she adjusted herself. "If your best friend had been in the driver's seat, how would it have gone differently?"

"Maybe he would have had more control," I said. "Of his emotions, of the car."

"You can never know that for sure," she said. "Even if someone appears to have it all together all the time, you can never predict the other factors that come into play. Road conditions, state of mind, other drivers' actions. Everything comes together to create those circumstances. That's what makes life so mysterious, so fragile, so precious."

I thought about how many times I'd driven with Bastian when he'd had one too many. It was the exact reason why I'd started laying off the booze and become the designated driver. I was afraid he'd kill us. And instead, I'd been the one to kill him. And I wasn't even drunk.

"Is that what bothers you—the fact that you lost control of the car?" Gabby asked.

"The uncertainty of what happened in that moment is probably what kills me the most."

"Uncertainty keeps a lot of people up at night," she said. "Tell me what you mean."

"My passenger . . ."

"The girlfriend."

"Yeah. She said that she noticed the truck veering close to our lane as we got on the freeway. So maybe it *was* my fault. I didn't notice or react in time," I said. "For days after, she blamed me, screamed at me, that her boyfriend was dead."

"It's natural for a person to direct his or her anger somewhere in a time of grief. Even you did that—you directed yours inward," she said, and I realized how right she was.

Still, I couldn't tell her that my parents had paid off the truck driver, that he'd admitted his guilt, because it didn't matter. I couldn't believe any of that was true. "It all happened too fast. I got on the freeway, the truck was in the lane next to me, and we sideswiped each other."

"What else do you remember, Daniel?"

"I remember seeing the truck in my peripheral view. But I also remember her fingers interlaced in mine and how that felt. And just being on automatic, driving along, and then boom," I said as my stomach clenched and the tears loomed at the corners of my lashes, threatening to splash down my face. "The impact. Our heads swinging forward and the car spinning. Her screaming . . . hitting the guardrail and the sound of glass shattering . . . metal crunching."

My throat closed up and my voice became ragged as I tried to suck in air through my teeth.

"And then silence. Eerie, ugly silence. For hours, it seemed, but it was probably only seconds," I whispered as I remembered all of it. "And then heavy breathing . . . groaning, as she and I tried to get out of the car. Then the blare of a siren. The sounds of voices . . . shouting . . . a commotion."

"And what did you think in that very moment, right before the rescue squad got there?" she asked. "What was the one thought that entered your mind?"

"I thought . . . I thought . . ." No one had ever asked me that question before, and, fuck, that moment was so crazy. It was like the very second before a tornado obliterated everything in your life. That's how singular that moment had felt. "I hoped—I *prayed*—that the worst thing that'd happened had been totaling my father's car."

We fell into silence, while I steadied my trembling hands, my shaky breaths. I'd just revealed my memories and feelings about the car crash. Something that for years had consumed, eradicated, and destroyed me to the very depths of my soul.

After another minute, Gabby asked, "And has that feeling you had in the car—that things might end up being all right—been smothered *completely*, Daniel?"

"That's why I called tonight," I said. "Because you asked me a question the last time we talked."

"Yes, I did," she said. "I asked what kept you alive."

"Yeah," I said. "And I recognized what it was the other day."

"What is it?"

"I realize that I still have a tiny sliver of hope buried deep inside me." It was the emotion I'd experienced the moment I stepped foot in my garage during spring break. Admitting that out loud was liberating. It loosened the mud, the grime, the cement that was caked around my guilt-filled grave.

"Hope for what, Daniel?"

"Hope that someday I'll be normal again, at least a little. That I'll feel something again, besides numb." I took a long and deep fortifying breath. One that I hadn't been able to take in so damn long. "Hope that maybe someday I can live again. Really live again."

I didn't mention that I also hoped that Ella could be in my life. To help me forget. And make me feel alive. But the thought was certainly there, at the forefront of my mind.

"That's awesome, Daniel."

"But . . . how can I live, if he's dead?"

"Because you just *have* to. For you. *You*, Daniel," she said, and I was beginning to believe her. "To make your life *mean* something. No matter how small. And it can't mean *anything* if you're walking around dead."

The weight of the world that had been living and breathing upon my shoulders was suddenly lifting. Gabby's voice had become the anchor to the new life I could possibly open myself up to.

"Daniel?" she said. "That's what I hope for you, too."

CHAPTER NINETEEN

ELLA

uinn came to Easter dinner with your family?" Avery asked, primping in the bathroom mirror. "Damn, why did Adam and I have to miss it this year? I would have enjoyed watching the show."

I rolled my eyes. "Mom said to tell you hello, by the way."

"I certainly missed her food. My mouth is watering just thinking about it," she said, smacking her pink lips together. "Did your mom have the potato-and-cheese pillow things again?"

"Pierogies? We made a fresh batch of them that morning," I said, applying my mascara. "Of course, I brought some home for you. They're in the freezer."

"I knew I loved you for a reason, bitch," she said, her eyes twinkling. "Now tell me about Quinn."

"He was great. And he seemed to really appreciate being there," I said, opening my blush compact. "I guess he was raised by nannies and cooks since his parents were always traveling. I was bummed to hear that."

"Everyone's got their own brand of shit to deal with," she said.

"No doubt about that," I said, thinking about Avery's miserable upbringing, too.

"I had Bennett do some investigating for me," Avery said, cutting her eyes at me.

My blush brush stopped midstride as a cold dread seeped into my stomach. "What do you mean?"

"I told him to ask Nate about Quinn." Nate was always at the frat house. He'd be the guy equivalent to our player friend, Rachel. They had so much in common I'd wondered why they never hooked up. But maybe that was the problem. The challenge would all but disappear for both of them.

"And?" I was almost afraid to hear what she had to say. I gritted my teeth so hard my gums hurt.

"Apparently Quinn's a good guy." She winked through the mirror at me and I pumped out a breath. "On the quiet side. Since he comes from a political family, the guys think that he's been in the spotlight for so much of his life that he just wants to be invisible for a while."

"That seems to fit. He's definitely a private person," I said. "The only time I saw him get really animated was talking about his beloved cars."

"Bennett mentioned that. Guess he asked Quinn about restoring the paint job on his Jeep when it got keyed last year. Quinn seemed really knowledgeable about it."

"He seems really *good* at it, too," I said, trying to keep the pride out of my voice. "Sounds like he's only getting his business degree to make Daddy happy."

"Is his dad a real prick?"

"I don't know, maybe," I said. All I knew was that his parents weren't around a lot. Were they shitty to him, too? My stomach clenched at the thought.

"So, did Nate say anything about any . . . girls?" I bit my lip and tightened my fist.

"You know I'd never leave you hanging." Avery brushed her hair into a low ponytail. "I guess he's only hooked up with a couple girls at Zach's Bar. And it was always on the down low."

I huffed out a breath and sagged against the counter.

"Feel better?" Avery asked.

I nodded. My instincts about him had been right so far.

"So . . ." Avery met my gaze in the mirror. "Did anything else happen between the two of you?"

I shrugged, trying to act nonchalant. "We walked to Seymour Park and ended up by the pond."

"You're kidding, you asshead," she said. "And you didn't tell me this information sooner?"

Heat climbed up my neck. Instead of looking her in the eye, I acted like I was cleaning up my mess on the counter.

Her hands went to her hips. "You were alone at the park?"

"We were alone when we went back to his house for him to change, too, and nothing happened."

"And at the park?" Avery asked in her impatient, I'm-going-to-kick-your-ass voice.

"He kissed me." There. I'd said it out loud.

"Shit! Tell me everything, dickhead," Avery said, gripping my shoulders. "No holding back."

I spun out of her grasp and strode out of the bathroom. "It was the best kiss of my life."

She followed me into my room, where I threw myself across my pillows.

"Seriously?" She scooted up on the bed. "So what's the problem?"

"The problem is: I don't even know what we're doing." I turned on my stomach and buried my face in my pillow. "He goes from telling me nothing can happen to an all-out groping session."

"That's understandable," she said. "There's been buildup for weeks."

"You've got that right." I hadn't been able to think of much else since. "And he said the most amazing things to me. I've never . . . had these kind of feelings before."

"Like what?" Avery said. She picked up a pillow and whacked me with it. "Talk, bitch."

"He told me I was sexy," I mumbled into the sheets. "No guy has ever made me feel that way before."

"No one?" Avery asked, her voice falling an octave.

"No one," I admitted. I took a deep breath, sat up, and crossed my legs in front of me.

"I knew it," she said, her voice all smug. "I could totally sense some crazy-good attraction between you two."

"What kind of crazy-good attraction?" I asked, a giddy smile tugging at my lips. "The kind where, if I ripped off all my clothes, he'd look at me like I was his last meal?"

"That's the kind I mean," she said, and glanced away wistfully, possibly recounting her crazy-good-looking boyfriend and the chemistry between them.

"What the hell do I do?" I said, gripping my bedsheets like a woman possessed. "Maybe it was just an impulse. Maybe he didn't mean it. But I can't imagine never kissing those lips again."

I jumped up and started pacing. I felt like I was losing my mind. "I mean, *damn*, have you seen those lips?"

"Someone's got it bad." Avery laughed. "It's okay to live in the gray for a while, Ella. I know you like to have your life all planned out."

Avery stood to pull a pair of jeans from a shelf in the closet. "Take it from me, I know."

She and Bennett had quite the roller-coaster ride last fall. Avery had only wanted a one-night stand. Bennett had wanted more and her feelings had gotten all messy. The end result was that she fell hard. They both did.

She tugged the denim up her tiny legs. "Plus, you might get some good sex out of it."

Just thinking about getting physical with Quinn made all my girl parts shiver. "I've never done that before."

She zipped up and then looked at me. "Had sex with a guy you weren't in a relationship with?"

I nodded and squirmed. The thought of Quinn's lips on my neck. His hard-on against my skin. *Hot damn.*

"Guess you haven't," she said, pulling a black shirt over her head. "Do you want to have sex with him?"

"God, yes," I said, probably a little too quickly.

"So just roll with it," she said, like it was the simplest thing in the world.

"Even if it means this guy has the potential to wreck me?"

Something constricted in my chest at the very thought. How was I going to protect myself from this gorgeous guy whose kisses had me panting for more?

"Maybe you have the potential to wreck *him*—ever think of *that*?" she asked, nudging my chin so that I looked at her. "You are a gorgeous and sexy beast, and you better start recognizing that about yourself."

"I'll try my best," I mumbled, and dipped my head.

And maybe she was right. Maybe Quinn was protecting himself as well. That much might have been obvious. He'd said he wasn't with Amber and wasn't in love with her. But I just knew something had happened between them, even if he was unwilling to share exactly what it had been. He'd said in his frat house bedroom that he didn't want to get involved *again*. Did I remind him of her in some way?

Nate had said that Quinn was rarely with any girls, so what was holding him back? At first I thought maybe it was his lack of attraction to me, but after the kiss at the park, it was pretty evident that wasn't it. You could still lust after someone and not want to date them, that was for sure. So maybe that's all it'd been.

"Avery?" I figured I'd ask since I had her full attention on this topic. "What does it feel like to be in love?"

I'd never been in love before. I'd thought I was falling for my boyfriend in high school. But looking back now, it just seemed juvenile and superficial.

"Love can seem so damn messy. You might not get there at the same instant or even want to admit it at the same time," she said, staring off into the space of her own thoughts. "But one thing's for certain. When you're together—and actually trusting your feelings and the honesty of the moment—you'll feel calm inside. *Still.* It'll feel *right.* Like . . . *magic.*"

She walked over to the window and watched the traffic out on the street. "And you'll know you're there because the very thought of being without him shakes you to your core."

Then she turned back to me. "And when he's in the room? Everything else fades to black."

"Listen to you," I said, staring at my friend in wonder. "What a difference a year makes."

"I know," she said, shaking her head. "I have no idea if my brain's been invaded by aliens or what. Trust me—I had no expectations of this ever happening. I didn't believe in it, and I certainly didn't want it."

That was for sure. She'd fought it practically the whole way through.

"But hope is a funny thing," Avery said. "It reveals itself in different forms, even when you're trying to squash it down."

Her mention of the word *hope* made me think of Daniel and our conversation the other day. "Remember that guy I've been telling you about who calls the hotline?"

"Yeah," she said. I was careful not to give away too many details about my callers. It was against the confidentiality agreement that I'd signed. "Did he call again?"

"Last night," I said. She didn't know his name or what his specific issue was. Just that he reminded me of Christopher and that he was suffering from extreme guilt over something he'd done. "We talked about hope. And, damn, it was an amazing conversation."

"If I didn't know any better, I'd think you had a crush on that dude, too."

"Ew, no, Avery. This is my job. We aren't allowed to get messed up with the people we help," I said. I didn't have a crush on Daniel, did I? While I marveled at Daniel's bravery, his resilience, and his determination, it wasn't in a romantic way.

I didn't know anything about him except how his voice sounded during the different emotions he'd expressed. How it was rougher when he was on the verge of tears. Had a dignified inflection when he was more optimistic. There was an undeniable familiarity between us. And in some cathartic way, he helped me work through some residual feelings I had about Christopher. Feelings I might continue to have on and off for the rest of my life.

And maybe in my subconscious somewhere, I was healing my brother, too.

"I know. I'm just messing with you," Avery said, pushing playfully at my shoulder. "It's just that you get this look in your eyes when you talk about him."

"I admire him. For hanging in there. Trying to make it through. And on a very basic level, I understand him." I turned toward my dresser and located the family photo I had placed there. "Because of Christopher."

"I can understand why you'd have a connection with this guy. And it sounds like you're helping him," she said, slipping into her thong sandals.

"My supervisor said that some callers will affect us more than others because our own experiences or emotions might register in some way. The important thing is to keep a level head and use our familiarity to help them."

"Makes sense." Avery shrugged. "You should feel proud of yourself. You're going to make a great psychologist someday."

"Thanks. I hope so." I grabbed my phone off my side table and sat back down on the bed.

"Speaking of Christopher," Avery said and then cringed, "how did Mom and Dad take the news about Joel?"

"You know, they were pretty cool about it," I said, scrolling through my messages.

I finally told my parents the night of the dinner, after all of our guests had left the house. And after my amazing kiss with Quinn. I didn't know why I thought they'd be upset. It was *me* who had held on to that connection Joel had with Christopher.

"My father actually looked relieved," I said. "He said he wasn't sure if Joel was the kind of guy to settle down with. Wonder what made him say that."

I could tell Avery was biting her tongue, waiting to say something as she gripped the keys in her hand.

"Out with it, asshead," I said. "There's something you want to say about Joel. So get it over with already."

She moved backward toward the door, her face a map of worry. I knew she had plans with Bennett, but she wasn't going anywhere until she told me what was on her mind. "Please tell me you always used protection?"

"Always. I'm no dummy." I threw my hands up in frustration. "Why?"

Her back rested against the door. "Something else Nate told Bennett."

I groaned as my stomach went into a tailspin. What the

hell was she about to tell me? Did Joel have a venereal disease that he picked up from one of those girls I'd always wondered about?

"He said that Joel was a pretty big flirt when you weren't around," she huffed. "The guy hooked up with different chicks while you were together."

My head fell into my hands. "How could I have been so stupid?"

I wondered if Quinn knew about Joel, too. I must have looked like an idiot. Why hadn't I listened to my gut? I knew there was something off about our relationship. And now it looked as if it had never been real.

"Don't you dare beat yourself up about this! That's the exact reason why I wasn't sure whether to tell you." Avery's strong voice broke me out of my pity party. She sat down facing me on the bed. "Don't go blaming yourself about something *he's* done. Sure, you were probably too loyal—but he made you believe he was, too."

"Maybe," I said, biting my lip. "But I think I ignored some warning signs."

"We all make mistakes. We've just got to learn from them." She brushed my hair from my forehead. "If this thing with Quinn goes anywhere, I have a feeling you'll let him know exactly what you want. You won't stand for this again. We've all been naïve at one time or another."

I lay back against my pillow, resisting the urge to curl into the fetal position. "But what about your whole living-in-the-gray thing with Quinn?"

"That's different. That's having fun without any expectations," she said. "From there, if you decide you want to move into more serious territory, I'd hope you and Quinn agree on a few things. Like what that means for both of you."

I turned onto my side and hugged my stomach. "After what you just told me about Joel, living in the gray sounds more doable right about now."

Avery kissed the top of my head before leaving me to my own thoughts.

I wasn't sure if I could trust my own judgment anymore.

Who was I kidding—I needed to start listening to my gut. *Really listening.*

CHAPTER TWENTY

QUINN

hadn't seen Ella since our kiss in the park, but since that day spent with her family, I could think of little else. She was in my thoughts every night before bed and at the very moment I awoke each morning.

The business and psychology buildings were on opposite ends of campus, so I hadn't even caught any glimpses of her in between classes. I was hoping she was still into me as much as I was into her.

But even through text conversations these past couple of days, Ella seemed different. More quiet, standoffish even. Like she had stuff on her mind. So I didn't want to push her.

Except I was going out of my fucking skull. It felt like it was a constant push and pull between us. I was finally feeling free, hopeful, and ready to take the next steps with a beautiful girl. And now she was the one who seemed to be putting on the brakes.

Possibly because I'd been talking out of two sides of my ass. At first, I'd told her that I couldn't be with anybody. And then I'd gone and kissed her—who was I kidding, practically mauled her—beneath the pine trees at the park.

And damn if that girl didn't turn me on in ways I never would have imagined. I mean, the way she was kissing me. Those lips, that body, the sexy noises. *Fuck.*

I was probably confusing the hell out of her, so I didn't know how to proceed. I figured baby steps were the smart way to go. So I'd finally broken down and asked her to do something. I was nearly desperate to see her. I didn't know what I'd do if she declined. Show up on her doorstep and beg her to see me, or something.

> Me: Just leaving practice. Can you meet for pizza at Luigia's in Eaton Center?
>
> Ella: Um . . . sure. Just finished studying for my psychopharmacology test at the library. I'm a block away, so I'll walk. See you in a few.
>
> Me: Psycho what? ;-) See you soon.

I was so relieved that she agreed to meet me. We were close enough to campus that we might be seen by friends, but maybe at this point it was time to figure out what we were doing.

If she still wanted to do *anything* with me.

I parked in the restaurant's back lot, far enough away from any cars that might nick my paint job, and then waited for her at the entrance. She walked up wearing a short denim skirt, some sort of flowy top, and sexy sandals that showed off her painted red toes. She had a brown leather messenger bag slung across her shoulder and she nearly stole my breath away. Her hair hung in delicate waves past her shoulders, unruly locks curling against her neckline, and she looked hot as fuck.

"Hi." Her voice sounded small and shy.

"Hi," I said. My hungry gaze wandered on its own accord over the curves of her cheekbones, to her distinct jawline, and down to the exposed skin in the scoop of her blouse.

As red flooded her cheeks, her eyes darted away from mine. I considered pulling her against me for a kiss. But I wasn't sure what was going on between us, especially since she'd been pulling back. So I'd decided to just follow her lead.

"Where'd you park Fury?" Concentration edged her brow as she looked around the parking lot. "In an open field somewhere, so no one could dent her?"

It took me a second to recall what in the hell Fury was until I remembered that she'd named my cars. Damn, she was cute.

"Not a bad idea, actually," I said with a laugh. "But no, just around back."

Her mouth lifted at the corners. "In the farthest space in the lot?"

I angled my head to the side. "Maybe."

When I opened the door to the pizza joint I couldn't help placing my fingers on the small of her back as she stepped inside. I could tell she didn't mind because she shivered against my touch. Plus, the air felt charged the moment our bodies were in close proximity. There was no denying that.

We sank down in the booth and my knees brushed against hers as I tried to stretch out my legs in the squashed space. But she didn't move away, so I was feeling even more certain that she still felt the same way about me.

"You got enough room, Tall Boy?" she asked, her cheeks glowing with a pretty rose hue.

"Tall Boy?" I smirked. "That's a new one."

I thought about how I'd had to bend down to reach her mouth and how seductive she'd looked when I'd arched her head up to connect with mine.

Now she was chewing her lip while studying the menu and I wanted to yank her over the top of the table to sit on my side of the booth. To hold her, feed her, kiss her. Wipe that worry off her face.

But I didn't want her to think I only wanted something physical. I really enjoyed her company, too. She was funny, smart, and passionate. I'd never felt this for someone in my life—a girl I could truly talk to and feel comfortable with, regardless of our crazy chemistry.

I still felt exposed under her scrutiny, even though she didn't know about my past and what I'd done. Maybe I'd finally bridge that gap and tell her all of it—my secrets, my wants and needs—everything that was real. Share which parts of me were the fake things I made up to please other people.

The thought still terrified me, so I needed to ease into it slowly. I figured if I kept her talking about herself tonight maybe she wouldn't ask me too many questions. At least not yet.

I wanted to know Ella, to see everything inside of her, to somehow become a part of her life. That terrified the shit out of me, but maybe she was also scared. Maybe we could overcome our fears together.

"So this crazy test you mentioned studying for?" I asked, playing with the salt and pepper shakers. It was a bad habit I had picked up, dining alone more times than I was willing to admit. Ella seemed mesmerized by the clear glass containers twisting in my fingers, leaving a smattering of salt crystals in their wake.

"Just a fancy name for the study of psych meds," she said, ripping off a piece of bread from the basket loaf and slathering it with butter.

As the server approached, Ella rested her fingers atop my hands and the shakers to still me and then proceeded to place our order for a half-pepperoni, half-mushroom pizza.

"For someone who takes such meticulous care of his car, you sure are messy in other areas," she said, motioning to my salt-and-pepper mess.

"Nervous habit, I guess." I shrugged. I wouldn't razz her about how she'd just cleaned up my mess at the table in ten seconds flat with a napkin. "You must be a neat freak."

"Pretty much." She shoved the balled-up napkin onto her plate.

"Maybe that's why you're so good at it. Your field of study, I mean," I said. Cleaning up people's messy lives seemed complicated. Perfect for someone more organized. Someone who had their shit together. "Have you always wanted to be a psychologist?"

I was afraid this line of questioning would've been too close of a reminder of her brother again, and I didn't want to upset her. She took her time answering while I sipped my beer.

"Maybe." She dipped her chin in a way that showed her vulnerability that was so appealing. "I've always been a helper sort of person."

"I could totally see that," I said. She had this soothing way about her, but she took charge, too. Like you could've gutted yourself right in front of her and she'd have taken the time to clean your wounds and stitch you back together.

"In high school, Avery joked that I must've had a sign on my forehead that read THE DOCTOR IS IN." When she laughed it was like I could see straight inside her soul. Like in that singular moment I knew her better than anyone else, even though I knew how wrong I was. But, damn, I *wanted* to know her. "Everybody seemed to come to me with their boyfriend troubles or whatever."

"So you were like one of those *Peanuts* cartoons?"

"Lucy, you mean? How she sets up her table and chair?" She twisted her lip, as if picturing it. "Yeah, pretty much. Too bad I can't take my own advice on relationships."

There was so much emotion behind those words I wondered exactly whom she was referring to. If it ran deeper than just her last asshole boyfriend.

"Did you know about Joel, too?" she asked, the words bursting forth with no warning. She bowed her head as pink crept up her cheeks. "That he was with other girls?"

And suddenly I understood why she'd been pulling away from me. Maybe she didn't trust herself anymore—or anyone else, for that matter. I hoped I could help her change that. I wanted her to trust me. For us to trust our feelings for each other.

Because I wouldn't hurt her. If anything, *I'd* be the one wounded, damaged, abandoned—but maybe that was the chance I was willing to take.

"I . . . had my suspicions," I said, working to keep my lips in a straight line. I wanted to keep my head. I didn't want her to see how entirely pissed off I was at Joel for making her feel that way. "Damn it. I'm sorry, Ella."

"Is that why it seemed like you wanted to pound him all the time?" she asked, taking a sip of her soda. A hint of frustration flitted through her eyes. Guess she knew, after all.

"Pretty much," I said. "He's an asshole, Ella. You deserved better."

"I'm not sure if I know what better *is* anymore," she said, her mouth turning down in a frown. "So I'm just taking it one day at a time."

I nodded and took a bite of my bread, even though it seemed to lodge in the back of my throat. That was Ella's way of telling me that she wasn't sure about me or even about *us*. So I needed to ask myself if I was up for the challenge. Was I finally ready to let somebody in? Even if it meant she might not want to stick around?

"So, how about you?" she asked suddenly, changing the subject. "Have you always played baseball?"

"I've played for a long time," I said, careful with how much I revealed, because a large portion of my baseball life involved Sebastian. "Started in Little League and then moved up from there."

"So, your parents come to games to cheer you on?" She looked away as if her question wasn't a loaded one. But I understood her curiosity. Maybe stuff I'd said at her family dinner didn't sit well with her. My family was different from hers and she wanted to know more. To understand.

"Sometimes. More my mom than my dad," I said. I didn't tell her that my dad never really came, and that my mom was more of a chauffeur in my younger years. But my aunt and uncle came, and Sebastian's parents always encouraged me and cheered me on.

"My best friend and I would practice throwing a tennis ball for hours sometimes, against the brick wall at the park so it would bounce back into our baseball gloves. Or even across our backyards," I said before I realized it had slipped out. It was hard not to associate baseball with Sebastian.

Her eyebrows quirked up. "Does your best friend play for TSU, too?"

"No, he doesn't," I said.

And then I was saved by the server delivering our pizza to the table. I dug right in and kept my mouth full so I didn't have to answer any more Sebastian questions.

CHAPTER TWENTY-ONE

ELLA

Quinn was as closed off as ever about his family and his past. He looked so uncomfortable whenever I asked him simple questions. He was holding on to something so tightly that seeing him struggle was a bit unsettling.

So we stuck to less threatening topics, like school, movies, music, and of course, video games. That was the place where we could find our middle ground. It centered us, in a way. Made us feel connected despite it all being make-believe.

What wasn't make-believe, however, was our attraction to each other. Every time he shifted beneath the table, goose bumps whispered a trail straight to my epicenter.

After we finished eating and Quinn walked me outside, he said, "Can I drive you back to your car?" I was parked in the library lot, but it was still light out, so I could easily walk back by myself.

When he saw my hesitation he said, "Or I could *walk* you back."

He looked so young and vulnerable right then that there was no way I could resist him. Besides, I knew that I wasn't ready to let him go just yet.

After I'd learned about Joel's cheating, I'd definitely taken two steps back. I'd decided that living in the gray was better than living with the knowledge that you were only a joke to your boyfriend and to maybe everyone around him. I obviously wasn't a good judge of character, so I'd just play along and get some of my physical needs met in the process.

My anger had built a protective wall around me, at least for now. And maybe I needed to take it slowly, make sure I fully trusted somebody. Unlike last time. I didn't know what Quinn wanted from me, but for now, I was fine with just living in the moment. Having some fun.

"Hmmm, I don't know," I joked. "It might take the same amount of time to walk to my car as it would to get to yours, parked over there in the boonies."

"Smart-ass." He swept me up in his arms, momentarily lifting me off the ground like he'd done at his parents' house. It seemed so natural that when I felt him temporarily waver, I tugged his arms more securely around me.

I felt his breaths against my hair and the hard wall of his chest. His heart rate had picked up speed and seemed to match mine beat for beat.

He released his hold and then grabbed my hand as he walked briskly toward his car, like he was on a mission. Fury was parked in the last row of the back lot, taking up two spaces, as usual.

When we got to the passenger-side door, his eyes fastened on mine with such concentration that I couldn't look away. His expression morphed into something deliberate, something that eased all the doubts I had locked up about him inside of me.

His head sloped to the side, his lips only a whisper away, and his gaze was so penetrating it seemed to devour me whole, beneath all the layers of my skin.

He was a living and breathing paradox. Laid-back and innocent just a moment ago and now so intense it left me defenseless, threatening to steal every last piece of my heart.

When his fingers grazed my jaw, I could barely catch my breath. I closed my eyes against the vulnerability I felt in this perfectly scripted moment.

His lips brushed mine so gently, in such contrast to the way he'd moved his mouth against me last time that I was momentarily transported somewhere else—maybe to the stars. There was something in his kiss. Something his lips were trying to communicate to me that maybe they couldn't—wouldn't— before.

I saw what was buried deep inside him—what reached far below the flecks of gold in his eyes, the rough pads of his fingers, the monosyllabic answers falling from his lips.

Something so honest and real that it left me bare, stripped, breathless.

My knees became weak and I sagged against him. He reached around my waist with one arm to pull me tight, while lightly tugging back my hair with the other to deepen the kiss.

His lips were so warm, his tongue so soft and tender, that my heart bloomed inside my chest in an array of bold and vibrant colors.

When he drew away he gazed into my eyes once more before pulling the door and holding it open for me. I stepped inside, still completely delirious over that kiss. But by the time he'd gotten into the driver's side, his demeanor had changed.

His eyes were dark and positively on fire for me. He trailed a tingly hand across my knee, my stomach bunched in anticipation, and all I wanted was for him to kiss the living hell out of me.

I didn't wait for him this time. I shifted forward and ran my hands along his biceps up to his neck. He inclined his head against my fingers and he huffed out a breath. "Ella."

I traced my tongue against his bottom lip and then pulled it into my mouth. He groaned and grabbed on to my waist, tugging me closer.

The noise tumbling out of his mouth was all it took to make me come unglued. I crushed my mouth against his in a greedy and hungry kiss. He yanked me against him and I pivoted across his body, straddling his hips. I could barely register that the steering wheel was digging into my back or that we were in a public parking lot.

We stayed that way for minutes or hours or days, our lips bruised and our breaths harsh. My hands were busy beneath his shirt appreciating the firmness of his skin and the hard planes of his muscles. My skirt had ridden up my thighs and his arousal ground against my bare skin. Suddenly I was thankful for his tinted windows.

He opened his eyes and inched his fingers to the clasps of

my blouse. Keeping his gaze glued to mine, he unfastened the first button. He kissed my bare skin as he continued down-ward, blazing a heated path as he went.

Parting the material, his fingers grazed the edges of my black bra, his thumbs slipping across my peaks. He palmed my breasts while he kissed the skin at my collarbone and then down the middle of my chest. I panted and moaned against his hot lips.

Focusing on the front clasp of my bra, he unhooked it with agile fingers. When I felt the cool air slink across my exposed skin, I bit my lip and threw back my head—half anticipation, half modesty.

"Goddamn. You're gorgeous, Ella," he whispered as he gazed at me in wonder. I'd heard guys compliment my breasts before, but this was somehow different. This was Quinn—yet again making me feel sexy. And powerful. And all woman.

His palms remained cupped against my breasts, his thumbs brushing my buds while he kissed me with such tenderness it was as if I were a fragile and delicate work of art.

It was intense. Mesmerizing. All-consuming.

We stayed that way—fingers splayed and lips joined—until the ball of light that had once shone high in the sky sank lower still, in the twilight of sleep.

CHAPTER TWENTY-TWO

QUINN

I t was a couple of hours before my next game and I lay on my bed thinking about my phone call with Gabby last night. Somehow in that conversation, I had told her about Ella.

Ella had never asked any further questions about the best friend I'd played baseball with. And when she finally did, I'd probably tell her that Bastian was dead, and I needed to prepare myself for that revelation.

"What's the worst that could happen if this girl *did* ask questions?" Gabby had asked.

"She'd want to know more—like maybe when and how it happened," I said. "And that scares me."

The accident happened days after high school graduation. The horror of seeing Sebastian in that wooden box at the funeral, in that black suit with the damn paisley tie, his hair neatly combed back, was second only to seeing him lying unmoving on the side of the road, caked in blood. My stomach bottomed out—my heart felt like it had been wrenched from my body—as I trembled and almost lost my cookies at his casket.

My father had given me a stern look as I stormed away from them—from Sebastian, from his parents, from everybody. But my aunt and uncle had intervened, told my parents to let me go. After the cemetery, I'd spent the rest of that day sitting on the side of the cliff, considering whether or not to jump in.

How could I tell Ella that?

"True, she might want to know more," Gabby said. "And you'd have to be brave enough to tell her. What scares you most about having to tell her?"

"My best friend's parents seem to have this unbelievable ability to forgive me," I said. "But maybe she won't."

I figured Bastian's parents were either going straight to heaven or they were good at steeling their emotions around me. Regardless, it was difficult to be around them for long. Their showing up at my games probably put them on the level of fucking sainthood or something.

"If his parents have forgiven you, Daniel," Gabby said, "is there a way you can finally forgive yourself?"

"I . . . I don't know."

"I have a feeling you will," she said. "Someday. And maybe this girl will be the one to convince you that you're worthy to live the kind of life you're hopeful about. I think you should give her a chance. I bet she'll surprise you."

Spilling my guts to Gabby again had made me feel better. Or maybe just empty.

Ready to fill myself back up again with something new. Something different.

Something better.

If only I'd given myself permission to let that happen.

I threw the ball back to Smithy on the mound and positioned myself behind home plate. No parental units were here to root for me tonight, and by the seventh inning I was beginning to feel some respite. I'd been able to get lost in something else for a while. No expectations to live up to except my own. I didn't know what would happen with my newfound lease on life, but for the first time in a long while, I wanted to try.

To live. To do something more meaningful. For me.

Outside of Gabby, Ella had gotten closer to me than anyone else—she'd been to my parents' house, and she knew stuff about me that others didn't. Even though she didn't know *everything*.

But I was working up to that. I was feeling more comfortable with the idea. Because the alternative was worse. Being without her. And if I didn't take that chance I'd never know. And I'd already had too many regrets in my life.

Ella and I had texted every day since our pizza date. And, of course, my fantasies were ramped way up since our insanely hot make-out session in my car, while the windows steamed up around us. I mean, *fuck*—the girl made me want to worship her, revere her, build a fucking altar in her name.

Nonetheless, Ella was still holding back. I could feel it. Not in her kisses. If anything, that's where I felt her emotions were on display. Instead, it was in her *heart*. Like maybe she'd decided that we'd just be friends with benefits and she'd be all right with that.

Except *I* wasn't okay with that. It might've taken the pressure off—but not enough for me to live with the idea of just being a fling to Ella. I had this intense need for her to know that I could barely go five minutes without thinking about her. If I could only get the words out. It's like they got lodged in the back of my throat and the only way I knew how to get beyond it was to *show* her instead. With my lips, my hands, and my body.

I was hoping to see her before the team hit the travel bus in two days. So I had texted her that morning.

Me: Fury got a flat tire last night.

Ella: Poor thing. Sounds like your baby needs some TLC.

Me: Absolutely does—from a certain brunette with beautiful blue eyes and kissable lips.

Ella: I'd be happy to offer up some lovin'.

Me: Hopefully soon? Fury's owner has one home game left before he hits the road.

My frat brothers and the girls from our sister sorority were hollering in the stands because McGreevy had thrown a player out at first. When my eyes darted over to them, I spotted her. Ella had shown up to my game and somehow having her here bolstered me. Made me want to work harder to finish this game on top, just so I'd be proud of myself when I saw her afterward.

She was sitting between Tracey and her friend Rachel.

I watched how Joel had looked behind him and waved at her. And how Ella's jaw had ticked as if she was clamping down tight on her tongue—holding herself back from telling him off or whacking him in the head. Maybe I'd knock him the fuck out for her.

I hadn't considered how it'd go down when Ella and Joel first saw each other again. But Joel seemed oblivious as usual, like the huge blockhead he'd always been. Besides, he had a blond chick sitting next to him. Apparently his new conquest.

The other night at poker he'd been a drunken sloppy mess again. He'd spouted off about Ella's amazing tits, how he missed looking at them, and I'd basically lost my mind. I jumped up, the chair clattering to the ground behind me, and had my fist drawn back ready to pummel him. Brian had to plant his hand on my arm to stop me. He yanked me into the other room to play *Call of Duty* and talk.

He hadn't asked me straight-out what was going on between Ella and me, but I got the impression that he and Tracey had figured it out. Probably along with everyone else by now.

I hated that Joel treated Ella like she was only made of

body parts. There was no denying that Ella had a beautiful body, but she was also perfect in every other way, too.

She was plain amazing. And I wanted more.

Maybe I wanted *everything*.

The game ended with a pop fly at home plate. I caught it, tossed it to the umpire, and headed for the locker room to change. Before leaving the field, I looked up at the stands once more and locked my gaze on Ella. I'd expected her to have waited for me in the parking lot with the other family, friends, and fans, but that hope was obliterated when she wasn't anywhere near the team bus.

Instead, I saw Ella up at Zach's Bar, drinking a beer at a back table with Tracey and Rachel. We made eye contact, but she looked hesitant to come up to me. It killed me that we didn't know how to be around each other yet. What we were to each other. I think she was as scared and confused as I was.

Plus, there was Joel to contend with. Not that I gave a shit what he thought. It was more that I wanted to respect Ella. Didn't want people to think she'd left him to be with me. Girls got a bad rap when it came to that kind of stuff—it was a ridiculous double standard. Guys could do whatever the hell they wanted, but girls were immediately called *sluts*.

I ordered two beers at the bar, hell-bent on joining Ella at her table, everyone else be damned. We were friends first and foremost and it wasn't like I planned on groping her in public, no matter how much I wanted to.

While we were waiting on our drinks, I got pulled into a discussion with some baseball fans. They'd asked about our upcoming schedule and whether we could keep ahead of our competition. When I next looked toward the back of the bar, Ella was nowhere to be found.

Her friend Rachel had moved to a table in the corner with one of my teammates. When my eyes skated past Brian's girlfriend, Tracey, I saw the tiny movement of her head.

I raised an eyebrow at her. She motioned to the parking lot. Her way of telling me Ella had taken off. *Shit.* I nodded in thanks.

I chugged back my drink, deciding what to do. At about the same time, my phone buzzed with a text message.

```
Ella: Headed home. Sorry, don't
feel like being in the same room
as Joel.

Me: Understood. It won't always
be this awkward. I won't let
it be.

Ella: I know.

Me: I really liked having you at
my game, Ella.

Ella: I liked being there.

Me: Wish you would've waited. Was
looking forward to spending time
with you.
```

Ella: Actually, I was hoping . . .

Me: Hoping what? Maybe it's the
same thing I'm hoping. . . .

Ella: Maybe it is. Apartment 1A.
34 Carmine Street—you know the
building. I'll be waiting.

I could barely contain myself on my barstool. I waited a good two seconds before bolting out the door. The urge to see her was nearly blinding.

I parked on her street and tried not to jog all the way up the walk. When I rang her apartment, she didn't even bother to ask who was at the door; she just buzzed me in. I decided I'd have a chat with her about that later, before I realized that she probably saw me pull up through her front window.

As soon as she swung open the door, I grabbed hold of her face and kissed her. I couldn't help myself. I wanted to smell her, taste her, hold her. And damn if her lips didn't feel so soft and pliant and ready for me. Her breath tasted like mint mixed with alcohol from the beer I'd seen her drinking at the table.

I backed her into the room and shut the door with my foot. "Are we alone?"

"Ye—" When she opened her lips to speak, I took advantage with my tongue, sliding it deep inside her mouth as she grasped at handfuls of my T-shirt. I couldn't get enough of her. She shoved her hands in the back pockets of my jeans and hauled me against her. In an instant I was hard as a block of fucking ice.

She moaned as I gathered up the back of her hair into a makeshift ponytail and gently tugged it down to gain better access to her mouth. I backed her in the direction of her room and though I could see her bed in my peripheral view, I wanted Ella in a different way.

When her back hit the door, I pinned her hands above her head, in much the same position we'd found ourselves in before. She closed her eyes, tilted her neck, and I took full advantage, practically devouring her skin. It was smooth and silky and smelled faintly of her almond scent.

"We always seem to end up against a door," she breathed out. Her words faltered as I licked and nipped my way down her collarbone to the scoop of skin above her breasts.

"I have fantasies about what I want to do to you against this door."

Her breath hitched as she squirmed, grinding her hips against the front of my jeans.

"You keep doing that and I'm going to come like a horny teenager," I breathed into her hair, attempting to steady my racing pulse. "That's how hot you make me."

She made that little noise in the back of her throat and I nearly lost my load.

"Want to know what I plan on doing to you?" I growled against her neck.

"Yes," she breathed out. "Please."

Shit. She did *not* have to beg. At this point, I'd probably walk across flaming coals if she'd asked me to.

I let go of her hands and trailed my fingers down to the sliver of stomach peeking beneath her shirt. I felt her shiver while I ran my tongue along her earlobe and then claimed the patch of skin below it. She fisted the back of my hair and tugged my lips back to her mouth. Her kiss was frantic and deep and, goddamn, this girl knew how to rock my world.

When she sucked on my tongue, I couldn't fucking take it anymore.

I needed to see her. *All of her.*

I inched her shirt up her torso to remove it and she lifted her arms to make it easier. I threw the thin material on her bed and then trained my gaze on her amazing tits.

I thumbed the lacy part of her bra and her nipples pebbled beneath the material. I sucked one nub straight through the fabric and when I moved to the other breast she whimpered and clawed at my back.

Fuck, this girl was hot.

She yanked off my shirt and traced her fingers over my arms and chest and then down the trail of hair above my belt loop. "Quinn," she said all breathy.

I closed my eyes and reveled in the feel of her hands on me. They were soft and smooth and warm. And when her nails lightly scratched across my abdomen, I inhaled sharply. It felt so damn good.

I let out a shaky breath before I opened my eyes and flattened my body against hers, practically molding her to the wood. This kiss was reckless, bordering on dangerous, and I wanted to keep my tongue in her mouth for all of eternity.

She peeled one bra strap down her arm and then the other, eyes glued to mine, like this was our private striptease. She reached around her back to unclasp her bra while my dick tried to spring free of my pants of its own accord.

Damn, this girl was perfection. Her breasts were perfectly

round, her nipples pink and standing at attention, and I was desperate to put my mouth on them so she could feel me. *Really* feel me.

I wanted to show her how beautiful she was.

"I want to kiss this gorgeous body." I strung my fingers through the ends of her hair. "Will you let me?"

Her only response was a low moan as she shut her eyes and knocked her head against the wood. My fingers skimmed across her stomach and then up to her breasts. I held the weight of them in my hands and thumbed her taut nipples before pulling one of them into my mouth.

I took my time sucking, licking, and nipping her warm peaks while Ella whimpered and murmured my name over and over again. I'd have kept going if only to hear her throaty pleas. Her breasts were bare, her buds hard and wet from where my mouth had been, and I was sure this image of her would be permanently etched in my brain.

When I pinned her earlobe between my teeth, her fingers shot to the front of my pants. She gripped me through the thick material and I strained against her hand, wanting to strip naked for her.

But not yet. Maybe not even tonight.

I wanted to savor this girl. Show her how much I relished her. I didn't want her to think I was anything like Joel. This girl needed to be cared for, protected, and valued.

This was Ella standing before me, allowing me to touch her and taste her, and all I wanted was to make her feel good. Special. Exquisite.

I removed her hand from the front of my jeans and then knelt down and kissed her stomach, which quivered at my touch. I flicked open the button on her pants and then looked up at her. Her eyes were filled with so much desire, it was all I could do not to throw her on that bed and sink myself deep inside of her. Lose myself in her. Claim her as mine.

But she wasn't mine. Not yet.

"I want to see you, Ella. *All* of you."

When she threaded her fingers through my hair, that was all the permission I needed. I rolled her jeans down her hips and she kicked them off. I grabbed hold of her ankle, momentarily studying the dragonfly tattoo I'd wanted to ask her about.

I didn't want to break this spell we were under, so I kept going, kissing up her calf to her knee. She wore little blue panties and I wanted to rip them off with my teeth. My fingers traced up and down her thighs and then thumbed beneath the edges of her lacy underwear.

"You're so damn sexy, Ella," I whispered. I heard how her breath caught. "You make me want to do naughty things to you."

"Is . . . is this part of that fantasy you were talking about?"

"Fuck yes," I said, adjusting myself on my knees and then palming her sweet spot through the thin material. "I want to kiss you, Ella. Right *here.*"

"Oh God, Quinn," she said, panting.

I'd never been so desperate to taste a woman before. Only Ella. With other girls, I'd just wanted to fuck and get myself off. But I needed to savor Ella. Consume her. *Own* her.

I tugged her panties down and helped her step through them. I met her large and sparkling eyes before I studied her stunning body, on display before me. Her hips were shapely and her boobs were amazing. She didn't have a skeleton body like other girls I'd been with. Her stomach wasn't completely flat and that made her even sexier.

She was all woman and hot as hell.

"I hope you know how gorgeous you are, Ella," I said as I kissed her thighs. They quivered with eagerness and it excited me even more that I could stir this girl so much.

Her fingers gripped the door handle and her head sank back.

I repositioned my hands to the back of her thighs before grabbing hold of her perfect ass. And damn if that didn't do me in right then and there. I looked up at her just as I hauled her hips closer to my mouth. Her lips parted and her eyes clenched tight in anticipation.

"Look at me, Ella," I murmured. "I want you to see how much I enjoy kissing you down here."

Her eyes snapped open, like she couldn't believe the words that had fallen from my lips. And actually I had no earthly idea where they had come from, either. Never had I uttered those words to a girl before. Never had I wanted to or even cared that much.

Ella just brought out this unyielding passion in me. I was desperate to feel connected to her and right now that connection would come through my tongue making contact with that gorgeous patch of skin on exhibit before me. It was swollen, perfectly trimmed, and waiting on me to sample it.

Her eyes blazed with the same intensity I'd seen before and as I opened my mouth to taste her, she shuddered against me. I kissed her gently at first, taking my time caressing her outer lips before flicking my tongue against her opening and then trailing it up her center.

She tossed her head back in pleasure, her chest and cheeks flushed with a pretty crimson color, her skin hot and pulsing beneath my lips.

I adjusted my hold on her ass and spread her wider so that my tongue could have full access. She had a heavenly musky scent that infiltrated my senses and made me nearly ravenous for her.

I tasted her for a long time as she whimpered and made that insanely sexy noise in the back of her throat. She grasped at my hair and when I sucked on her bud she nearly unraveled right in front of me.

But I drew away and made sure her eyes were still on me. They were glossy and unfocused but she never looked away. She bit her lip and inhaled sharply as my tongue continued to map its pattern over her folds. And then deeply inside her.

Finally, I settled on her epicenter again, alternately sucking and swirling her into a frenzy.

"Yes . . . Quinn." Her voice was hoarse and gravelly as she reached her breaking point. "Oh God. Don't stop."

Her knees gave way and she nearly collapsed against me, but I braced her hips against the door. I licked her more slowly and gently to bring her down as my fingers grazed soothing patterns over her skin.

"You are so fucking incredible, Ella."

When she finally stopped quivering, she fastened her eyes on mine solid as steel.

And I swear I saw straight through to her center. Maybe to her soul.

So I gave her sweet pink bud one final, lasting kiss.

CHAPTER TWENTY-THREE

ELLA

I hadn't seen Quinn in a few days. But damn if I didn't still feel his tongue on me and fantasize about experiencing the sensation again. And maybe he'd finally allow me to return the favor.

After he had his way with me against the door, I could tell how aroused he'd been—but he acted like it was no big deal and refused anything in return.

Instead, he helped me get dressed, which almost made me ready for round two—until he pulled out the Xbox controllers. I kicked his butt in a *Sonic* racing game, and afterward, he held me on the couch while we clicked through the channels.

I almost fell asleep in his lap while he stroked my hair and kissed my forehead. It was such a comfort to have him there. I wanted him to stay over but I wasn't sure if I could ask him, or even if I should.

I had stood naked in front of him and not felt shy in the least bit. Hadn't even felt the need to hide my stomach or my ass. The way he looked at me with such reverence and passion was something I'd never experienced before. He asked me to watch him while he relished my body, and that was, hands down, the most erotic experience of my life.

But I still didn't know where we stood or how to define us. I was living in the gray and just trying to enjoy it, but I'd never done that before. Been with someone for the sake of being with them—with no parameters or definitions caging us in.

It felt unnatural, but also, in a way, *freeing*. There were no expectations about loyalty or communication, and Lord knew that boy could make quite a statement with his tongue.

I was free to do what I wanted with anybody else, really, but the reality was, I didn't want to. And I knew with an unspoken degree of certainty, neither did he.

And that right there was the difference between Quinn and Joel.

Even though Quinn had no claims on me, my gut told me he wanted me, and this time, I was listening. But something was holding him back. Something in his past that he needed to work through. Someone or something had hurt him, and that made me feel protective of him.

The problem would be letting him go. Defending my own heart would not be easy. If we kept going this way, I'd eventually fall for him. *Hard*. If I wasn't falling already.

The team had been on the road, and between work and classes, we'd only had time to text. But he was coming home today and my stomach buzzed with anticipation when his text came in.

> Quinn: Hey, sexy. Do you already
> have plans? If not, want to catch
> dinner and a movie?
>
> Me: Sounds like a plan. I can be
> ready in an hour.

I jumped in the shower and contemplated what to wear. I decided on jeans and a dressier top with my wedges. This would be the first time we were out in public together, but considering this was a large town, the chances of us running into anyone we knew were slim, unless we stuck to the regular college haunts.

Besides, did it matter anymore? Tracey said that most everyone had figured it out anyway. Although I wasn't sure exactly what they'd figured out if Quinn and I didn't even know ourselves.

Avery had come home from work and was changing in the bedroom when Quinn knocked on the door.

"I'll get it," she said, pulling her shirt over her head. Mischief blazed in her eyes.

"You rein it in, asshead," I said, still trying to figure out what to do with my hair. "I'll be out in a couple of minutes."

I heard Avery let Quinn inside while I started to tuck my hair up in a messy bun.

"So, is this, like, a *real* date?" Avery asked. No hello, no nothing.

What in the hell was she doing? She told me to live in the gray and then she went and asked him a *so*-not-gray question.

I knew she was just trying to feel him out, but talk about *Holy mixed signals, Batman.*

"I guess you could call it that," Quinn said, his gravelly voice rumbling up my spine and warming me in all the right places.

"What are you guys gonna do when you finally run into Joel?"

"Dunno," he said. I brushed back a piece of my hair, listening to his reply. "That motherfucker didn't deserve her anyway, so who the hell cares."

My hands stilled in my hair. I hadn't been expecting that response.

"Good answer," Avery said. I imagined her folding her arms across her chest like a surrogate parent or big sister or something. "Do you think *you* deserve her?"

A gasp caught in my throat and I sagged against the sink. I was going to kick her ass.

"I'm not sure," Quinn said, and I sucked in a breath. "But I'm sure as hell *trying* to be worthy of her."

Shit. What the hell had just happened? Everything suddenly seemed flipped around. Here I was just going with the flow, living in the unknown, and Avery had turned this into something heavy.

Something I wasn't sure if I had wanted to hear, because it was too perfect. *He* was almost too perfect. And if it didn't work out, my heart was going to have a long recovery time.

Joel had nothing on what Quinn had made me feel in just a handful of weeks.

I closed my eyes and inhaled a lungful of air. I needed to

get out there before Avery said anything else to embarrass me. Although maybe I should thank her. Maybe Quinn had been feeling the same thing—this compelling pull to be together. And maybe we should do something about it.

I opened the bathroom door and stepped out. Quinn looked stunning in relaxed jeans, a black fitted T-shirt, and canvas flip-flops. I could even see the manly hair on his toes.

He didn't have his Titans ball cap on today, and his copper hair was twisted upward in a kind of a modified Mohawk. Like he had run his fingers through the mess before walking out the door.

"Just trying to do something with my hair. Sorry," I said, and then shot Avery a look. She shrugged as if challenging me to be mad at her.

"I like when you wear your hair up," he said, his eyes gliding over me. "Shows off your cheekbones."

I felt a blush creep up my face. "Thanks."

"I'm headed up to five," Avery said, winking at me. "Have fun, kids."

She left us standing in the living room facing each other. I realized then just how much I'd missed seeing him all week. I felt like skipping our plans, pulling him down on the couch, and spending all evening groping him.

"So, um . . . any idea what movie you want to see?" he asked, shoving his hands in his pockets.

We definitely needed to do more than make out like a couple of teenagers. We needed to do real things, out in public, so we could see how we navigated the world together. What we had in common. How well we could discuss things. "I wouldn't mind checking out the new *Star Trek* movie."

"Really?" He rubbed his jaw as if this pronouncement had

made him more confused about me. "Video games. *Star Trek*. You really did grow up in a house full of brothers, didn't you?"

"Maybe," I said. "But remember, I'm the oldest, so *I* influenced *them*."

"Point taken," he said, holding the door open for me.

When I slid into the leather front seat of his car, I said, "So how's Fury holding up?"

"Pretty well," he said, his cheeks lifting into a grin. "But she doesn't like to park in busy movie-theater lots where people will touch her. So she may drop you at the door while she finds a spot away from the crowd."

I just shook my head and laughed.

At the theater, we bought popcorn, Milk Duds, and large sodas. After we settled in our seats in the crowded room, I opened the box of chocolate caramel confections and dumped them in the large tub.

"Um," Quinn said, scratching his chin.

"Sweet and salty—it's a must-have for movie watching."

"Seriously?"

"Yes, seriously." I picked up a Milk Dud, flanked it with two pieces of popcorn, and then brought it to his lips. "Here. I guarantee you'll fall in love. You'll never watch a movie without them again."

"If you say so. " He dragged the sweet and salty mixture into his mouth but kept my fingers enclosed between his lips. I held in a gasp while he ran his tongue over my thumb and then sucked on my forefinger before releasing my hand and chewing what remained.

"Agree," he said around a mouthful of popcorn. "Wouldn't want to be without them ever again."

Quinn's gaze latched on to mine. It felt like a bundle of feathers had been let loose in my stomach. "Guess you'll have to come to *every* movie from now on. So I don't forget."

Speechless wasn't even the word for what I felt in that moment. *Dumbfounded* might have been more like it, or maybe just *struck stupid*, because I couldn't even move my lips to form any coherent words.

When the movie previews began, he turned toward the screen and reached for my fingers, interlacing our hands. Then he leaned close to my ear and said, "I expect you to feed me just like that the entire movie."

I cleared my throat and finally found my voice. "If I did, we'd never make it through."

"I'm not sure I'll be able to concentrate anyway," he said, kissing the palm of my hand. "With you sitting so close and me not being able to touch you."

"Quinn," I mumbled. I didn't even know what I was going to say—it was just a verbal response to the millions of pinpricks overwhelming my body. Imprinting me with his words. And his voice. And their meaning.

As it turned out, the simple act of lacing my fingers through Quinn's in a darkened room for two hours straight somehow felt more intimate—real, overwhelming—than one of his kisses. Though I would have welcomed one.

We did, in fact, make it through the movie and proceeded to chat about the special effects all the way to the car, which he had parked in Timbuktu. He'd tried to insist that I wait at the entrance until he picked me up, but I'd refused.

We were so full from our drinks and the large tub of

popcorn that we decided to drive around for a while instead of getting dinner.

"Have you ever been to the cliff?" he asked.

"The one on Magnolia Street that overlooks the city?"

He nodded.

"Only once or twice," I said. "It's really pretty."

At the light, he curved around the bend and traveled in that direction. Turning off the main street, he headed toward the cliff. He pulled up alongside the guardrail that prevented cars from flying over. Parking was allowed in this area, as was sitting on the grassy hilltop.

"I come here whenever I can, actually," he said, and it kind of made perfect sense. It fit him and his gentle nature.

I took in the grass, the trees, and the rocky descent to the water. "You've been here a lot, huh?"

He shut off the engine and turned toward me. "Does that surprise you?"

"I don't know." I pushed open my door to exit the car and he came around the other side. "You seem so busy with baseball and classes and frat stuff."

"Right now is a busy time, but not always," he said, removing two thick blankets from his trunk. "And in case you haven't noticed, I don't get involved in too many frat things. Just when I need to."

We headed toward the hill. A few people were scattered here and there, mostly couples. He chose a more secluded area near an oak tree and laid a blanket beneath it.

"Why is that, Quinn?" I asked, kicking off my wedges and sinking down on the soft blanket. The night air was cool but not too chilly. The view of the city was breathtaking, with the silhouette of slim buildings, sailboats, and twinkling lights.

The water below was dark and murky. I noticed how Quinn intently studied the shoreline. I was curious what he saw in it. I wondered so many things about him. "What I mean is, why join a frat if you aren't really into it?"

"I . . . um . . ." he sputtered. But I didn't want to let him off easy this time. I desperately wanted to get to know him, and I didn't feel this question was too personal. He'd asked me way tougher questions. "It's complicated."

"I mean, I'll admit, it doesn't fit you. Doesn't seem to be your thing," I said, looking up at him. He shrugged and sank down directly behind me, sliding me between his legs. I couldn't see his eyes or his expression and I wondered if that was purposeful on his part. "Or is this another one of those Daddy wishes and you're doing the frat thing for someone else?"

"Yeah, something like that," he said, and then he sighed. "I look forward to the freedom of graduation, but I still have a year left. How about you?"

"I'm kind of on the five-year plan. I didn't do a full load of classes my first year, so I've been playing catch-up," I said. "I'm going straight into the master's program anyway."

His fingers lightly brushed my knees and my calves and then traced over my dragonfly tattoo. "Bennett did that for me," I said.

"Yeah?" he asked. "What does it mean?"

"It reminds me of Christopher. Of our childhood," I said. "Bennett said something to me that day, like—the tattoos people regret the least are the ones that have *meaning*. So I'm glad I got it."

His lips found my neck and I wilted against him.

"How about you—ever think of getting something inked?" I muttered, trying to rein in my jagged breaths. His arms came around and wrapped me tight. It felt protective and warm. His mouth brushed light kisses along my hairline, making my skin pebble. "Mmmm . . . you're trying to make me change the subject."

"Is it working?" he whispered. He tightened his hold, pulling me flush against him, barely allowing a millimeter of space between us. I felt his heartbeat strong and steady against my back.

"Kind of." I rested my head against his shoulder and snuck a glance at him. "Just trying to get to know you better, Quinn."

"I know," he said, his breath against my hair. "There's not much to tell. Right now I'm living under someone else's thumb and I don't like it. But someday, I hope to break free and do my own thing, be my own person."

He kissed the top of my head before resting his chin there. I wanted to crawl inside of his skin and stay all night, just like this, nestled against him. His arms acting as a cocoon, a shield, a defense. Us against the world. Like I belonged to him.

Except that I wasn't his. The circle of his arms provided only a temporary safeguard. Flimsy at best. Because there were parts of him he was keeping from me. Holding back. Parts he wouldn't—or couldn't—allow me to see.

Avery had told me to set parameters around what I wanted, if it came to that. And if Quinn and I kept going like this, I'd soon be ready to talk about those things.

Or I'd have to walk away.

But tonight . . . Tonight, I just wanted him to hold me.

"You gonna work on those cars you're so fond of—after you graduate?"

He stiffened briefly against me. Another wall erected. "Maybe. You . . . kinda helped me remember how important it was to me."

"Yeah?" I tilted my head sideways and his hot mouth feathered along my jaw. My knees instantly went liquid and I was glad to be anchored by him.

"Yeah." He lifted my chin and in another beat of my heart, his mouth was covering mine.

The tip of his tongue outlined my lips and I opened my mouth in a sigh. His mouth was hungry and wet and lingered against mine in a slow and sexy rhythm. He cast a seductive spell, completely mesmerizing me, and when his hands trailed down to my stomach, heat pooled low in my belly.

"Ella," he mumbled, "you're driving me nuts. Your lips, your smell, your skin."

I combed my fingers over his cheekbones and through the back of his hair as his lips captured mine again. As the sky grew darker, the full moon made its stunning debut. Our mouths were joined beneath it until they felt bruised, but I couldn't stop kissing him if I'd tried.

Quinn flipped me around so that I was straddling him, and his hardness was like a steel rod through his jeans. The heavy material separating us created a raw friction that was driving me out of my skull. I kept in mind that we were out in public and were only hidden by an oak tree. But as Quinn's fingers skimmed beneath my shirt, I moaned into his mouth.

"Ella, you are so fucking sexy," he said. "I can't wait to taste you again."

I bent my forehead to his lips and said, "I believe it would be my turn."

He braced my jaw to look directly into my eyes. "You don't even know what you're doing to me right now." I brushed my fingers against his zipper, and he hissed through his teeth.

I brought the second blanket up higher around our shoulders. "No one will see us."

His hand clamped down on my fingers to stop me. "Not here."

"Where's your sense of adventure?" When in the hell had I ever uttered those words to a guy? We were out in the open, for the love of all things sacred. Who had stolen my brain and replaced it with the pages of an erotic romance novel? "We'll concentrate on being quiet."

He let out a low growl before devouring my mouth again. His tongue probed deep, telling me just how desperate he was for release, and I couldn't wait to give it to him.

I unbuttoned his pants and lowered his boxer briefs until he poked out. Even in the shadow of the blanket, he still looked gorgeous. I ran my thumb along the moisture that had beaded along his tip and his breath hitched.

"Relax your legs a bit," I whispered.

He leaned back, positioning his arms on the blanket behind him. With his hands out of the way, he was in easy reach. He felt warm and solid in my palm. I hadn't been with that many guys, but I could tell that he was very long and thick and imagining him inside me made my underwear instantly damp.

"Christ, Ella." He closed his eyes and tried to control his breathing.

"Same deal you had with me," I said. "I want your eyes on me while I touch you."

I surprised myself with my boldness. Having the power to make Quinn putty in my hands was so completely heady.

I moved my fingers up and down in a steady and deliberate rhythm and his head sloped to the side. His eyes softened and his gaze never left mine. With my other hand, I reached below his shaft and grasped him there, teasing the area with my fingers. "Oh fuck, Ella. I'm close."

I lowered my lips to his. "Kiss me. I want to feel you when you come."

He sealed his lips over mine and with his tongue he mimicked the up-and-down motion of my fingers. He groaned his release into my mouth, his lips quivering with the effort.

It was the sexiest damn thing I had ever felt—let alone done with a guy.

As if I'd absorbed his passion and it'd ignited every nerve ending inside of me.

This was the type of physical connection I'd never had but always longed for with someone. It rooted something between us. Something that had embedded itself in my very center.

"Ella, goddamn," he panted out as he caught his breath. "That was amazing."

CHAPTER TWENTY-FOUR

QUINN

Ella had come to as many of my games as she could this past week when she wasn't busy with classes or homework or her volunteer work at a psych center.

We'd fallen into a natural routine where I'd show up at her place and we'd play video games, laugh, and hold each other. Ella did most of the talking—the sound of her voice comforted me—or we didn't do any talking at all.

We hadn't had sex yet, but we'd come close. Lots of grinding, touching, and kissing.

I knew I couldn't go there with her until I was sure. Sure that I could give her everything. Tell her everything.

Plus, the experience of being inside her might just do me in. Make it that much harder to leave if she decided she didn't want me. Once I told her all of it. I was feeling things for Ella that I'd never felt for a girl before.

I'd slept in her bed a couple times and those mornings had become my favorite. She'd be wrapped in my arms and I'd watch her sleep, so warm and sexy and beautiful. Her breasts would be bare and the curve of her neck would call to me. I'd nestle my lips against her skin and she'd make that noise. The noise that drove me crazy.

We didn't talk about what we were doing or what we'd become to each other, but I could tell the question was on the edge of her lips. Just dangling there. Waiting for me. She wanted to know. She *deserved* to know. And I was struggling to gain my footing, to hold on tight. Because she'd given me something I hadn't had in a long time, maybe even ever.

She made me feel happy. Normal. Whole. Like everything was possible.

Maybe even *love*.

She had this way of putting things in perspective—life, relationships, dreams. Even when she didn't realize she was touching on stuff that was significant to me. It was an intrinsic quality that she possessed, despite her psychology major. It made her special—that part of her that had a calming effect on me.

The other night I'd come so close to just spilling everything. But something still held me back. More than likely it was gut-wrenching panic. That she'd walk away. And then I'd have to find a new kind of normal again. And I really liked living in *this* normal, where I could get lost in her. Her smile, her scent, her skin.

A normal where I hadn't killed my best friend because his girlfriend was coming on to me.

But Gabby from the hotline had helped me to see myself

differently, even though I'd only talked to her a handful of times. Like maybe I *was* worthy. I had always lived in Bastian's shadow and thought I was worth crap without him. But maybe Amber truly liked me for me and had been going about it the wrong way. She was human, too, after all. I needed to re-member that.

Now I was perched at Ella's door, a bag from the local deli tucked beneath my arm, a couple of sandwiches inside. To-morrow, I was headed to a special dedication ceremony for Sebastian. His parents had donated a new scoreboard in his honor.

They'd requested I attend—my parents, of course, had insisted—and as the date loomed nearer, I'd become more of a wreck. About seeing all the people I'd wanted to avoid. Maybe forever.

I'd considered begging Ella to come with me, but then I'd have to tell her everything. And right now I was living day by day. Hour by hour.

When she swung open the door my heart strained against my rib cage. Stunning even in her cutoff jean shorts and plain white T-shirt. Her legs seemed to go on for miles and her boobs more than filled out the thin cotton material.

"Hey, baby. You look kissable," I said, and her cheeks flushed the color of her lips. My fingers wound around her neck to draw her closer and my lips brushed against her soft mouth.

Kissing Ella was like coming home. There was no other way to describe it. It felt natural, thrilling, *right*. I just wasn't sure if I was right for *her*.

Ella picked at her turkey-and-cheese sandwich and I

helped clean up her leftovers. Without another word, we sank down on her couch and picked up the controllers—as if we were one seamless unit.

We'd spent the bulk of the other night building a mansion in *Minecraft*. We'd compromised on number of rooms, placement of bathrooms, down to our luxurious back deck that housed its very own hot tub. Yeah, my mind had quickly gone to the gutter on that one.

It was as if we had built our dream home together even though neither of us breathed a word about it. But there was a connection there. Like we were united, somehow considering our future, planning it together.

"Where do you want this to go, Tall Boy?" Ella asked, her knee brushing against mine.

"How about here, Silly Girl?" I smirked and shook my head.

Ella had decided that a giant roller coaster needed to be erected right outside our make-believe home, which, obviously, I completely dug. Maybe it was her way of telling me that we could have fun together. Like she knew I was holding myself back and was giving me time to work it out.

"Ready to go for a test drive?" she asked, wiggling her eyebrows at me.

"Ooooh, yeah." I winked. "I love roller coasters."

We climbed up the length of the track and then slid down our imaginary amusement-park ride.

"Wheeee." Ella laughed and it was the greatest sound to my ears. "Maybe we could go for real one day."

"On a roller coaster?" I nudged her with my knee until she looked at me. "Sounds perfect. You name it and I'm there."

"It's a date, then." Ella's cheeks bloomed pink and she looked so damn pretty right then it made my heart hurt. I wanted nothing more in the world than to fulfill that promise to her.

After we tested out our roller coaster a couple more times, I threw down the controller and pulled Ella onto my lap. God, it felt good to have her in my arms. She trailed her lips down my jaw and then whispered my name in my ear. It made my stomach perform a dive-bomb—like I was really on that ride, holding on for dear life.

She stood up, reached for my hand, and walked backward toward her bedroom. "Will you stay again?" I nodded and she flashed me a wicked smile, knowing just how to produce the desired effect.

I jerked her top off and nudged her onto the bed. Flicking my tongue down her neck to her collarbone, I felt her nipples harden through her bra. She moaned and squirmed, bringing my dick to full attention.

I tugged the straps off her arms, unhooked the clasp, and dropped the flimsy material onto the floor. Curving my hand around a soft globe of her flesh, I drew the peak inside my mouth as she writhed beneath me. I moved to her other breast and indulged on her other pink bud.

"Quinn," she rasped out. "Take off your shirt. I want to feel you."

I did as she asked and then sank back into her arms. Capturing her bottom lip between my teeth, I nibbled and then swiped my tongue across the tender flesh. She whimpered beneath me and I plunged my tongue deep inside her mouth, completely turned inside out over this girl.

One of my hands tangled in her hair while the other one gripped her hip. Her breasts were like firm pillows against my bare flesh and I had the urge to get her completely naked beneath me. My fingers traveled between our bodies to unfasten the button on her shorts. I pulled back and used both hands to tug the denim down, along with her lacy white panties.

I slid them off her legs and then savored the view between her thighs. She practically knocked the goddamn wind out of me each time I had the privilege of seeing her nude and I prayed there would come a day when I could plunge myself deep inside of her.

But for now I needed to touch her, to show her how amazing she was. My fingers trailed down her stomach and I felt her muscles contract beneath my touch. I skimmed my fingers over her perfectly groomed patch of hair before sliding my fingers through her slick folds. "You're so wet, Ella."

Her forearms rested above her head and she moaned against her pillow. When I thrust one finger inside, her back arched off the bed. She was so ready for me and for one brief moment I considered letting it all go and falling into her.

But I knew this girl deserved more.

I plunged two fingers deep inside and hooked them upward, hoping to hit that magic spot that made her shudder against my hand. My tongue went to work on her inner thighs, trailing my way up to her sweet spot.

"Please, Quinn." Her gaze was tethered to mine, thick as a rope, pure abandon blazing in her eyes. "I need you inside me."

Hearing her beg for it almost made me lose my fucking mind.

"No, Ella." I struggled to find my voice through my blinding arousal. "Not tonight."

"Why not?" she panted out. "I want you. Right now. Like this."

I withdrew my fingers and she groaned from their absence. I crawled up her body, placing my knees on either side of her thighs. Her eyes widened in anticipation.

"Don't misunderstand, Ella. I want you. So *fucking* bad." I gathered her face in my hands. "The day I can finally bury myself inside of you is the day I know for sure that you're mine. *All mine. Only* mine. And anything other than that isn't good enough."

Her chest was heaving and her jaw was slack, but she didn't say anything.

"Do you understand me, Ella?"

"Yes," she whispered, her eyes full and glassy. "I know there are parts of you that you're holding back. And I . . . I want to know all of you."

I shut my eyes against her words. Against the honesty in them. And the pain.

"Damn it, Quinn." Her fingers gripped my thighs and my eyes snapped open. I looked at her. Really looked at her. Her vibrant blue irises. Her luminous wavy hair. Her velvet-soft skin. She was like a goddamn angel.

Her hand cupped my jaw. "I'd be *honored* if you shared yourself with me."

Honored? *Fuck.* I backed the hell away and sat down on the edge of her bed, hot and stinging tears gathering behind my eyes. If only she knew. She would *not* be fucking honored to know that I'd killed my best friend.

Shit. What was I doing here with this girl who deserved someone better?

My head sank into my hands and I considered fleeing from the room. From her life.

"Hey," she said, scooting off the bed and kneeling in front of me. "Quinn."

She tugged my hands from my face and locked her gaze on me. "Whatever it is, I know it's important. It makes you afraid. Afraid to share yourself completely with me."

"I . . . Shit. I don't deserve someone like you," I mumbled. "You shouldn't be . . . with someone like me."

Ella became still. The only sign of life was in her eyes, which were quickly welling up. *Fuck.* I swiped a stray tear from my cheek and looked away from her, embarrassment heating my face. Or maybe disgrace.

"No," she said, grasping for my hands, forcing me to look at her. "You . . . you're the best kind of person I know."

"No." I shook my head, hard and insistent. "I'm not."

"*I* believe you are, Quinn." Hearing those words tumble from her mouth triggered something. Something deep inside. It felt like I'd heard similar words uttered by someone else before. "And when you're ready to tell me, I'll be here."

I was so full of emotion for this girl that I yanked her mouth to mine and practically devoured her lips. She grasped fistfuls of my hair and then straddled my lap to get as close to me as possible. I greedily sucked her tongue into my mouth as a moan erupted from her throat. Our kiss turned frantic, impassioned, reckless. It was busting at the seams with unspoken feelings.

And so many unspoken words.

I told her everything through that kiss. Every single fucking thing.

I begged her to forgive me. And then I pleaded with Sebastian to absolve me. So I could be with this beautiful girl. And give her all the damn things she deserved.

Ella's hands rushed down my body to my shorts and she flicked open my top button.

"No, Ella." I halted her efforts with my hand. "You don't have to do this right now."

"Goddamn it, Quinn," she practically growled. "I want to. Let me."

And before I could protest and tell her how undeserving I was, she had my dick in her warm hands and I was panting from the contact.

She forced my shoulders back and yanked off my shorts. Then she knelt down, grabbed a solid hold of me and trailed her tongue in circles along my head. And, damn, if I wasn't hard before, the sudden rush of blood to my nether regions made me solid as fucking marble now.

She pumped me in and out of her hot mouth, expertly licking and sucking, and I collapsed against the pillow from the sheer eroticism of seeing her lips around me. I completely lost myself in her again. In this gorgeous girl who wanted to know me, please me, and be with me.

As much as I wanted to be with her.

With her wide blue eyes settled on mine, she ran her tongue up the length of me, drew my tip between those pouty lips, and I was ready to explode.

"Oh God, Ella," I groaned as the milky liquid shot out, running down my shaft and onto my stomach.

Ella left my side momentarily only to return with a wet washcloth. As she dabbed the warm rag on my abdomen, my fingers traced over her cheekbone. "You're incredible, Ella."

Something had passed between us tonight. Something powerful. Commanding. Profound. We were on the cusp of exclaiming our deepest feelings and intentions to each other and both wholly aware of it.

We were standing on the cliff together, ready to take the plunge.

And most of it hinged on me.

Ella climbed into bed and reached for her shirt. I seized it from her grasp and tossed it back on the floor. "I want to feel your skin against mine all night."

I pulled Ella against me, her back to my front, and I floated into peaceful slumber with her almond scent wrapped all around me.

CHAPTER TWENTY-FIVE

ELLA

I woke up hot and sweaty, and I quickly realized that Quinn's body was swathed so tightly around mine that I didn't know where our limbs began and the twisted covers ended.

I pulled my arms out from under him, stretched them above my head, and shifted onto my back.

"Mmmm, good morning." His voice was hoarse and deep and I wanted to stay wrapped up in his embrace all day.

"Good morning," I said, giving him a chaste peck on the lips. His fingers latched on to the back of my head and he pressed his lips firmly to mine. His tongue flickered against my mouth momentarily before pulling away and leaving me breathless.

"So, you hitting the road this morning?" I knew he was headed to his parents' house for a couple of days and I was already missing him. But yet again, he was acting mysterious.

Said he had stuff to take care of at home. And those kinds of answers made me pause, instead of begging him to go all the way, like I had last night.

I was still trying to live in the gray like Avery advised, even though I knew we were beyond that. But we'd never get any further emotionally unless he trusted me enough to let me in. I couldn't imagine what he could be holding back.

And then my thoughts turned to Daniel. He considered his secret to be pretty big. So large in fact that he wanted to kill himself. He figured he was a disgrace—contemptible even—and the idea of that made my heart crumble.

Daniel's accident was nobody's fault. A simple nudge of the steering wheel, a failure to look into traffic one last time. Studies showed that guys tended to hide their low self-worth and loneliness, often leading to higher rates of depression or even suicide.

That very thought roused me straight out of bed. Whatever skeletons Quinn had in his closet, he needed to realize that living was so much better than simply existing.

"I'll be here when you get back," I said, sliding into sweat shorts and a T-shirt. "And then maybe we can . . . talk."

He didn't even question me, just nodded like he knew it was inevitable. And in my own way, maybe I was giving him a sort of ultimatum. That we needed to lay everything between us out there. In the open.

Because there was something bigger happening here and I didn't feel like being on the fence any longer. If he wasn't sure about me, then fine. I'd have to accept that. But, based on what he'd said to me last night, I suspected it had more to do with him than with me.

After Quinn left, I jumped in the shower. Avery and I were meeting Rachel to do a little shopping and girl bonding. It was such a sunny day that we decided to walk to Vine Street to meet her.

"So how was last night with Quinn?" Avery asked.

"Dreamy," I said. "Damn, he's so hot."

"Have you guys gotten freaky deaky yet?" She tucked a smirk in the side of her cheek.

"I want to. Bad," I said. "I've been trying to just go with it, like you said. But he's holding back and I'm not sure why."

"You do realize that I understand that kind of logic completely," she said.

I nodded and let her continue. "He has to feel comfortable enough—ready enough—to share stuff with you, whatever it is," she said, lacing her arm through mine.

"I know," I said, frustration seeping into my words. "It's just annoying because it feels like it's the one thing holding us back."

"I can tell that boy is hot for you," Avery said, leading us across the street as the light changed to red. "So it's only a matter of time."

Rachel stood outside of a new shop called Threads. We gave brief one-armed hugs and then turned toward the shop's window display. It contained gigantic paper mums in pastel colors that were only eclipsed by the colorful vintage-inspired clothing on display.

"I've been dying to shop here since this place opened," Rachel said before we stepped inside.

After the owner greeted us, we perused the racks along the wall and agreed that the prices were reasonable. I was probably the most girly of my two friends. I rarely saw them in skirts or dresses. Rachel found a rack of vintage T-shirts and piled a few on her arm before heading for the dressing room. Avery grabbed two pairs of skinny jeans that she could squeeze her tiny butt into, and I followed behind with a couple of sparkly tops.

"So, have you gotten that boy in your bed yet, bitch?" Rachel said over the dressing-room door.

I pulled a black top with sequins over my head. "Not yet, but I'm working on it."

"He's in my marketing class on Tuesdays," she said, both of us stepping out to check ourselves in the large three-way mirror. "Pretty much keeps to himself. A couple of the girls in the class are hot for him, but he doesn't give them the time of day."

I understood that logic now. He didn't talk to anybody because he somehow felt unworthy.

"As a matter of fact," she said, tugging the thin material over her belt loops, "I've never seen him with anybody."

"Oh, he's so into Ella," Avery called from over her stall. "You should see the way he looks at her."

"Good to know," I said in the most laid-back voice I could muster, despite a thrill racing through me. He didn't seem to notice any other girls besides me. But that still didn't mean we'd end up being together, not if he wouldn't allow himself.

And what he'd said last night about not having sex unless I belonged to him. Holy hot damn! That had turned me into a complete mushy mess. No guy had ever uttered those words to me before. It only made me want him more. If that was possible.

"Not sure what that pretty boy's deal is, but he does seem to be into you," Rachel said. "So I need to hear the dirt when you finally let him in your pants."

Little did she realize that it was the other way around.

CHAPTER TWENTY-SIX

QUINN

Sometimes when I walked into my childhood home, it was like stepping back in time. Pamphlets and flyers strewn across the kitchen counter. Mom and Dad prepping for their next event or fund-raiser. Advisors plotting strategies on the campaign trail. Various personalities gathered around the kitchen table, welcomed into our home like close friends.

How was it possible to be surrounded by so many people but still feel completely alone?

It hadn't always been that hectic or eventful. It was quieter in my younger years. Gentler moments could be plucked from my memory, when my parents were becoming savvier—the idea of politics was just taking hold. When it had all been grassroots and our involvement in the community didn't feel like a game.

When the campaign trail became our way of life, everything began to blur. We were always on the road, in planes, visiting city after city, the skylines smudging in the background. I'd latch on to other politicians' kids because they seemed to get it—get me.

That was the exact reason Sebastian and I got along so well. At least in the beginning. He would have made a great politician. All charm and skill and bullshit. He knew how to build you up, and with the simple flick of an eyebrow, tear you back down. He could command a room just by stepping into it—and everyone gravitated to him like he was the fucking sun or something. Including me.

I'd lost my virginity to a senator's daughter in the backseat of her daddy's Range Rover. There was nothing romantic about it. We were both lonely and horny and fulfilling a need. By that time, Sebastian had taken the virtue of more than a few willing girls.

When I stepped inside the quiet of my parents' home this morning, I realized we were completely alone, just the three of us. And now I'd welcome some sort of distraction. Because my parents had become strangers to me.

My mother was already dressed in her white pearls and crisp cardigan. It was a rarity to see her in anything other than a skirt. She was always *on*—as if a fucking camera were following her around, documenting her political life or something.

Was it any wonder how paranoid I'd become about revealing too much of myself to outsiders?

"Hi, honey," she drawled, setting a steaming cup in front of my father, who was standing at the kitchen counter in his shirt and tie. "I laid out your best suit for the event."

"Yep," I mumbled, and nudged past her to get to my room. But my father's large hand latched on to my shoulder.

When I looked at him, I saw irritation hidden behind his eyes. The same impatience I'd seen countless times when I didn't do what was expected of me. "I hope you'll have an attitude adjustment by the time we get to the dedication."

"Yeah, sure, whatever," I said, stepping out of his grasp.

"Don't you think of anyone but yourself?" he growled. My shoulder slumped against the wall, my back to him. "He was your best friend. These people lost their child that night."

My fingers balled into tight fists and I considered using them on him.

"Are you fucking kidding me—you think I don't know that?" I turned to glare at him. "You think I don't live with that every single day?"

"Don't you raise your voice to me, young man," my father said, his top lip quivering.

"Or *what*, Dad? What will you do to me?" I challenged him. "Take away my college funding?"

"Don't get smart with me." His voice had lowered, his anger taken down a notch. I had thrown him off by confronting him. He was unsure where this was headed. *Good.*

"You can't punish me anymore than I've already punished myself," I said, my rage deflating, sliding out of me into a puddle on the floor. To be quickly replaced by self-loathing. "I mean, *shit*, Dad. Almost every night, I consider driving myself off a bridge."

My mother gasped, her hand crashing down on her mouth. And I'll admit, I liked hearing that sound. Of her being shocked. Maybe it meant she still cared.

If not, then maybe I'd done my job of ruining her perfect façade.

"Why would you say such a thing?" my mother said in a low and horrified voice. "What would be so bad that you'd want to tarnish our name?"

I snorted. It always came back to that: soiling our family's goddamn reputation.

"I took someone's life that night, don't you get it?" I threw the words in her face and it felt so damn good. So fucking perfect. "How do you think people see me? As a pathetic kid or a murderer?"

"Don't you dare say that, *Daniel Joseph*." She only used my middle name when she was serious. When something was important. "He did it—Jacob Matthews—that man who drove the truck. He admitted it and we took care of it."

I hunched forward like I'd been punched in the gut. The air had trouble making its way down my lungs. I braced the wall and sucked in air.

"T-tell me what happened that night," I panted out. "The night all the adults met with Sebastian's parents. What was said?"

"We won't talk about that night," my dad said, as if he was having trouble swallowing. "What's done is done."

"So it's okay if your son—your only child—walks around with all of this guilt. Wants to kill himself for it. That's *fucked* up, Dad."

"Watch your mouth," he muttered, more out of habit than anything else.

A bitter laugh escaped my lips. "Right, because not using profanity is so much more important than the truth."

Mom and Dad shared a look. The same look I'd seen countless times when they were deciding whether I was mature enough, *worthy* enough, to be privy to their useless information. Then Mom gave Dad a slight nod, like they were letting me in. Letting their pathetic child inside their fucked-up lives with their fucked-up logic.

God, how the hell had I been able to stomach this for so long?

"Daniel," my mom said. "Jacob Matthews admitted that he fell asleep at the wheel."

My body became numb and my vision blurred, like I was in some fucked-up *Twilight Zone* episode. That was the first I'd heard that version of the story. What the *hell*? I had the sensation of falling, falling, falling, down the side of a giant mountain.

"He was scared," Mom said. "He apologized to Sebastian's parents, signed the plea agreement along with *other* legal documents, and we moved forward from there."

I moved my lips in a fuzzy haze. "What you mean is . . . you paid people off so that the public didn't hear about it again."

"We did what we needed to do to protect our families," she whispered. I saw how her hands shook as she gripped the counter. "We didn't need that kind of publicity."

My father took a step toward me and for the first time in a long while, I didn't feel the need to cower. I felt dead, numb— weightless, even. Like I'd just been gutted and my remains lay in a heap on the floor and I couldn't do a damn thing about it. "You have nothing to feel guilty about, son."

My gaze leveled on him. I could tell how uncomfortable I'd made him, glaring at him like that, but he didn't look away.

"Don't you get it?" My voice was soft, defeated even. "This entire time I thought you paid him off because it was *my* fault. You didn't think I deserved to have that information?"

My hands tore through my hair as the resentment surged to a crescendo again. "You're my parents, for God's sake."

A choking, garbled sound burst from my mother's lips. "I . . . I wish I'd known you'd been suffering like this." When I looked up at her, tears were spilling over her cheeks in waves.

But I couldn't handle it. Not now. Maybe not ever.

It was too late.

I stormed down the hall to my room and slammed the door.

I lay in my bed and stared up at the ceiling, my body convulsing in shock waves. I'd spent so many years trapped in a prison of my own making.

My thoughts naturally wandered to Jacob Matthews. Did this arrangement keep *him* awake at night as well? Would *I* have taken what'd been offered to me? Maybe Matthews knew as well as I did that you could never run far enough away from your own damn self.

There was also a small a part of me that wondered if Matthews's hands had been tied—that he'd felt forced to confess. That maybe somebody had dug up dirt on him—I'd seen it too many times to count on the campaign trail.

It was that kind of uncertainty that Gabby said I'd face for the rest of my life. And there was nothing I could do about it, except try to move on. Try to make something meaningful out of my life.

I pulled myself out of bed, changed into my suit, and soon enough there was a knock on my door.

"It's time to head to the dedication, Daniel." My mother's voice sounded small and quiet. Filled with regret. And uncertainty.

And I could only hope that she got it. *Really* got it now. Got *me* now.

Understood that she'd once held me in her arms, whispered soothing words into my tiny ears, and shaped me into believing all things were possible. And then gradually, over time, the rug had been pulled out from under me. It had all been hollow. Useless. Disingenuous.

And then the night of the accident—it was all taken away. Just gone.

My hopes. My desires. My dreams.

And she—they—did nothing to make me feel otherwise. Only considered themselves. Their reputation. Their political standing.

And it was wrong. So goddamn wrong.

And in that moment, I decided never to allow anyone I cared about to feel that small. That worthless. That insignificant.

When we pulled into the crowded parking lot, my stomach had tightened into a fist. I realized how many of the people from high school that I had severed ties with would be here. Including Amber.

And in that moment, I wished that Ella was at my side.

I saw Amber's shock of red hair from the backseat of my parents' car, and I knew I needed to say something to her before I chickened out. "I'll meet you inside."

I walked faster to catch up with her. "Amber, wait up."

She turned, her eyebrows meeting in the center of her forehead.

"Hi, Quinn." She motioned to her parents to keep going. "What's up?"

She was gorgeous, with a flowing head of curly hair and pouty red lips. And I realized that the two of us had been high school students with almost-innocent crushes. I wasn't the first and I wouldn't be the last. And someday she would find a guy who'd feel for her what I already felt for somebody else.

I'd made mistakes. We all had. And it was time to remedy them. Right here and now.

"Listen, I'm sorry," I said, and her lips parted in surprise. "That I keep pushing you away. I've been broken up about this for years. Living with my own guilt and I'm ready to be done with it. Move on from it."

"I'm glad," she said, a small smile lifting her cheeks. "I've had my share of guilt, too. For liking you. Being attracted to you. When I was with someone else."

"This whole time, I figured you were using me to get to Sebastian," I said. "I mean, he was the king, the boss, had girls lined up around the corner."

"And he knew it, too." We both laughed about our lost friend and it felt good. Too bad he wasn't here with us, so we could rag on him. But maybe he was somewhere, listening. Ready to pound his fist into my arm or wrestle me into a headlock like he'd done countless times on his front lawn.

I couldn't blame him for having all of that charisma, unless he was abusing it—like I'd been fearful would happen if he kept traveling down the same path. I'd always hoped that reality would slam into him one day. But not in the way it had. And not at my own hands.

In retrospect, I was jealous of Sebastian. I'd wished whatever it was that he possessed would rub off on me. That I could be as luminescent as he'd been. As beautiful and magnetic.

But maybe it only mattered if *one* person felt that way about you. That you were the moon, the stars, and maybe even the whole damn universe.

"Anyway, Quinn," Amber said, bringing me out of my thoughts. "I liked you for *you*. Sure, Sebastian was a superstar— gorgeous and charming and good at everything he touched. But so were you—in your own quiet way. And there was something so attractive about that."

I closed my eyes at the sound of her words. Because Gabby had been right. There was a glow inside of me, too. Incandescent. This entire time. I just hadn't recognized it.

"Thank you for that." I grabbed Amber's hand and squeezed. "I hope we can start over and be friends."

"Just friends?" Her eyebrow quirked up.

I nodded and dipped my head, hoping I wasn't hurting her again.

"I could do that," she said, and then smiled. It was a genuine smile that helped unraveled that ball of worry in my gut. "Let's go."

She threaded her arm through mine and we walked up the stairs to the building. This time, I held my head high and saw things a bit differently from the way I had a couple years ago. People greeted me and slapped me on the back. I didn't see pity or disgust in their faces. I realized now that what I had seen back then was my own emotions reflected back at me.

We slid into the front row of seats near our parents, but not before walking past Bastian's family first. This time I looked his parents in the eye. Really looked at them. And I saw their sorrow, their grief, their forgiveness shining back at me.

And I showed them the depths of my emotions, as well. Because that was the singular place we were joined. Connected. In our heartache over losing someone that we'd loved.

I found the empty seat next to my mother, faced the front of the stage, and straightened my tie, ready to take on the day. That's when I felt a pair of small hands grip my shoulders.

I turned to look into the eyes of my aunt Gabby. Uncle Nick stood beside her and he reached for her hand, his gaze never leaving mine.

"We came to support you. We figured you'd need it," Aunt Gabby whispered in my ear. "Please stop shutting us out. We want you in our lives, Daniel."

I nodded and allowed her to encircle me in a hug, while Uncle Nick clapped me on the shoulder. I felt something warm and wet slip down my neck onto my hand, so I looked up at her.

And that's when I realized that the tears that had fallen were all my own making.

CHAPTER TWENTY-SEVEN

ELLA

'd been lying on the couch trying to get my thoughts in order about Quinn when my phone buzzed with a text. I hadn't been able to sleep very well the night before, like there had been a dark shadow looming over me. Over my heart.

Quinn: Heading home from my parents' house. Can I stop by?

My pulse thrummed in my veins. I was desperate to see him, if only to hold him again. I loved the weight and feel of his arms around me. And I was scared of the possibility that that would be all I'd ever get from him. That he'd only be able to show me how he felt through his touch, and with his body—and never with his words or his emotions. That I'd have to make the difficult decision to walk away. Before I fell even deeper.

Me: I'd like that. Don't have to
be at work for a couple of hours.

Quinn: See you in a bit.

I brushed my hair into soft waves, sprayed it, and then changed into the clothes I'd be wearing to work—a simple black skirt, a plain lilac T-shirt, and a chunky necklace.

When I let Quinn inside, he didn't waste any time gliding his fingers around my waist and resting his forehead against mine. "I've missed you."

My heart threatened to burst through my chest. "Me, too."

I pulled away and headed toward the kitchen. "You hungry or thirsty?"

He tugged at my hand to sit next to him on the couch. "Only for *you*."

Then his lips met mine and I felt something warm and comforting in the center of my chest. Something that felt a lot like coming home.

I raked my hands through his hair and his fingertips fluttered against my thighs. "I like this skirt you're wearing. Your legs are so sexy." His fingers teased farther up my thighs beneath the cotton material. I let out a sigh as he kissed my neck.

"So, how was your visit?" I asked between breaths, hoping he'd open up, but also hoping he wouldn't—so his hands would keep working their way to my panties.

His fingers stilled on the undersides of my legs and he pulled his lips away from my jaw to look me in the eye. "It went okay."

It was as if I'd doused him with a cold bucket of water. He

sat back against the cushions and rested his hands in his lap. The air in the room had changed to something thick and suffocating. I tried to swallow but it was as if fear had replaced my saliva and I couldn't wash it down. It infused my skin and saturated my bones.

He seemed distant and isolated and anxiety rolled off of him in waves.

This was it. The moment he'd finally tell me something. Maybe everything. It was like a boulder that sat wedged between us. One that needed to be pushed to the side so we could get to the path beyond.

I ground my jaw and tried to still my reaction. Nothing he told me could possibly make me react as badly as he'd imagined. I almost wanted to coddle him like a mother would a small child and tell him it would all be okay.

"Listen—" he began, but I cut him off.

"Wait," I said, rolling out my shoulders, working up the courage. "Quinn, I love being with you. I want you to know how much I look forward to whatever comes next . . . for you and me. That is, if you want the part that comes next."

I dipped my head, suddenly shy and anxious, like maybe I'd been presuming too much.

I heard how roughly he swallowed. "I'm pretty sure that next part is going to be up to you," he whispered.

I grabbed hold of his hand, laced our fingers together, and gave him my full attention.

"Ella, I went home yesterday because my best friend from high school . . ." he said, and then squeezed his eyes shut. "He . . . his parents dedicated a baseball scoreboard in his memory."

"Oh." I waited to see if he'd offer anything more. After another beat, I asked, "Did he pass away?"

He nodded, fingering the blanket folded on the arm of the couch.

"I'm sorry," I said. "In high school?"

He looked up at me. "Right after graduation."

I felt a stab of melancholy for his parents and those that loved him. Why did senseless things like that happen? And when they happened to someone young, in their prime, they felt even worse.

Was this supposed to be the big secret he was holding on to? "You must miss him a lot."

"I do," he said. His voice was raw and throaty, sending a shiver racing through me. I'd never heard him sound that way before and something in the back of my mind was niggling at me. A memory. One I couldn't quite put my finger on. "I have many regrets."

Regrets. So that's what this was about. He felt remorse over something he'd said to him before he died. Maybe they had a fight. Or maybe he lamented *not* saying something to him.

"How . . . how did he die?"

And now his face contorted into something grief-stricken. It made my heart slam into my throat. "In a car accident."

"Oh," I said, and suddenly things began rearranging themselves in my head. Bells and whistles were going off. But still I didn't know what it was that I was supposed to be remembering.

"Was he . . . was he alone?"

He shook his head violently and his eyes looked red and

tortured. "We, um . . . we were at a party together. I was the designated driver."

My stomach seized up as I tried to recall where I might have heard this story before.

The next part flew out of his mouth in a jumble of words and breaths and unease. "I drove Sebastian and his girlfriend, Amber, home. She was in the front seat and he was in the back, passed out. We sideswiped a truck, and Sebastian . . . He died instantly."

And all of a sudden the sound whooshed out of the room. I couldn't hear or see anything, only the memory washing through me like déjà vu—this same conversation played out a couple weeks back on a hotline call. The exact story that haunted me, the identical voice that left me unsettled—and it all fell into place in my mind.

That poignant, agonizing, emotional voice was now *here* in the same room. I sprang up and backed away, unsure if my brain was messing with me.

My lips were immobile and I wasn't sure how my features had arranged themselves. All I could notice was Quinn's response to my reaction. His eyes were wide and afraid. Terrified, in fact. And then they transformed into something else. Sorrow and regret and dejection.

He bounded off the couch and then backed away from me.

"Just forget it . . ." He sounded like he was talking through a tin can. Like his brain couldn't get his lips to form the right words. "Fucking forget *everything.*"

And then he was out the door and gone. Just *gone.*

And still I stood there and stared at the wall, at the ceiling, out the window, and only one thought was ticking through my brain. *Quinn is Daniel?*

Suddenly the sound rumbled back into the room—along with my breath—and I gasped and sputtered and almost puked right there on my floor.

"DANIEL IS QUINN!" I rushed for the door.

"Quinn!" I called, despite knowing he was long gone. I sprinted outside to my stoop and looked both ways down the street, tears already streaming down my cheeks.

I needed to find him. I needed to explain. He thought I was disgusted by him—just like he'd always feared. *Fuck.*

I ran back inside to slip on my shoes and grab my phone and purse. I had an hour before I needed to be at the hotline. I'd find him before then, apologize, and explain that I was in shock.

Maybe I could explain without having to disclose the confidentiality of the mental health facility I volunteered for. I might be in a world of trouble for nearly having sex with one of my hotline callers.

Wasn't there some kind of client-patient rule against cavorting with each other? How in the hell was I supposed to know that he was Daniel? This was totally coincidental. Did something like this even happen in a million years?

The first place I ended up was the frat house. I hadn't been there in weeks. I didn't see Quinn's car, but still I yanked open the door and rushed inside. Joel was sitting at the table playing poker with a couple of the guys. A blond girl was in his lap, slobbering kisses on his neck.

Joel's eyes practically bugged out of his head upon seeing

me. "Ella, what are you doing here?" I must have looked like a wreck, a tangle, a maze of emotions. Because that's how it felt in my head and in my chest. And most of all, in my heart.

"Is . . . has . . . has Quinn been here in the last thirty minutes?"

"Quinn?" Joel said. "Why are you looking for Quinn?"

I ignored Joel and looked at Brian instead. "Has he?"

"I asked you a question, Ella," Joel said, pushing the blonde out of his lap.

"No, I asked you first," I practically snarled. "So answer my fucking question."

He stood up. "Are you screwing Quinn?"

"Fuck you, Joel," I said, and some of the guys whistled. Exasperated, I turned to dash out the door, figuring I wouldn't get anywhere, anyway. But then I swung back around and faced Joel again.

"No, you know what?" I said, finally able to fit my jumbled thoughts together. "I *wish* I had been screwing Quinn instead of you for all of those months."

He barked out a laugh. "You want to screw Quinn? I'm pretty sure he doesn't even know where to aim his dick."

"See, that's where you're wrong," I said, gripping my fingers into a fist. "He's more man than you'll ever be, Joel."

I angled back my arm, wanting to take my anguish out on someone. Joel would have been the perfect candidate. I wanted to punch the astonished look off his face.

Jimmy came bounding around his seat to hold me back. "I should probably grab *him* and let you take a good shot, but you'd do more damage to your hand than his face."

"He hasn't been here, Ella," Brian said now, in a soothing

voice. "We haven't seen him since he went home for a couple of days."

"Thanks." I sagged against Jimmy's arms. "If you do, please tell him I'm looking for him and . . . and I'm sorry."

I jumped back in my car and drove past Zach's Bar, the pizza place Quinn and I ate at the other night, and then the movie theater, hoping I'd spot his car. I texted him twice, but he never responded. I told myself that maybe he just needed time to cool off.

I pulled into the parking lot of a drugstore and tried one last time.

Me: Please let me explain.

And then the only thing left to do was to head to work. I wasn't sure how I'd make it through the next three hours, but I didn't know what else to do. I sat at my desk wondering how in the hell I had even driven here—my mind was a patchwork of conversations between Daniel and me.

How he'd sounded when he'd cried—like an injured animal. How the last time we'd spoken he seemed hopeful.

Had that optimism come from meeting me or was I being too presumptuous? To think my very presence would do the trick when his problems were so ingrained. I had known better than that. Psychology 101.

I'd told Quinn all about Christopher at his parents' house that holiday weekend. Had he felt the same connection despite not understanding exactly how very real it had been at the time?

My mind drifted to the pictures in Quinn's room. Oh *God*. Sebastian and Amber had been in that group snapshot.

And they had been in that car that fateful night, with Quinn driving.

And Amber. She'd been the girl in the parking lot at Zach's. And he wanted her, felt something for her. No wonder they'd seemed to have such a bond as they held each other. They'd experienced something so tragic, so life-altering, together.

Now my brain was reeling. Spinning. Like wheels on ice.

When my supervisor checked in tonight, I needed to tell him that I'd inadvertently befriended one of my callers. More than befriended. I had fallen for Daniel. For Quinn.

Was Daniel his first name? *Daniel Quinn.*

My phone line lit up and I was reluctant to answer it. What advice could I possibly offer anyone tonight when I couldn't even figure out my own problems? I was going to have trouble getting out of my own head. But I needed to push through. This was my future, after all.

"Suicide prevention." I took a huge breath. "This is Gabriella."

"Gabby." His voice sounded husky and filled with bitterness.

I panicked. Completely fell to pieces. My hands were shaking and my heartbeat was thundering in my ears. What did I do? Blow my cover? Play along until I could talk to him in person, or speak to my supervisor?

Yes, that was it. I needed someone—a superior to give me advice. I needed to play by the rules here. Fess up that I had made a mistake. And be professional about it.

"Hello?" he said.

"Daniel," I said, my fingers nearly dropping my water

glass. "Sorry . . . um . . . I know my voice is a little hoarse. G-go on."

I heard something distinct in the background. Something familiar I couldn't place.

"No problem," he said, sounding a bit unsure of himself. "Um . . . so, remember our conversation about hope?"

Long pause. I tried to move my lips. I was sure he'd notice something was off about me tonight. I gulped down my fear. "Yes, of course."

"I think I hoped for too much." I could hear the pain in his voice and I wanted to reach out to him. To tell him he hadn't. That it would be okay. I couldn't get any words out and I was blowing it big-time. Blowing it out of the damn water. And he knew it. He *so* knew it.

"You know what?" he said in a low voice. "Just . . . FUCK IT."

"No, wait!" But the line was already dead.

And I was done waiting for someone to tell me what to do. I needed to decide for *myself* what was important. What mattered in my own damn life. Screw the rules!

I needed to do the right thing. And this time it didn't mean showing up to my job and doing everything by the book.

I needed to find Quinn and I think I knew exactly where he had gone. Despite the flashing red button, I stood, grabbed my purse, and clutched my stomach. Pretending I was sick wouldn't be that far-fetched.

I perched at my coworker's door. "I think I might have the stomach flu. I've got to go now before I throw up or something."

I was pretty sure, given the sympathetic look on her face, she seemed convinced.

I didn't even wait for her response. I just flew out the door and headed for my car, one thought racing through my head on repeat.

I need to get to you, Quinn. Before you break.

CHAPTER TWENTY-EIGHT

QUINN

sat on the side of the cliff staring into the murky water. Something was off about Gabby tonight. Maybe she had problems of her own. I knew nothing about her but she knew everything about me. Everything that mattered.

I was pretty sure I made her night that much more miserable by hanging up, but I'd decided in that moment that I didn't need her anymore. I needed *me*. Myself. I needed to get my shit together and start living again.

Even if it had to be without Ella. I didn't need a girl in my life, even though Ella had made me feel so many things. I'd be good on my own. Besides, I'd never be able to forget that look on her face when I'd bared my soul to her.

I'd decided right here and now that I would finish my degree and then talk to my uncle about working for him so I could then open my own shop someday. I'd remembered talking endlessly to Sebastian about it our senior year of high school and even he'd encouraged me to pursue my love of cars. Hadn't even made fun of me or acted like it was a lesser career choice. Even he'd known I was good at it.

I'd come to realize that since the accident, I'd been in pursuit of the truth. About his death. About my feelings. About life.

And what I'd discovered about truth was that it wasn't constant or objective. It was messy and uneven and sometimes unattainable. I wasn't going to finally kill myself in that water down below, but I did need to find a way to get through my days.

Car lights appeared on the street corner, but I was hidden by the oak tree. The same tree I'd sat beneath with Ella. I'd miss her lips, and her arms, and her laugh. How she made me feel so alive. But I didn't feel like dying anymore, so maybe I needed to thank her for that, too. It hadn't just been Gabby helping me.

I heard footsteps trudging through the grass behind me and I turned to see Ella standing there. She'd said she had to work, so I hadn't expected her to show up. Tears dotted her eyelashes and she looked relieved. Like the weight of the world had been removed from her shoulders.

And that didn't really jell—it didn't make any sense. Was she happy to have found me?

Back at her apartment, she'd thought I was pretty awful. So why would she come here? To clear her own conscience? Make *herself* feel better?

I turned away from her. "What are you doing here?"

She took another step forward and peered around the tree

at me. And now pain crossed over her features. "What the heck happened to your face?"

"You should see the other guy," I said. Even if Ella and I would never end up together, it had been sweet justice giving Joel a pounding. And all it had taken was one hard blow to break his nose and lay his ass flat on the ground, after he'd sucker punched me in the forehead. "You should thank me. Joel finally got what he deserved."

Her breath caught and she knelt down beside me. Her fingers reached for my face before falling short. She looked defeated and fisted her knuckles in her lap.

But, hell, did she have to be so damn beautiful? I'd miss looking into those blue eyes that were like the ocean, deep and powerful—yet peaceful and familiar.

She looked down at my hands, one of which was red and split at the knuckle. She inched her fingers toward mine, but I shoved my hands beneath my thighs. No way did I need the torture of feeling her skin against mine.

"I'm—I'm so sorry," she croaked out, and her voice broke on the last word.

And something shattered inside of me, too. A piece of my heart had chipped away, leaving me with something so small, so trivial—I wasn't sure it would have been enough for her, anyway.

"It's fine," I said, hardening my voice. "I knew it was a long shot, so I took a gamble. And it didn't pay off."

And now the last piece of my heart receded to the dark corner of my chest. I wouldn't let her have that piece, too. I needed to save something for things I still looked forward to.

Like my cars, my aunt and uncle, and the idea of being free. I needed her to get whatever she had to say out of her system and then be gone. As far away from me as possible, so I could start getting over her.

Another example of that slippery slope of truth.

"Daniel." Ella had said the word so softly, I didn't know if I'd heard her correctly. My head snapped up to meet her eyes. "Is that your real name . . . your first name?"

I nodded, not sure where she was going with this.

"Daniel," she said again, more sure of herself this time. And I hated that I liked the sound of my name falling from her lips. "I . . . I'm Gabby."

At first what she'd said hadn't even registered in my brain. It was as if I was under water where everything was fuzzy and dark. And then, as it all snapped together, I broke the surface. I found my air and started breathing again.

Ella was *Gabby.* Gabriella. The girl to whom I had poured out my soul. No wonder she'd always seemed so familiar. So memorable. So comfortable.

But that also meant that she had deceived me. That she'd been messing with me this whole time. I sprang up so fast from my sitting position that my back scraped the tree trunk behind me. My skin was on fire, and I welcomed the burn.

"Get the hell away from me," I said. "You've been lying to me. Is this some kind of sick fucking joke?"

"No, Quinn, please. I swear to you." She moved toward me, her eyes wild and untamed and filled with desperation. "I didn't know until tonight, when you told me about Sebastian and Amber. That's when I put two and two together."

How was that even fucking possible? The coincidence was

too great. I knew that she did some sort of psych work, but I had no clue that it was the hotline. *Fuck.* I'd told her some deep and dark stuff. Stuff that maybe no one should confess—unless they were anonymous.

"That's why I responded that way, Quinn." She latched on to my arm, but I yanked it out of her grasp. "Not because I think less of you."

"I need you to leave me alone." I started trekking down the hill toward the water.

"Don't you see, Quinn?" she called out to me. When I glanced behind me she had sunk to her knees in the grass. "I think so much more of you. I think you're *amazing.*"

I froze for a split second from the sheer implausibility of her statement. I was angry and embarrassed and miserable and I needed to get the hell away from her.

When I spoke to her, I didn't think I'd ever heard my voice come out so quietly. "Please. Please just leave me alone."

And she didn't come after me. She just let me go.

CHAPTER TWENTY-NINE

ELLA

watched as Quinn—Daniel—whoever the hell he was, moved farther away from me into the blackness of the night. When I came upon him on the hill, I expected to find a distraught Daniel. The same one I'd talked to on the phone.

But there'd been something different about *this* Daniel. He had grown and healed, and he seemed almost numb to me. Maybe resigned. That last part hurt the worst.

I didn't see how any of this could be resolved. Could even work between us. And now I understood why there were rules about this very thing in mental health facilities. Because it's essentially a one-sided relationship. One person was the wounded and the other person was the healer.

Even still, there was always a give-and-take. After infusing someone's sorrow inside your soul, it was nearly impossible not to come away transformed. And sometimes there was that one person who changed you so much, that you were altered for *life*.

Because you held their very essence—their very sanity— in the palm of your hand. And there was no way you could be left unscathed.

And I'd decided right in that moment what I absolutely, without question, *had* to do.

I needed to place my soul in the palm of Quinn's hand and force him to make a decision. Either to ignore it or nurture it. Maybe then he'd understand. And maybe then we could heal, *together*.

I stood up, dusted myself off, and silently made my way down the hill. Quinn was standing close to the water's edge, and for a split moment I wondered if he'd considered walking right in. Or maybe he'd prefer that *I* did in his place. I couldn't gauge how much anger and disappointment he was feeling right then.

When he heard twigs snapping beneath my feet, his back stiffened. Even still, he didn't turn around. I picked up the nearest stick and began marring the pebbled sand below me. Prepping myself for what I was about to say.

I moved closer behind him and then let my words flow out.

"The night that Christopher took his own life," I began, and he twisted slightly toward the sound of my voice, "I was supposed to come home earlier from a party I'd attended with my high school friends."

I had never before uttered these next words to anybody except my therapist, in the small confines of her office, over a box of Kleenex. I noticed how Quinn stood motionless now, as if anticipating my next confession. And I realized just how difficult it must have been for him to tell me all that he had over the phone lines those few times.

"But there was this guy at the party. Someone from another school," I breathed out. "I'd seen him before and he was really cute and cool."

I turned and stepped away even though Quinn hadn't turned to face me. It was so difficult to admit that you'd done something so trivial while your brother had lain dying.

Or your best friend lay sleeping in the backseat of your car.

"So I stayed at that party an extra hour, just so I could talk to him out by the bonfire," I mumbled. "And while I was flirting and smiling and feeling all heated from his attention, my brother was killing himself."

I turned back toward the water and noticed how rigid Quinn's shoulders had become.

"I could have gotten home early and maybe stopped him or caught him or talked him out of it," I said, louder now, using the anger that had lain dormant inside me. "Something— anything—other than being hot over some guy that I never saw again."

Quinn finally turned around—gaze locked on mine—and took a step toward me. Something was hooded there in his eyes. Sadness, pity, camaraderie. I didn't know.

"I've never told anybody that story," I said with a very confident voice, so that he'd know how much I trusted him with my vulnerabilities. "Not one person. Except the therapist who helped me through my grief afterward."

He moved closer. And then closer still. He was a breath away and I wanted him to envelop me in his strong arms. But

still, I waited. I wasn't sure what he was feeling. If he was beginning to understand that we weren't so different. Or if he
was still confused and angry.

"We all have moments we wish we could take back," I
said. "Our actions may change the course of somebody's life,
without us even realizing it."

And now we stood toe to toe, Quinn's rapid breaths against
my hair. His gaze was soft, genuine, caring, and all at once I
was gripped with the knowledge that I had been blessed with
two parts of a whole. The Daniel part and the Quinn part had
merged to become the most incredible guy I'd ever met. And
he was standing right before me.

Even if I never got to spend any more time with Daniel
Quinn beyond tonight.

"But you seem so with it. So together, Ella," he muttered.
And then a deep growl emerged from his throat. One of pain,
frustration, and isolation. "How in the hell did you move
on? Become the strong person you are today?"

He dropped to the sand, picked up a rock, and flung it
across the water.

I sat down next to him but refrained from touching
him. I didn't know what he wanted from me right then—
physically—so instead, I became his emotional anchor, again.

"First you talk to a professional . . . one whom you haven't
kissed. And I can help you find the right one."

He nodded but remained quiet.

"And then you have to allow yourself to truly feel everything. All the emotions. The anger, the loss, the shock, the
sadness. Don't run from it, become numb from it, or just go

through the motions," I said. "And don't become somebody *else*. Whether it's with noble intentions or *not*."

He thrust his head in his hands. "Goddamn, how do you *do* that?"

My fingers raked through the sand. "Do what?"

"See inside me," he whispered. "See me for who I really am?"

"This isn't one-sided, Quinn." His head jerked up and there was awe in his eyes. "You make me feel things I've never felt, see things about myself no one has ever made me see before. And I have you to thank for that."

"You don't have to thank me," he muttered. "It's easy to be with you, Ella."

I felt the knot that had been lodged in my chest loosen just a little more.

"You seem to have it all together," he said. "And you've made me feel like maybe it's possible for me, too."

"It wasn't always that way for me," I said. "Sometimes, I still need to sit with my grief and let it shred me to bits and pieces over and over again. But I know that life is beautiful and I know that I've got so much to be thankful for."

He squeezed his eyes shut like my words were too impossible to absorb.

"Those nights on the phone with me. You were already doing it, working through it," I said. "And that's why you've changed. I could tell the difference in your words, the tone of your voice."

"Even still," he said, his voice husky. "I'm afraid if I start . . . if I *really* start feeling everything—I won't be able to stop."

BEFORE YOU BREAK

"No, that's not the way it works. You'd get through it and come out the other side." I reached for him, tentatively weaved my arm through his—and he let me.

"You'll learn to be normal again. You will. It's already begun," I said, my face at his neck, breathing him in. "It'll be a new kind of normal, but normal just the same. It'll be a *Daniel Quinn* kind of normal."

His lips lifted at the corners and our eyes met in one long unblinking look. And that's when I knew. Really knew. That we'd be okay. That we'd work through all of this, *together.*

He scooted closer, his thigh brushing against mine. "How do you live with the what-ifs?" he asked.

"Neither one of us will ever know if our actions would have produced a different result. Or maybe delayed the inevitable," I said. "We'll *never* know. And we need to learn how to live with that."

He nodded and looked at me with tenderness in his eyes. "I'm beginning to believe that."

"Had you never called the hotline, I wouldn't have known this amazingly gentle side of you yet," I said, reaching out and brushing my fingers against his cheek. He closed his eyes in relief. "For what it's worth, Daniel Quinn, it is a *gift* to know you. Every single part of you."

His eyes sprang open and there was panic visible in them again. "You don't feel differently about me now?"

"Yeah, I do." His face fell and I nudged his knee with mine. "My feelings for you are much *stronger* now."

His breath caught and he dipped his head. My fingers

253

grazed his hairline and he shuddered. He brought my hand to his mouth, his lips resting at the center of my palm.

I felt his tender kiss all the way down to my toes.

"And what about me?" I asked cautiously. "Do you feel differently?"

"Sometimes I'd lie awake at night, fantasizing about the Ella part of you." He traced his fingers against my jaw. "But I'd be desperate to talk to the Gabby part of you. So now I've got them both."

"Quinn," I mumbled, overwhelming affection coursing through me.

"Gabriella's a pretty name," he said, trailing his fingers through my hair, as if combing away my worries. "For a pretty girl."

He moved his face toward mine and then tenderly brushed his lips across my cheekbone. I trembled in the wake of his touch as his fingers stroked where his lips had just been.

"Am I allowed to kiss Gabby?" he said, nuzzling my ear. Every nerve ending in my body pulsed against him.

"Please," I whispered. "She wants you to."

When his lips finally moved over mine I sighed against his mouth. I was so thankful to feel his skin next to mine again. His tongue fluttered out to meet mine and I got lost in his deep and powerful kiss.

I pulled away to catch my breath. "For the record, Daniel kisses better than Quinn."

"Is that right?" His forehead creased, and I realized I'd come to appreciate that little line that appeared smack-dab in the center of his eyebrows.

"Yes," I said, kissing his ear. "Because now I can feel *all* of him."

He tugged me down on the sand and we kissed until our tongues were swollen and our lips were bruised. But our eyes remained open and our hearts became full.

CHAPTER THIRTY

QUINN

We pulled up to Hartford Memorial Cemetery as Ella clutched her bouquet of yellow daisies. She looked anxious even though she told me that she'd been there last month on Christopher's birthday. So maybe her nervousness had everything to do with me being with her this time.

After our night at the cliff, I felt insanely closer to Ella. It was like we'd clicked on many different levels. I still don't know how it was possible that I'd met someone like her, let alone called her on the hotline, too.

When Ella said it was fate, I just bit my damn tongue. But maybe she was right. And maybe if I'd never called that hotline, I'd still have been inspired by Ella to become a better version of myself. It was like I'd been drowning and she'd come along and saved me. But she wouldn't have agreed with that summation. She'd say that she'd encouraged me to save *myself.*

And she was right. Because I had. But she'd been the catalyst, that was for damn sure.

And maybe, just maybe, I had found some small way to save her, too.

"You ready, pretty girl?" I said, slinking her hair away from her neck. I restrained myself from kissing her soft skin, because then we'd never leave the car.

She gave me that adorable smile that softened my insides. "Let's go."

She led me toward the row of tombstones across the way until she found her brother's. She smoothed her hand across the stone where his name had been etched. And then she sank down to her knees and I followed suit.

"Hey, Christopher, I want you to meet someone very special. His name is Daniel Quinn."

I had trouble finding my voice. Suddenly this had become very personal and very real. I squeezed her hand. "Hi, Christopher."

"You would love him, Chris." She swiped a tear from her cheek and I felt the back of my eyes prickling. "And guess what? The dude will play *Minecraft* with me for hours."

I grinned at her comment. "She practically forces me to, Chris."

We sat on the ground for maybe twenty minutes more while she told Christopher about school, the suicide hotline, how we'd met, and how the family was holding up.

As we headed out of the graveyard, my stomach tightened in anticipation for our next destination. I hadn't been there since the funeral, and I didn't know how I was going to deal with it now. But I had Ella with me. She provided me with strength and hope and incentive to face my demons head-on.

The ride to Lakeside Cemetery was mostly quiet. It was a comfortable silence as Ella held my hand and sang softly to the songs piping through my stereo system. It reminded me how much I looked forward to plugging in my earbuds and working in my garage later. Ella kept pushing me to fix Fire so we could take her for a ride.

My parents were out of town for the weekend and Ella planned on staying the night. And it felt so damn good to have her with me.

As I pulled in the driveway of the cemetery, I inhaled a deep breath. I knew the section and lot number, but it hadn't occurred to me that the patches of grass would have filled in around his plot and the tree planted near it would've grown taller.

"Do you want me to wait in the car for a bit to give you time to yourself?" Ella asked. I wanted to say, *No, please, I need you.* But the fact of the matter was that I did need to do this by myself.

She traced her thumb across the inside of my wrist, over the tattoo I'd gotten from Bennett at Raw Ink the weekend before. It was simplistic—a baseball with Sebastian's number, seven, inked inside. But it was a huge and powerful step for me—to acknowledge him in a way that hadn't brought forth a tremendous amount of guilt.

This was getting easier. Better. I was finally able to breathe more freely.

I nodded. "Give me a ten-minute head start."

As soon as I saw his name imprinted in the stone along with his birth and death dates, my legs practically gave way. It all came rushing back to me, and I heard a roaring in my eardrums that ended up being my own heartbeat.

I remembered how they'd lowered his casket into the ground to be sealed for eternity and how the very idea of that had been *staggering*. Now I sank to the ground and allowed all of the memories to flood my brain.

How none of my classmates seemed to be able to make eye contact with me that day. Maybe they sympathized or even pitied me. And they should have, because I was pretty damned pitiful. I was lost and broken and hadn't even known how I'd get through the rest of the day.

The rest of *any* day going forward.

"Bastian, I loved you like a brother," I told him. "I'm so sorry. So damn sorry that you're not here anymore. And for as long as I live I will never forget you—you'll always be with me."

Shudders rolled up my back and pulsed through my shoulders until all of that emotion transformed itself into ugly sobbing. My whole body shook as I remembered everything.

Every damn thing. Just like Ella had encouraged me to do.

"But I've got to move on. If anything, to honor *you*," I panted out. "Because right now, I'm just doing whatever it takes to get by."

I placed my head in my hand and rocked forward. "It's fucking hard trying to be you. But you were good at it, Bastian. And I need to get better at being my *own* damn self."

I felt Ella's heat behind me, so I tugged her onto my lap,

encircled her in my arms, and held her tightly against me. "Thank you," I said against her ear, more than once.

I felt Ella's tears dripping onto the back of my hands, her gaze fixed solidly on Sebastian's grave.

"Thank you, Sebastian," she whispered. "For bringing Quinn into my life."

CHAPTER THIRTY-ONE

ELLA

At Quinn's childhood home, we cooked burgers and ate them on the deck along with the margaritas he'd concocted for us, with salt around the rims. We sat together in a reclining chair, me propped between his legs, looking out at the view together.

His parents' property extended into the woods and when you sat back here you felt like you were in a secluded oasis. Even though Quinn grew up lonely in this house, its gardens that were filled with lush hydrangea bushes, dogwood trees, and weeping willows were impressive. Lined along the back of the land were strapping pine trees that acted as a barrier between properties.

Between us and the outside world. And there was no other place I'd rather be. Maybe tonight could be the beginning of new memories for Quinn. For us. Here. Together.

Quinn's mouth swept over mine while the crickets chirped, coyotes howled, and the fireflies lit up the night sky. I licked the salt from his lips and tasted the tequila on his tongue and felt so relaxed and at peace with his arms around me. Protecting me. Keeping my heart safe.

But he didn't own me completely. Not yet. Nor I him. Not according to the conditions he had set before he'd made his confession to me. And mine to him.

But if he wanted to take me right here in this chair, I wouldn't object.

He removed the margarita from my hand and set it next to his on the side table. Then he flipped me around so I was facing him, my legs dangling on either side of his thighs.

"Before we head out in the morning," he said, nuzzling my chin, "would you mind stopping at my aunt and uncle's?"

"I'd love to meet them," I said, honored that he'd even ask. I knew how much they meant to him and now that he'd begun forgiving himself, maybe he'd let them back into his life.

He cupped my cheeks and stared deeply into my eyes. I felt a fluttering in my chest, like a hatchling testing its new wings.

Brushing his thumb against my lips, he said, "Gabriella Abrams?"

He was distracting me with the lips and the eyes and the breaths, so my voice faltered a bit. "D-Daniel Quinn?"

"I'm in deep. So very deep," he whispered against my lips and a bolt of lightning shot straight to my core. "With this girl—who rocks my world with her amazing lips and her brilliant mind and her generosity."

Now that baby bird was swooping and soaring, thrashing against my rib cage, and bursting out of my chest.

"I want to be with her." His hot breath mingled with my own. "I want *everything* with her."

This boy—this man—was asking for the moon and the stars. And I was willing to shoot us straight off the map. And offer him the entire universe.

"I'm . . ." I cleared my throat, trying to swallow the tears that had begun to form there. "I'm in deep, too."

He closed his eyes as if savoring my words. His long eye-lashes brushed against his cheeks and his full red lips remained perfectly still, waiting on me.

"With this boy—whose kisses, bravery, and tender heart make me melt. Plus, he's damn hot and I want him more than I've wanted anyone else in my life," I murmured. He opened his eyes and fixed his gaze on me. "I want everything with him, too."

Those were the last words uttered between us for a long passage of time.

Because all at once he stood up, taking me with him. I wrapped my legs around his waist and secured my arms against his neck. His lips claimed mine, his tongue deep in my mouth—probing, penetrating, searching for his *everything*.

Sliding open the screen door with one hand, he walked us down the hall. He paused outside his room, which contained a queen-size bed, more lush and firm than the one I slept in at home.

Propping me against the wall, he flicked his tongue along my jawline and then moved up to my ear, where he pinned the fleshy lobe between his teeth. His body pressed so firmly, his groan reverberated so deeply, that I almost became liquid beneath him.

His hard bulge drove against my center and a loud moan burst from my throat. I clenched his hair in my fingers and thrust my hips against him. His eyes grew dark—so dark—as overwhelming desire coursed through them.

He laid me down in his soft sheets and then took his time undressing me. He lifted off my shirt and tugged down the straps of my bra. His tongue stroked my hard buds before he pulled each breast into his mouth and sucked gently. My back curved off the bed and my nails bowed against his back.

The only sound in the room was of our breaths and moans. And whereas we'd always been so vocal before—boldly telling each other what we needed and how much we wanted each other—this time seemed different. Tender. Attentive. *Reverent.*

Our silence felt like a necessity as we touched, tasted, discovered, and worshipped.

His shirt joined mine on the floor and I licked the toned muscles on his chest and tasted the smooth skin on his stomach. He made swift work of unbuttoning his shorts and removing them. He knelt on the bed completely naked before me— allowing my gaze to trail over every ripple, curve, and angle. I slid my fingers down the center of his chest, in awe of how gorgeous he was—inside and out.

He flicked open the button on my pants and tugged them down, depositing them to the floor. Then he twisted me onto my stomach. I felt exposed to him, just like that first night in the bathroom—the first time I'd felt a flicker of desire for him—and now I wondered if he was thinking about that same moment.

But I didn't want to breach our silence—this quiet serenity—to ask him.

Tonight was too special. Too perfect. Too *right*.

He swept my hair to the side and I felt his hot breath in my ear and then on my neck and I quivered in anticipation. He trailed his tongue between my shoulder blades and his hands snaked down to my underwear, outlining the curve of my ass with his fingers. I was hot and throbbing between my legs, sure that my underwear was already soaked.

His lips slid down the center of my spine and his fingers curved beneath the elastic of my panties as he tugged them down. I squirmed in arousal, muffling my moans into his pillow. Once he'd pulled the material from my legs, he continued kissing downward, while I writhed beneath him.

Quinn using his mouth and tongue and fingers so intimately was hands down the most sensual thing I'd ever experienced. I was dripping wet for him, thrusting my ass toward him, practically begging for him to take me from behind.

His fingers slid over my thighs to my stomach and I felt myself trembling beneath his touch. He positioned me onto my knees, his fingers found my sweet spot, and I nearly exploded from the contact. While he rubbed my slick center, I felt his head move under my thighs.

Then all at once his hot tongue swiped against my opening. I groaned loudly and sank to the bed—but he held me up, anchoring me with his forearms.

I whimpered and moaned as his tongue tunneled inside me and his fingers worked their magic from the front. His tongue mapped circles against my swollen flesh and then moved down to close around my extremely sensitive bud. And that's when I was driven over the edge.

Light and heat danced around the corners of my mind, while the world caved in around me. He stilled his lips and clung onto my thighs while I throbbed and panted and quivered.

As I floated back down he licked me tenderly before finally releasing his hold on me.

I collapsed onto the bed and then curled onto my side into a tight ball, mumbling incoherently, still throbbing in pleasure. He reached for my chin and stared into my eyes.

Stroking my slick hair away from my face, he shattered the silence by uttering his first words, in a shaky, almost desperate voice, "Ella . . ."

"Please, Quinn . . ." I rasped out. "Now."

He bent over and picked his shorts off the floor, pulling a condom from his wallet. He slid it over his very stiff erection, trembling with need. I turned and raised my hips with eagerness, but still he took his time. He bent down and kissed me, forcing his tongue so deep into my mouth that I gasped for air.

His eyes were fixed on mine as he pushed his tip in tentatively. The feeling was so intense, so personal that I struggled to keep my tears at bay. Quinn briefly closed his eyes like he couldn't handle all of the sensations at once.

When he opened them again he gazed at me in wonder.

"You feel amazing," he murmured. "Christ, so incredible."

He rocked into me, going deeper before pulling almost all the way back out. He repeated the motion, finding a rhythm that had me writhing with pleasure.

Having him fill me so completely was incredible. Gratifying. Profound.

I had fallen so hard for this boy. And I saw the same reflected in his eyes.

He cradled my head in his hands in an almost-protective gesture right before he plunged inside me again. I brought my legs higher around his waist and his thrusts became harder and deeper. His groans filled the room as he drove into me again and again.

He leaned down and pulled my breast into mouth, sucking it eagerly. His tongue swirled around my nipple before biting down. That was my tipping point as he sent me skyward again.

The feeling was beyond words. Beyond colors and lights. It was the sky. The universe.

A pure and exquisite slice of heaven.

"Fuck, Ella." He became still, watching me. Waiting. Marveling.

And then he drove himself fully inside of me, deep and solid.

As solid as my bones. As liquid as my veins.

To the very depths of my core. And maybe even my soul.

His release came in a breathy and curse-laden chorus.

He collapsed on top of me and kissed my neck and ear and jaw all while whispering unintelligible words. Tangled together in a sheen of sweat—we lay panting and recovering.

"You're so beautiful, Ella," he said, before gathering me in his arms and kissing me tenderly. "I've never had this . . ." The words escaped him, his throat clogging with emotion.

As the first tear spilled from my eye, I said, "Me, neither."

His thumb came up and swiped my cheek. Then he pulled me tightly against him, my back to his front. Our breaths were soft and steady against the stillness of the night.

"I guess this means you're all mine," he breathed against my ear.

"For as long as you'll have me," I mumbled, in the haze of sleep.

And just as we drifted off into the land of bliss, I heard him whisper, "Forever works for me."

Despite this book being a work of fiction, suicide is a very real epidemic in our country. If you need to talk to someone, if only to hear an empathetic voice, please consider calling the National Suicide Prevention Lifeline: 1-800-273-8255.

ACKNOWLEDGMENTS

First, I want to say how grateful I am for my ten plus years as a clinical social worker, where my experience in child and family therapy taught me a great deal about humanity. I learned about empathy, vulnerability, and the resilience of the human spirit. The thing we all share regardless of our race, gender, or socioeconomic status is the need to be loved and to belong. Kindness goes a long way in helping someone keep their dignity. It might actually be a lifeline.

Thank you to Jane G. for assisting me with hotline details. You are truly one of the most gifted and compassionate people in my former field. And in *life*.

Thanks to Greg P. for teaching me the ins and outs of college baseball.

To my rock star agent, Sara Megibow. You are like the voice of reason inside my head.

To the entire Penguin team, including the art department for my amazing covers, and the savvy publicity team: Erin

ACKNOWLEDGMENTS

Galloway and Nina Bocci. To the editing department: Laura Fazio, your keen eye helped make this book so much stronger. I'm so glad to have you in my corner. Special shout-out to Jesse Feldman, who helped shape this story from the beginning.

To my family and friends for your constant unwavering support: I love you.

To my first readers: Kate, Stina, Lindsay, Deb, and Alina. Thank you for believing in Quinn and Ella's story.

To the book bloggers and reviewers out there—there are too many of you to list here. Please just know I appreciate all that you do for the simple love of books. Because when it comes down to it, all of us are first and foremost *readers*.

A special shout-out to the Sub Club ladies for making my debut book tour rock.

An additional thanks to Neda, Angelica, and Christine for those extra things you did to make my debut launch more special.

Last, to the readers. Thank you for taking a chance on my books and reaching out to talk to me about them. For an author, there may be no better feeling.

Read on for a sneak peek from the third book in
Christina Lee's Between Breaths Series,

WHISPER TO ME

Available wherever e-books are sold.

"N ot even going to talk to you," I said through gritted teeth. "But I'm not letting you leave alone. You haven't had more than one drink, right?"

She nodded.

"So just start driving, goddamn it."

"Shit," Rachel grunted, and then she pushed down on the gas pedal, causing her to fishtail through the grass. I kept my mouth shut like I'd promised and gripped the door handle instead. She turned the wheel and straightened out the car as she came toward the road.

Being with Rachel like this again made it all rush back. Not one great middle-school memory didn't include her. Rachel had always been so damn cute with that dark hair and those sea-green eyes. And now this body of hers that had blossomed since her illness—she'd developed shapely legs, narrow hips, and tits that I couldn't stop noticing in that thin tank top of hers. Fuck me.

When she started dating that douche bag Miles, she'd changed. She became meek and humble, lost her smartass retorts and sarcasm. She hadn't been my Rachel anymore. She'd been his.

But now. Now she was her old self to the *extreme*. They say your personality can change after a head injury. But this was something altogether different. This was Rachel shutting down, closing herself off completely. And I got it. I so got it.

I had looked for someone like Rachel in Amsterdam. I'd actually dated girl after girl trying to get that feeling back that I had when I was around her. In her space. But it had never returned. Until now.

Rachel grumbled and huffed and smacked the wheel. I just shook my head and looked out the window, allowing her to work it through in her own head. I wanted to know what that motherfucker had said to her, but a promise was a promise.

Did Miles want her back? Would she actually consider it after all this time? He was like her Kryptonite. I clenched my jaw until it ached. I wanted to push his teeth through his skull.

As we drove past Lucy's bar, her foot let off the gas in a moment's hesitation. Maybe if I hadn't been with her, she would have pulled in and drunk herself stupid. Gone home with some random guy. I wasn't an idiot. I knew what my cousin Nate was getting at when he'd given me reports about Rachel.

She'd become someone different in college. It sounded like she was using guys who reminded her of Miles to get lost in for a night. Just like I'd used girls who weren't Rachel in Amsterdam.

I figured at the very least I was saving her from making a dumb-ass decision tonight. Not that there was anything wrong with having an active sex life, but she seemed to be exercising it for the wrong reasons. I pushed away the thought of just how many guys she might have been with at college. The idea of any number of dudes pawing at her body made me want to slam my fist through the windshield.

But then a heavier thought flitted through my brain. *At least she was at the university.* At least she was living a life that had once threatened to be taken from her.

I noticed the tears welling up in the corners of her eyes and knew she was on the verge of losing it. So I turned up the radio and let her be alone with her thoughts. If I tried to speak she'd ream me a new one anyway.

Yep, she was definitely alive and letting everyone know it.

She pulled into the underground garage and thrust the car into park. I wanted to yell at her for bashing on my brakes, but I held my tongue. She slammed the car door and charged up the stairs to the bank of elevators in the lobby. I caught up to her just as the metal doors ground open. I allowed her to pass in first, and she jammed the button to our floor before sagging against the far wall.

I could hear her heavy breaths as she attempted to keep her emotions at bay. I tried to keep my gaze off the vein throbbing in her neck as her gaze skated over my body as if she was memorizing me or discovering me all over again. I didn't know which. Maybe she just wanted to use me as a punching bag. I pushed away the thought of what angry sex with Rachel would feel like. Her on top, riding me with wild abandon in her eyes. *Fuck.*

I bolted out of the elevator as soon as the doors parted, and then turned the key in the lock. She pushed open the door and stormed past me, heading straight for the bar. She rummaged around before finally pulling out a shot glass and a bottle of Patrón.

She sat down hard on a barstool and poured herself a generous shot. Swirling the tequila in her cup, she looked lost in deep thought. I made my way behind the bar and pulled out a glass of my own. I began prepping the lime slices and salt but she didn't wait for me. She threw back her head and gulped the strong drink, wincing as it went down.

Then she started pouring herself another one.

Her eyes slid up to meet mine in quiet determination. She looked woozy yet still defiant.

"Well, damn," I said, finally breaking the silence that had been building up between us.

A bark of amusement shot out of her mouth before she covered it with her hand. It was like being back in middle school all over again. My lips twitched as I tried to hold back my own grin. I downed my shot and heard her break into the same kind of hysterical fit that, when we were kids, would become contagious.

She stopped laughing long enough to knock back one more shot, and then choked and coughed after it went down. She rested her head on the edge of the bar, her shoulders shaking with laughter, and I couldn't hold back any longer. I laughed long and hard right along with her.

After a couple of minutes her chuckling slowed into sputtering gasps. She lifted her head and heaved out a gloomy sigh. Her eyes welled with tears that had nothing to do with the laughter from moments before as she tried keeping her trembling lips in a neat straight line. But she failed miserably after two seconds more as the floodgates opened and she began bawling.

Fat trails of tears rolled down her cheeks, and she tried swiping at them unsuccessfully.

Her emotions were all over the map tonight.

"Hey," I said, my own voice rough with compassion. "Come here."

I pulled her into my arms, and she cried even harder against my shoulder. My cotton T-shirt was soon soaked from her tears, but I didn't give two shits. This was the kind of weeping she'd done in the hospital over that same piece of garbage, and I fucking hated hearing it again.

"It's gonna be okay," I said, rubbing circles on her back. I wasn't sure what to say at this point that wouldn't hurt her worse.

Her arms, which had been hanging limply at her sides, came up to grasp my shoulders, as if I were her anchor. She was breathing heavily into my neck, and I felt her tears slide onto the skin at the base of my throat.

My fingers trailed down her back to grasp her waist, and I could feel how lean she was. Not as lean as she'd been in the hospital. This was shapely, sexy, all-woman lean. My fingers rested on the sliver of bare skin that had become exposed when she'd raised her arms to embrace me, and I relished the softness there.

Her head moved to the crook of my neck, and I felt her shudder, so I drew her even closer, my fingers sliding up her bare back in an attempt to comfort her. The next moment I felt a tentative brush of her lips against my skin. Right above the neckline of my shirt. I became perfectly still, wondering if I'd only imagined it.

But then she trailed her soft lips across my neck to my throat as I swallowed roughly. It felt so damn good that I couldn't help the groan that escaped my lips shortly thereafter.

I grabbed hold of her shoulders and pushed back to look into her eyes. There was alarm there at what she'd done, certainly. Like her body had been on auto-pilot and she couldn't stop herself. Yet there was something underneath as well. Need. Passion. Desperation.

At that realization my brain lost all logical function. I gathered her face in my hands and whispered, "What are you doing, Rach?"

She shook her head, maybe trying to clear the doubt, the shock. "I . . . I don't know."

My thumbs slid over her cheeks and I asked the more direct question. The one that maybe she'd been waiting for, given how she'd dealt with her emotions the past three years. "What do you *need*?"

In response, she closed her eyes and let out a whimper. Her hips thrust forward against mine and my dick immediately responded.

Then I felt her fingernail trail up the back of my neck, and she fisted my hair tightly in her grasp, which only lit a fire inside my chest. I realized just how fucking much I wanted her in that moment.

Except, she didn't want me in the same way. She just wanted the idea of me. She wanted the escape I could give her. And given my history with the female population, she probably thought I knew damn well how to deliver it to her.

Sure, after downing those two shots she probably wasn't thinking too clearly. But neither was I, because she was touching me and her hands were warm and her sounds were sexy and her eyes told me she needed me. Just for tonight.

And I'd give her whatever the hell she wanted, even if I had to forget it ever happened tomorrow. I'd do that for her. And suffer the consequences.

Before I could reason any further, she brought her other hand up and stroked the pad of her thumb across the flesh of my bottom lip. I let out a soft growl and flattened my body against hers.

Her back angled above the lip of the bar, and I positioned my groin against her smooth center as she spread her knees to adjust. And, shit, being this close to her was amazing. Fucking unbelievable. To smell her soft scent and hear the heightened arousal in her harsh breaths.

A moan tumbled from her lips and her nipples pebbled through the thin material of her shirt. I flicked my tongue along her jaw to her ear and mumbled, "Is this what you wanted?"

"Yes." She panted out a breath, and then opened her eyes to look at me. Her pupils were clear. So damn clear in that moment. *"Please."*

No question about it. I was *so* fucked.

ove was like a loaded gun. You slid your bullet inside the cold metal chamber as a safeguard for the inevitable day that everything went to shit. At the first sign of trouble, you blew your opponent to pieces, long before their finger found the trigger. At least that's what my mother's string of failed relationships taught me.

I downed the warm beer and scanned the frat party from my armchair perch. The low moans drifting from the next couch over awakened a longing inside me. My best friend, Ella, and her boyfriend were going at it again. Our other friend, Rachel, an even bigger player than me, was in the far corner making out with another university jock. And I wasn't about to be the only one leaving empty-handed tonight.

Guys were easy to figure out—at least in the hormonal sense. You needed only appear helpless or horny, and their pants instantly dropped to their ankles. Except none of the guys here tonight appealed to me. Maybe I'd text Rob for a booty call on my way home. He was always good for one, unless he'd already hooked up with someone else.

My gaze landed on the guy entering the back door through the kitchen. A red baseball cap was slung low on his head and inky black curls escaped beneath it. His arms were muscular, and his charcoal T-shirt hugged his lean chest. He was Grade A Prime Meat and probably knew exactly how to put those full lips to good use.

I watched as he high-fived one of the guys and then propped his forearm against the counter. His smile was magnetic, and I pictured him using it on me in another five minutes, when he sweet-talked me. I stood up and straightened my shirt so that it revealed more of my cleavage—the little I had—and strode toward the keg with my plastic cup.

As I drew nearer, I saw how alarmingly gorgeous this guy really was. The one hand fisted in his pocket tugged at his jeans, revealing a small sliver of a taut stomach. The trail of baby-fine hairs leading downward made heat pool low in my stomach.

I tried catching his eye, but he wasn't going for it.

His friend was a different story, though. He practically growled in my direction.

The friend was cute, too, but paled in comparison to Hot Boy. But maybe his friend was my ticket in. Too bad I wasn't the type to take on both of them—that might be entertaining.

Bile scorched the back of my throat. *Hell, no.* Two meant more testosterone, less power. No telling what might happen, even if I *thought* I was in control. There was a reason I only did one willing guy at a time.

When I stopped at the keg, I overheard Hot Boy telling a friend that he was moving in the morning. Hopefully not out of state. No matter; I only needed him for tonight. His voice was low and gruff, sending a ripple of satisfaction through me.

Hot Boy's friend reached over and grabbed hold of my cup. "Let me help you with that."

Hot Boy looked up and our gazes meshed for the first time. Warm chocolate eyes pinned me to my spot. They raked over me once before flitting away, sending my stomach into a free fall.

He pushed aside the messy bangs hanging in his eyes and resumed his conversation.

I wanted to run my fingers through those unruly curls at the nape of his neck. I made a mental note to do that later, when he was lying on top of me.

His friend handed my cup back, filled to the brim. Hot Boy didn't look my way again.

"Thanks." I clenched my teeth and worked to keep my lips in a neat, straight line.

"So, what's your name?" he asked as he stepped closer. His breath was sour with beer and cigarettes and I knew I could've taken him oh-so-easily. As simple as the arch of my eyebrow.

But I didn't want him. I wanted Hot Boy. Just for one night.

"My name's Avery," I said, loud enough for Hot Boy to hear.

Hot Boy only paused at the sound of my voice without looking my way. *Damn.* Maybe he had a girlfriend, or maybe he was gay. The pretty boys always were.

"Nice to meet you, Avery. I'm Nate." His friend slid his hand to my hip, and I considered giving up the hunt and taking him upstairs. But for some reason, I just wasn't feeling it.

"I'll be right back." I left him swaying unsteadily on his feet.

I headed back to Ella and Joel, who were still hot and heavy on the couch.

"I'm going to head home," I said, close to her ear.

Ella came up for air. "No prospects tonight?"

"One." I glanced over my shoulder to the kitchen. Hot Boy's friend was still waiting for me. "But I'm not really into it."

"Bitch, you're always into it." Her lips curved into a devilish grin. "Gonna hook up with Rob tonight instead?"

"Maybe." I didn't want to disappoint her. I was ready for a good time most weekends. And, even though she didn't really approve, she was ready for all the gritty details the next day. Ella hadn't gotten me to change my ways in high school, and she wouldn't now. But if I wasn't in the mood, I didn't feel like explaining it to her.

I looked around for Rachel to say good-bye, but she was already somewhere private with jock boy. Ella went back to ramming her tongue into Joel's mouth.

She'd probably felt stranded by Rachel and me too many times to count, so seeing her with Joel actually thawed a corner of my frozen heart. A real live boyfriend was what Ella had always wanted. Someone who *got* her, she'd said. Whatever the hell that meant.

Hopefully Joel would keep treating her right, or he'd have to answer to me. I wasn't opposed to grabbing hold and yanking those balls down hard. My self-defense classes had taught me well.

I decided to give Hot Boy one last shot as I passed by him on my way out the door, luring him with my sexiest voice. Unfortunately that meant passing his friend, too.

"Excuse me." My mouth was close to Hot Boy's ear, my chest brushing past his arm. He smelled like coconut shampoo. Like warm sand, hot sun, and sex. I wanted to wrap myself inside of his arms, but I kept on moving.

"No problem," he said without even a glance.

Damn. Rejected again. That made me want him twice as much.

Just as my foot crossed onto the landing, I felt a warm hand reach around my waist. I almost fist pumped the air. *Got him.*

I turned to greet Hot Boy, my breaths already fluttery. But the smile slid from my lips and slumped to the floor when I realized it was his friend who'd grabbed me instead.

"Hey, baby, where you going?"

"I'm leaving." I twisted away, hoping to break his embrace.

But he kept in step with me. "How about you hang with me awhile longer?"

"Maybe another time."

His hands frisked around to my stomach, and normally I'd accept that kind of action—initiate it, even—but for some reason I couldn't shake Hot Boy's rejection.

I was more of an emotional train wreck than even *I'd* realized. Despite Ella reminding me almost every fucking day.

And just as I was chastising myself and changing my mind about hooking up with his friend, I heard Hot Boy's low rumble of a voice. "Give it a rest, Nate. She said she was leaving, and I'm pretty sure that means without *you.*"

I blinked in shock. Maybe he'd noticed me after all.

His friend backed away with his hands raised. And then turned to the keg.

Hot Boy gave me a once-over. "You good?"

"Yeah, thanks."

Wait a minute, this was backward. I was thanking Hot Boy for being all chivalrous. And the boys I hooked up with were *so not chivalrous.*

Hot Boy nodded before turning on his heels and heading out of the room, leaving my ego collapsing on the cold hard tile.

Chivalrous Hot Boy was so not into me.

I walked the two blocks back to my apartment alone.

I tossed and turned, imagining Hot Boy's lips on mine, a fire blazing across my skin.

My cell phone buzzed from the nightstand.

```
Rob: You in the mood?

Me: Not tonight.
```

Christina Lee lives in the Midwest with her husband and son—her two favorite guys. She's addicted to lip gloss and salted caramel everything. She believes in true love and kissing, so writing romance novels has become a dream job. She also owns her own jewelry business, called Tags-n-Stones, where she hand-stamps meaningful words or letters onto silver for her customers. Christina loves to hear from her readers. Visit her online at www.christinalee.net.

CONNECT ONLINE

christinalee.net